Palace Green

Kingsgate footbridge

North Bailey

South Bailey

Prebend's Walk

Watergate

Matthew McClements

Also by Denise Robertson

THE LAND OF LOST CONTENT
A YEAR OF WINTER
BLUE REMEMBERED HILLS
THE LAND OF LOST CONTENT: THE BELGATE
TRILOGY
THE SECOND WIFE ✓
NONE TO MAKE YOU CRY
REMEMBER THE MOMENT
THE STARS BURN ON
THE ANXIOUS HEART
THE BELOVED PEOPLE
STRENGTH FOR THE MORNING
TOWARDS JERUSALEM
A RELATIVE FREEDOM ✓

ACT OF OBLIVION

DENISE ROBERTSON

SIMON & SCHUSTER

LONDON · SYDNEY · NEW YORK · TOKYO · SINGAPORE · TORONTO

First published in Great Britain by Simon & Schuster Ltd, 1995

Simon & Schuster Ltd
West Garden Place
Kendal Street
London W2 2AQ

Simon & Schuster of Australia Pty Ltd
Sydney

A CIP catalogue record for this book is available from the
British Library

ISBN 0-671-71857-6

Typeset in Goudy Modern 15/16pt
Palimpsest Book Production Limited, Polmont, Stirlingshire
Printed and bound in Great Britain by
Butler & Tanner, Frome & London

Afterwards, whenever Claire looked back on that October day, she could pinpoint the exact moment when she became afraid. But that afternoon, as the light faded and the street-lamps sprang to life outside, she felt particularly at peace. Piled in front of her drawing-board were swatches of next year's materials: raw and slubby silks, soft, mottled jaspé yarns, close-fit jersey, fine openwork ribs in soft, milky tints and bold vibrant colours for contrast. There was a bunch of loopy terry knits and coarse open-weaves, and a range of dark, earth-stained colours to reflect ethnic origins, as well as satin and velvet. It was an exciting collection to work with and she sketched with a will, keeping the lines fluid, the skirts short and floaty or long and clinging.

She smiled as she worked, thinking of Sammy Gold's reaction whenever she delivered designs.

'The best,' he would say, his pink jowls quivering with pleasure. 'The best ever.' But it was Sorrel, his wife, whose shrewd approval mattered most to Claire.

Sammy knew costings but Sorrel knew the customers. If Sorrel approved, the collection would sell.

Claire finished the detail on a skirt, sketching in each fold, each dart, before pinning on the appropriate sample of cloth and laying it aside. It was ten to six when she laid down her pencil and flexed her weary shoulders.

Michael had promised her that the debate on North Sea fish stocks would finish early, leaving him free to eat at home for a change, so tonight was special. Claire had been an MP's wife for eight years so she was used to her husband's late nights, but sometimes she was lonely. Michael was a PPS, a Parliamentary Private Secretary: the lowest rung on the ladder of government. If it was like this now, how would it be later?

She dismissed this uncomfortable thought and moved to the mirror above the mantel, tucking her dark hair behind her ears. In the looking-glass her face seemed ghostly; she was seven pounds underweight and it showed. She touched the shadows under her eyes with a gentle finger and pursed her lips, trying to improve her appearance. The casserole would be ready at seven-thirty, so there was time to take a shower and paint on some roses before Michael arrived. She wanted to look her best tonight.

In the kitchen she turned up the thermostat on the boiler and switched on the small television set. The Conservative Party was in the limelight once more as the row over money for asking parliamentary questions rambled on. Three Labour MPs had quit the Privileges

Committee – which was to investigate the allegations – in protest at the fact that hearings were to be held in private. Claire listened for a moment, hoping the furore would not delay Michael's journey home, then opened a bottle of 1991 Château Tour to breathe and checked the oven.

The recipe for Boeuf Bourgignon had come from Debbo and if it tasted as good as it looked and smelt it would be heaven. She felt herself begin to salivate and closed the oven door quickly, before she was tempted to taste and spoil her appetite.

She was laying out a change of clothing when the telephone shrilled in the bedroom. It was not Michael ringing to apologise and postpone dinner, as she had feared. 'Hello Perdy,' she said, relief flooding over her as she recognised the familiar voice at the other end of the line. 'When did you get back?'

'Only an hour ago and this place is in chaos. I should've come back earlier – I'm in court tomorrow – but there was so much I wanted to do there. It was fabulous, Cleo; hard work but I did get to see the city, and I learnt a lot about the American legal system. We flew in at night, and when the plane was coming in to land I looked down and there was Los Angeles looking like handfuls of diamonds thrown on to black velvet. It was lovely.'

'It sounds it,' Claire said, rubbing one bare foot against the opposite calf. 'So it was worth going?'

'Definitely! I mean it wasn't flawless; the traffic is unbelievable – they don't have a rush hour, it's always snarled up – and they've terrible air pollution, but I liked the climate. They say everyone who can has moved out but it looked pretty well-populated to me. Not that you wouldn't need a lifetime to work the place out. I saw Sunset Strip and Chinatown – wonderful food; everything from burgers to Thai cuisine. I couldn't go anywhere alone after dark, it's not the best of cities for a woman on her own . . . but you and Michael must go soon. I've a sheaf of contacts . . . you'll adore it.'

Claire had been friends with Perdy and Debbo since their first week at university, when they had walked Durham's narrow streets together, sporting their new scarves, talking animatedly to hide the fact that they were homesick and scared. Perdy was blonde and unfairly good-looking but Debbo was the luckiest of them all, with a good marriage and three lovely children, in addition to two well-reviewed books on Elizabethan theatre behind her. Perdy seemed happy enough and was spoken of as a rising barrister; there was no one man in her life but she was never short of an escort and never would be. 'I'm happy too,' Claire thought, but visions of the fertility clinic threatened to intrude and she gave her attention back to Perdy, who was still raving about all things American.

Claire was always pleased to hear from Perdy but it was a relief when at last she could put down the phone and scuttle for the shower. At any moment Michael's key might turn in the lock and she wanted to be ready; nothing must spoil their first romantic evening together in longer than she cared to remember. At the moment the Government was under pressure because of the sleaze row, and Michael needed a break.

As she set the table and put the vegetables on to the hotplates she thought once more of Durham in those far-off student days. They had lived in college for two years and then shared a flat, which looked out on to the River Wear beyond smoke-blackened chimneys. At night they pored over books and scribbled essays, and then — duty done — one of them, usually Debbo, would cook a huge pasta and serve it straight from the stove. Afterwards, feeling virtuous and replete, they had sipped whatever alcoholic beverage they could afford and dreamt out loud. Perdy was the most ambitious. 'The Woolsack,' she would say, narrowing her eyes and squinting at her glass. 'The first woman on the Woolsack ... that'll do for starters.' Even then she had had the patina of success; straight dark brows contrasting with smooth blond hair, and penetrating eyes of a peculiar greeny-blue.

'It isn't fair,' Debbo would moan each time another diet failed. 'A figure like that and she can eat whatever she likes.' But after one consuming passion in the third year, Perdy had never had a relationship that lasted longer than six months and sometimes Claire sensed that she was lonely.

Claire had intended to teach, picturing herself in some leafy girls' school, filling young minds with the ascent of man. She had never thought of marriage, except as some far-off dream.

They had talked about love in those days and all

professed a desire for children. 'But not yet,' Perdy had said firmly. 'Not till I'm thirty-eight, then I'll produce three in three years and have my tubes tied.' Now Debbo was thirty and Claire and Perdy were twenty-nine. Debs had married in her final year and given birth seven months later to the day. 'And I am barren,' Claire thought, remembering the dismal rounds of fertility clinics with their misleading odour of optimism.

She had married Michael two months after graduation and their picture had adorned the front page of the *Express* because Michael had only recently won his seat and a wedding made a pretty picture. 'By-election victor weds,' said the caption and her father bought twelve copies of the paper. That was 1985. Now she moved between the flat in Kensington and a converted vicarage in Michael's Yorkshire constituency. She had never bothered to take her post-graduate certificate of education, never used her degree in anthropology. Instead she had turned her hobby, designing clothes for herself and her friends, into a vocation.

It was Perdy who found the Golds. 'They admired my suit and said they were in the rag trade themselves. I said it was exclusive but I represented the designer, and they want to see more. Ask a lot, Cleo—' The others had christened her Cleopatra because she had sported a fringe in her first year at Durham and the nickname had stuck. 'Better still, ask for a royalty on every garment. I'll do the contract. You'll make a bomb.'

In the event it had been a bomb of World War II proportions rather than atomic, but it had given Claire a degree of independence and in the long days of waiting to conceive, designing two collections a year had kept her sane. She had spent time with the Golds and in their two factories, learning the trade, discovering what could and could not be done with each fabric, and learning how to cost designs. She owed the Golds a great deal but they seemed happy with her work so it was a mutually productive arrangement.

She chose strings of ivory beads tonight, to complement her A-line, paprika silk shift. Her legs were still tanned from the summer but she rolled on sheer stockings and suspendered them carefully to avoid runs. Sitting in front of the dressing-table mirror she hastily smoothed in foundation, but once she had applied eyeshadow she began to relax. Even if she heard Michael come in now, she could be ready in time. The addition of blusher gave her a glow and she dusted it over her forehead and chin, then outlined her lips with a pencil, filling them in with Rose Sable. A liberal application of Opium and she was ready.

She took one last satisfied look at herself and went through to the living-room to give the table a final flourish with a single, long-stemmed carnation in a cylinder vase. Eight-forty. Michael was going to be late again, and not only late but tired, so they would hardly exchange a word before he tumbled into bed, asleep. 'I must do something about it,' Claire thought. 'We can't go on like this.'

As she checked her make-up once more she listed the possibilities. They could go up to the cottage one weekend before Christmas, if constituency affairs allowed, but Cumbria was not at its best in October or November. The autumnal landscape was magnificent but the days were short and the weather harsh. Perhaps they might manage a weekend in Paris . . . even one night would do if they were both alert and glad to be together. And Paris was enchanting at any time of the year. Sitting on the steps of the Sacré-Coeur, drinking in the sun. That would do them both good.

The first time she had seen Michael he had been standing, head bent, listening to a woman in a flowered hat. Her parents had dragged her along to a cheese and wine party.

'It's the least you can do, Claire . . . Daddy is the Constituency Chairman. If he can't get support from his own family—'

She had wanted to point out that her brothers had been excused family responsibilities so why was she different? In the end, though, she had ducked a confrontation and changed into her well-worn blue silk suit, with pearls at her ears and throat.

'You'll meet the new candidate,' her mother had said once she had passed muster. 'For heaven's sake make him feel welcome. Daddy says we're lucky to get someone of his calibre. He's ear-marked for big things.'

Devening had always been a safe Conservative seat and probably always would be, but the sitting Member had angina and wanted out at the next election. Michael Griffin, rugger blue and advertising executive, was to be his replacement. Claire had imagined him, fair and chinless with a bright blue tie and weak blue eyes, chortling too much and turning even the mildest of observations into an oration. And then he had looked up from his conversation and smiled at Claire as though he had been waiting for her arrival.

Now she switched on the TV in search of diversion but it was a waspish professor from the LSE who was always making a fool of himself on the box, and when she changed channels it was to see an earnest ex-children's TV presenter sailing down an unattractive river. She switched it off and crossed to the window, in the hope of seeing a cab draw up in the street below.

There were people moving about, their faces briefly illuminated as they passed beneath the street lamps. There were cars too, plenty of them, but no black cabs nosing in to the kerb. She let the curtain fall back into place and put her hand on the radiator. It was almost too hot to touch but she felt a sudden chill. Autumn was giving way to winter and she had only just noticed.

At nine-thirty she turned off the oven and telephoned Michael's secretary. 'Maeve? I'm sorry to bother you but Michael was so certain he'd be home tonight—'

'And he isn't?' The smooth secretarial voice sounded a trifle surprised. 'The debate finished hours ago, at least it was drawing to a close as I came away. I expect he's gone up for a drink — you know what it's like.'

'Yes,' Claire said dryly. 'I do know what it's like. Oh well . . . as long as it's over, I expect he'll be here soon. How's Timmy?' Maeve was a doting single parent and the description of Timmy's glowing health and winning ways took nearly ten minutes. Claire went back to her drawing-board after replacing the receiver but she wasn't in the mood for work and it was a relief when the phone rang.

'Debs? No, no you're not interrupting anything. I'm on my own. As usual.'

'Well, I did warn you.' As ever, Deborah was practical. 'Come over here for an hour. Hugh is glued to some documentary and I've a lovely Chablis in the fridge. I could do with some girl-talk, actually. I've just read *Postman Pat* to Emlyn, cover-to-cover three times. It numbs the brain in the end. They should use it to anaesthetise for neurosurgery.'

Claire chuckled, thinking of Deborah's two-year-old and his passion for bedtime stories. 'Thanks, but I ought to stay here. Michael should be home at any moment. Talking of home, have you heard from Perdy? She's back.'

They talked for ten more minutes about Perdy and her LA trip and then finally Debs sighed. 'Well, if you're sure I can't persuade you—'

'No,' Claire said firmly. 'I'll come over soon, or you and Hugh must come over for a meal — not that I can promise you'll find the host *in situ*. He was sure he'd be home on time tonight.'

'He's probably on his way,' Debs said soothingly. 'Ring if he doesn't turn up . . . but he will. Give him my love.'

*   *   *

It was almost ten-thirty. Claire had eaten nothing since lunch but the thought of a solitary casserole did not appeal. She opened the fridge and surveyed the contents with a pessimistic eye, settling in the end for a piece of Port Salut and the remnants of an M & S pasta salad.

She drank coffee as she watched 'News at Ten' and then 'Newsnight'. There was no mention of crises or late-night conferences in smoke-filled rooms. 'Why doesn't he ring?' she thought, feeling sudden anger as she imagined him coming through the door eventually, his blond hair ruffled over his brow, his eyes crinkled in a charming politician's smile.

'Darling, why did you worry?' he would say. 'I couldn't ring . . . and when I got away it made more sense to come straight home.' Well, he wouldn't get away with it this time. She stalked into the kitchen and poured herself a glass of the Château Tour.

She was half-way down the bottle when the black-and-white movie on BBC2 came to an end. It was twelve-twenty-five and she kept watching until the BBC clock disappeared and the screen went blank. She used the remote control to flick through the channels but she was too distracted to watch anything. Michael was often late but he always telephoned.

She looked across at the ivory instrument. Who else could she ring? Who would know what had happened tonight? She could ring any one of several colleagues but what would Michael say if she did? No news was good news. If he'd been in a road accident the police would have been on her doorstep by now. She thought of ringing Debbo or Perdy and sharing her anxiety but some instinct for privacy stopped her. It would make Michael look so uncaring . . . and even if he was being inconsiderate this time, she didn't want to advertise it, not even to her closest friends. As for her parents, she imagined the impatient intake of breath at the other end of the phone if she rang home. 'Aren't you making a fuss about nothing, Claire? Michael's a busy man. And he's an hour or so late? Don't be silly, dear.' No, of all the people in the world she could turn to now, her family were last on the list.

'It's OK,' she told herself. 'It's probably nothing . . . and even if it isn't, I can cope.'

She felt better when she had put on her dressing-gown and pinned up her hair. In a moment she would hear a key in the door and he would be here, contrite. Once before, when he had had to let her down, he had arrived hidden behind an enormous bunch of garish flowers, bought at a late-night garage. Claire smiled at the memory and put the remains of the wine in the fridge. Might as well be standing up when he arrived.

The casserole had cooled and she put it in the fridge too. Everyone said casseroles were better for standing – they would have it tomorrow with fresh vegetables. She munched two sticks of lukewarm broccoli and tipped the rest of the vegetables into the bin. It was ten to one and she ought to go to bed but she still felt wide awake. She picked up the handset to hear the comforting buzz on the line and make sure it was working. Michael would ring soon or else he would come through the door and laugh away her fears.

She made a small plate of ham sandwiches liberally spread with French mustard, Michael's favourite, and covered them with a second plate, before going through to the bedroom. Eventually she fell asleep on top of the duvet while the World Service burbled away in her ear.

When she awoke, blinking in the glare of the harsh ceiling light, it was a quarter to three. She shivered a little and was suddenly afraid. Outside in the street tyres screeched on tarmac, marking the exact moment that fear replaced anxiety. The engine noise waxed and then receded and she was left alone in the bedroom, knowing that there was no simple explanation for her husband's absence. Whatever had detained Michael, it was something serious. She set the alarm for six o'clock and then put out the light but not even darkness could give her respite from her fears. In the end, she bunched up the pillows and sat up in bed, her arms round her legs, her cheek resting on one knee — every fibre of her being willing the world to wake up and help her.

2

By five-thirty Claire's eyes felt on fire and her head ached. All through the night she had set herself deadlines. If Michael didn't appear by three she would ring the police. If he didn't ring by three-thirty . . . four . . . four-fifteen. Always something held her back. To Michael, discretion was everything: he hated anyone knowing anything about him, his life at home or their relationship with one another. He had even found it difficult to respond to the gynaecologist who had treated her infertility. In the consulting-room he had been affable enough, even made jokes. But his eyes had signalled, 'Do we have to do this?' so that in the end she had come to feel guilty, not only for her inability to conceive but for even wanting to in the first place.

They had used contraception in the first year of marriage. 'Let's enjoy one another,' Michael had said. And they had done just that . . . their love-making had been frequent and intense — or as frequent and intense as the House would allow.

At first she had resented politics and the almost feverish look it had brought to her husband's eye but eventually she had become resigned. 'You accept it or it breaks you,' another wife had told her and it was true. But with resignation had come yearning for a child . . . something of Michael's for her to hold on to in his absence.

They had tried for eighteen months before she sought help. Michael had given reluctant approval and winced visibly when she told him he would have to have a sperm count. They had sat side by side in the consultant's waiting-room and she had almost heard him tap out each wasted minute. Alone now, in the silent bedroom, she willed herself to stop thinking about it: 'Get Michael back,' she told herself. Time enough for everything else when that was done.

She reached out to the phone once, at quarter to five, but a mental picture of newspaper headlines intruded. 'MP's wife blows whistle. PPS in dog-house over late night with colleagues.' Worse still, 'Which honourable member is carpeted for night on tiles?' alongside as unflattering a picture of Michael as the newspaper's library could provide. There would be a resumé of his career to date and details of his family background. He would be 'tipped for promotion' but, in the light of his wife's obvious mistrust, 'subject to grave doubts'. Every other PPS who had fallen from grace in the previous decade would be listed, together with speculation about the party's fate at the next election and the Prime Minister's chances of surviving a back-bench revolt.

Not a good idea when the Government was in so much trouble and the 'cash for questions' issue unresolved.

'You know what they're like,' Michael had told her over and over again. 'Give them the slightest excuse and they'll build it into a 10,000 word exposé.' He had made her afraid to show the slightest spontaneity in public. Now she withdrew her hand from the telephone and settled down again to wait.

At six o' clock the alarm shrilled and she switched it off but at half-past she knew the time had come for action. If Michael had had an accident, was even now lying unconscious in some accident unit, her very inaction would be seized on and distorted. 'Wife fails to raise alarm over Government rising star.' They were always rising stars if scandal loomed. She could see the front page of the tabloids even now. She reached for the phone and dialled Perdy's number.

As she waited for an answer she gazed at the reflection of the table, still set for last night's dinner, in the mirror outside her bedroom door. She had had such hopes about that meal. The two of them together for once, with time just to talk. And afterwards . . . they hadn't made love for a long time – she was counting days that turned into weeks when Perdy's voice, heavy with sleep, spoke at the other end of the line.

'Perdy, I'm sorry to ring so early when you're just back—'

'It's OK.' Already Perdy's voice was more alert. 'What's wrong?'

'I'd've rung Debbo but I thought she'd be busy with the children—'

'Stop havering, Cleo. You wouldn't ring at this time – God, is it only half-past-six? – unless you were pushed. What's wrong?'

'Michael hasn't come home.' Even as she said it Claire felt foolish. He would turn up at any moment and she would have egg on her face.

'Hasn't he telephoned?' Perdy didn't sound as though she thought it silly.

'No,' Claire said gratefully. 'And he always does if it's an all-night sitting. And anyway, it isn't – I checked with Maeve, and there was nothing on "Newsnight" . . . no row . . . no crisis.'

'So he should've been home for bedtime?'

'For dinner . . . we were going to have a meal. A special meal in a way because he knew he'd be home and that's rare. I thought he'd call and say something had cropped up but he hasn't. Now I think I ought to let someone know . . . or something.' Her voice trailed off. You didn't report people missing after less than twelve hours – not sensible, powerful people like Michael, who had never had the merest kind of instability attached to him and could handle any situation.

'I'm coming round,' Perdy said. 'Put some coffee on and sit tight. We'll decide what to do when I get there. He'll be all right, so let's not panic. I'll be half an hour.'

She was there in thirty-five minutes, face bare of make-up, blond hair still wet from the shower.

'You look ghastly,' she said briskly. 'Now, where's that coffee?'

Claire felt tears of gratitude well up in her eyes. Everything seemed more normal with a fellow human being there, especially when that one other was Perdy. 'Ta,' she said. 'You're a brick.' It was almost seven-thirty and the world was awake and everything seemed somehow better. 'He's probably stayed somewhere for the night,' she said apologetically. 'He'll slaughter me when he finds I bothered you.'

'We won't tell him,' Perdy said. 'I'll make up a story when the time comes. Now, get the coffee and then we'll make an action plan.' Claire was coming through the doorway with the loaded tray when she heard Perdy's voice. She was speaking softly but there was something in her tone that brought Claire's fears rushing to the surface once more. 'Yes. As soon as you can. I'm due in court at ten so if you can make it by nine . . .' She turned, sensing Claire behind her. 'That was Debbo,' she said, replacing the receiver. 'I thought she might as well be in on it.'

'You think something's happened, don't you?' Claire said. Perdy's chin came up and her eyes, when they met Claire's own, were apologetic.

'I think it might be . . . difficult,' she said. 'Michael knows you worry, so there has to be a reason why he hasn't rung you.'

They drank their coffee quietly, each busy with her own thoughts, making polite remarks about the coffee or the autumn weather or the news items that spilled out from the radio on the coffee table while they struggled to decide what to do for the best.

'Right,' Perdy said at last. 'I've thought it over. I don't think we should involve the police at this stage. If he'd been involved in a road accident you'd've heard by now. He's bound to have identification on him and they can get your life history from a credit card. It's just possible that he's concussed somewhere – not enough for someone to step in; they always assume dazed people are drunk and give them a wide berth – but somehow I don't think that's it.'

'Then where is he?' Claire interrupted, unable to contain herself any longer.

'He may be being held under duress, Cleo.' Perdy spoke quietly as though in awe of her own words.

'Duress?' Claire shook her head in puzzlement. 'Do you mean kidnap?'

'Sort of . . . he *is* an MP . . . some group could hold him, just to make a point – they wouldn't hurt him. He's not important enough . . . Well, you know what I mean. If they were going to make a martyr of someone they'd go higher. And if it was the IRA they always make contact so you'd know by now.'

'You keep eliminating things,' Claire said. 'What's left?'

'I don't know.' Perdy's brow was furrowed. 'He's not the type to have run off, whatever problems he might have. My guess is it's some kind of crisis. Not his probably. His boss or some bigwig . . . and he's had to stick his finger in the dyke and can't ring.' She smiled reassuringly but Claire was not comforted.

'He'd ask someone else to ring. I know Michael. He'd find a way.'

Perdy glanced at her watch. 'Seven-thirty. If he hasn't turned up by eight I'll ring someone I know at Bow Street. He'll make some discreet enquiries. In the meantime, why don't you ring his secretary again . . . she might have heard something. It's worth a try.'

But Maeve had no new information and when she heard Michael had not been home she was aghast.

'I'm going in to the office now,' she said. 'I'll ring if he's there. Not that he will be. He'd have phoned you if he was able to. Still . . .' A forced cheerfulness entered her voice. '. . . there'll be some logical explanation. We'll laugh about it later on.'

The doorbell rang as Claire replaced the receiver. It was Debbo, looking a little flustered, her face shining clean but devoid even of the minimal make-up she usually wore, her brown hair scooped up into an untidy tea-cake that threatened to come adrift from its flowered rouleau. 'You shouldn't've come this early,' Claire said. 'What about the children?'

'The children are fine.' Deborah shrugged out of her jacket and pushed up the sleeves of her woollen sweater. Her arms were plump and dimpled, like a baby's, and suddenly Claire wanted them around her, soothing, patting, just as she did her children. But all she said was 'Well, at least let me get you some tea or coffee.'

Perdy was ahead of her. In the kitchen the kettle was boiling and Perdy was rattling a tray together with typical efficiency. 'We'll drink this,' Perdy said. 'Then by the time we've finished he'll have rung . . . but if I have to, I'll ring my Bow Street man.'

They were lifting their cups when the doorbell rang again. There was a swift exchange of glances between the two friends and Claire felt a sudden drying of her mouth. She meant to get to her feet, to answer her own front door, but strangely her legs refused to move or her arms to lever her up from the chair. She could not even turn her head to see through into the hall. There was a murmur of voices, and for a moment she contemplated covering her ears but she didn't even have the strength for that. She raised her eyes to the mirror and registered the navy uniforms, the chequered hat-band of the policewoman. She saw the girl's hair, neat above a whiter-than-white collar, and the gold braid on the policeman's shoulders. It was that, more than anything, that told her they were bringing portentous news.

Perdy had moved behind her and was resting a hand on her shoulder. Across the coffee table, Deborah's eyes had widened into dark and anxious pools.

'Mrs Griffin? Mrs Michael Griffin?' It was the man who spoke. He had removed his uniform hat and was holding it in front of him.

'Yes. Have you come about my husband?'

His eyes dropped and then he lifted his head and spoke.

'My name is Chief Inspector Maynard, Mrs Griffin. I'm afraid I may have some bad news for you. Some very bad news.'

'Is he dead?' She heard her own voice as though from a distance. The man's face softened suddenly and he bit his lower lip.

'We have reason to believe . . .' He cleared his throat and started again. 'Acting on information received this morning we went to an apartment in Kennerley Street, off the Edgware Road. We found a body there which we believe to be the cor . . . the body of your husband. There was identification in the room, . . . and your husband is a public figure. One of our officers knew him from—'

There was a ringing in Claire's ears, a ringing and a rushing of air. And then the peal of the doorbell and Debbo rising from her chair to answer it.

'It can't be Michael.' Someone said that and she didn't recognise the voice as her own but everyone was looking at her. 'Michael can't be dead.'

A man had come into the room, thin and elegant in a melton overcoat. 'Gavin Lambert, Central Office,' he said crisply to the policeman. 'Your Superintendent telephoned me.'

Perdy was bending over her. 'It's all right darling. We're here. Do you want a drink?'

'He can't be dead, Perdy. Tell them he can't be dead. They've made a mistake.'

'We'll make sure, Cleo. Try not to worry. We'll find out very soon. Shall Debs get you some brandy?' Debbo was hovering in front of them, her plump, be-ringed fingers intertwined in anguish, but Claire suddenly remembered something the policeman had said.

'Information received? What did you mean by that? What information?'

'There was a call to the Police Emergency line earlier this morning. It gave an address and said we should go there.' On the sideboard the onyx statuette of the 1920s dancer seemed to sway and Claire felt herself sway in unison.

'Was Michael murdered? Was it the IRA?'

He was shaking his head. 'I can't say with certainty until we get the ME's report but it would appear that Mr ... that the man concerned died of natural causes.'

Claire felt a sudden elation. It couldn't be Michael. You didn't die of natural causes at thirty-seven. She looked up and smiled. 'You've got the wrong name for your body, Chief Inspector.' Her voice was high and bright now. 'My husband is only thirty-seven. And now if you'll excuse me.' She was on her feet but the bedroom door suddenly seemed a mile away.

She could hear muttering behind her, between the man in the melton overcoat and the Inspector. She heard the Inspector say, 'We only need someone with personal knowledge of the deceased.' And then the man from Central Office was buttoning his coat and turning to the door.

Again her own voice, the voice of a stranger, high and indignant. 'Whatever it is you're arranging, I want to go myself. If it *is* Michael, I have a right. I know you've made a mistake but it's up to me—' And then Debbo was shrugging her into her trench coat as she would a child, whilst Perdy wound a scarf around her neck, and then they both guided her towards the door as though she had suddenly lost all sense of volition.

She didn't believe it was Michael until she saw the small brown mole above his left eyebrow. The face beneath was waxen, the teeth unduly prominent beneath his lips, the eyelids dark and sunken. But the fair hair was breathtakingly familiar, the mole unmistakable.

'Is this Michael Griffin? I'm afraid I must ask you formally. I'm sorry.' The Chief Inspector's face was anguished, as he tried to remain phlegmatic.

'Yes,' Claire said. There was a faint suggestion of a smile on the dead face and she put out a finger to touch it but the skin was cold, the flesh beneath turned to stone.

'Come on, Cleo,' Perdy said. 'Let's go home.'

It was then Claire noticed the smell; death and disinfectant in equal measure. She choked, her tongue suddenly feeling large in her mouth as Perdy guided her out into the corridor, where Deborah and the man from Central Office were waiting.

'Darling?' Deborah was looking hopeful.

'It's him,' Claire said flatly. 'It's definitely Michael.'

'Mrs Griffin . . . Claire—' The melton overcoat was touching her arm. 'Leave everything to me. I'll fend off the Press as long as I can.'

'Press?' Claire asked, suddenly bewildered.

'Newspapers,' Perdy said. 'The tabloids. They'll be interested because of Michael's job . . . but don't let it worry you. We'll see to everything.'

'It's best if you say as little as possible, even to family, Mrs Griffin.' The Central Office man was pulling a rueful face. 'I'm afraid they'll be after everyone as soon as this gets out – family, friends, even old schoolmates—'

'Can't this wait?' Debbo's voice was hostile as she interrupted.

'I wish it could,' the man said wearily. 'But bitter experience tells me we have no time at all.'

They were looking at her, and again she could hear her own voice. A single sentence. 'What was he doing in Kennerley Street?' she asked and saw discomfort dawning in all their eyes at her question.

3

There were people crowding round the door to the flats when the police car rounded the corner. Claire heard Gavin Lambert's tongue click against his teeth in annoyance but his face betrayed no emotion when he turned from the front passenger seat to face her.

'I'm sorry about this . . . but I was expecting it. We'll get you into the house, don't worry.'

Claire looked at him blankly. 'Who are they?' But before he could tell her, she saw the cameras, the notebooks, the shoulders hunched to support a plethora of gear that meant the media were gathering for a kill.

'Can't we go to my place?' Debbo asked desperately but before Lambert could answer Claire shook her head.

'I'm going home.' The car was drawing to a halt and she clutched at the neck of her coat and leant towards the door, wishing that Perdy had not had to leave her at the mortuary to appear in court.

'Don't say a word,' Lambert said. It was an order rather than a suggestion. 'Don't speak at all. Give me your key. That's right. When we get out, just put your head down and follow me.' And then she was out in the street and they were calling her name from all sides, so that she felt assaulted. She knew she must not meet their eyes — that would be fatal. Deborah struck out left and right, her face contorted with fury as she elbowed her way through, Claire behind her within the circle of Gavin Lambert's arm.

'For God's sake,' Debbo said, turning as she reached the step to look back at the mob that pressed around them. She was about to say something worse but a look from Lambert and a shake of his head silenced her. And then the door opened and they were in the cool sanctuary of the hall, but not before one reporter, taller than the rest, his shoulders hunched inside a tweed overcoat, had caught Claire's eye.

'When you're ready,' he mouthed. His eyes were somewhat softer than the others focused on her and she let him press a card into her unresisting hand.

'Right.' Gavin Lambert closed the door and blew out his relief through pursed lips. 'Some tea, I think . . . and then we need to talk. I wish I could spare you this but if we're to get them off your back we must give them something.'

Deborah helped her assemble cups on a tray while they waited for the kettle to boil. 'Earl Grey, I think,' Debbo said, selecting the right caddy. 'He looks an Earl Grey man.' She carried the tray through to the living-room and Claire poured, marvelling that her hand was shaking only slightly. Michael was dead. The very earth should shake.

Lambert accepted a cup and raised it to his lips. 'Ah, Earl Grey,' he said appreciatively and Claire felt wild laughter bubble up, which she managed to turn into a strangled cough.

'Have you a fax machine?' Lambert asked.

'There's one in Michael's study,' Claire said and raised her own cup as though the fragrant brew would somehow be a panacea.

The statement they concocted was brief and held nothing with which Claire could disagree.

'The family of Michael Griffin are grief-stricken and ask that they be left alone to deal with their tragedy. The circumstances of Michael's death must be subject to a coroner's investigation but the family have been assured that there were no untoward factors and that his death was peaceful and swift and due to natural causes.'

'I'll fax this to Central Office and then I'll read it out to that mob outside. No need for you to appear.' Suddenly Claire thought of all those stoic Conservative wives who appeared on doorsteps when the packs gathered. But they had had husbands to support while she had none. This was not a scandal. It was a tragedy. Except . . .

She was saved further consideration by the ringing of the doorbell. It was her GP, full of concern and professional warmth but he failed to meet her eyes. How had he got here?

'I'm going to give you something . . . just a little sedative—' He was already fumbling in his bag so he had come prepared.

'I don't want anything.' She was proud of how quietly she had spoken.

'Don't you think it would help, Cleo?' Debbo's face was anxious. 'I'd take it like a shot. Just for a little while . . . the next few days.'

'Can't you see, I need to think?' Suddenly her voice was shrill, her words spat out like bullets. 'There's something going on here. Something you're not telling me – all of you – I'm not a fool. Who made that phone call? Why didn't Michael ring me? What was he doing in that street? Whose house was it? You must at least know that?'

'Please—' The doctor took hold of her wrist, his fingertips cold and dry against her skin. 'It does no good to conjecture at this stage. If you lie down for a while . . . you didn't sleep last night—'

'Who told you that?' Suddenly Claire felt betrayed. They had been talking behind her back . . . what else had they talked about besides her broken night? Had they told him she had been struggling to preserve her marriage? But how could they, when she had only just realised it herself?

'I told him, Claire.' Deborah was standing up, looking suddenly dignified and firm. 'I told him when I rang and asked him to come round. You need some help;

you've had a shock on top of hours of anxiety. Please accept the doctor's help . . . and then, when you feel better, we'll find out exactly what happened. I promise you we will.'

'I won't take drugs . . . but I will lie down for a while,' Claire conceded. She couldn't fight all of them. 'Call me if anything happens, Debs, please.' She was in her bedroom, unfastening her blouse which had suddenly grown constricting at the neck, when she asked herself what could happen that hadn't happened already. 'Michael is dead.' She said it aloud, softly at first and then louder.

His picture looked up at her from a dozen angles, snapshots placed carefully under the plate-glass top of her dressing-table. Michael smiling, throwing back his head to laugh, frowning at a road map, his hair tousled by wind. She sat down and placed her hands, palms down, either side of the pictures. 'What happened?' she asked but his face looked back at her, smiling, and no one answered her question.

She contemplated getting out of the flat but when she peeped around the curtain, the news-hounds were still there, huddled in groups, shifting their feet occasionally, sometimes letting out a raucous laugh. What was so funny? If she went down into the street would they tell her? Could she walk past them and melt into the passers-by? 'I could take the boat to Greenwich,' she thought, suddenly longing for air and space and the feel of the age-old Thames beneath her. And just as suddenly she was filled with horror that she could think of such a thing at such a time. 'Perhaps I'm going mad?' she wondered aloud and cringed anew at the further sign of madness.

In the end she lay down on the bed, removing her shoes, and slipping under the duvet. She was lying there, wide awake, eyes open because when they were closed her eyelids burnt from lack of sleep, when Debbo peeped around the door.

'Are you OK?' Debbo closed the door behind her and moved to sit on the edge of the bed. 'I wish I knew what was going on. I don't think anyone knows. Not really.'

'You're keeping something from me,' Claire said. 'All of you, even you, Debs – look at you now, you're being shifty.'

Deborah's lips closed for an instant and then she pushed back the sleeves of her sweater as though gearing up for action. 'It's only because I don't actually *know* anything. If I'm being devious it's because I don't want to feed you a story and then find out it's untrue.'

'So you do know something?' Claire raised herself up on the pillows, not taking her eyes from her friend's face for a second.

'I know what they think ... but they're far from sure.'

'For God's sake tell me, Debs. Whatever it is. Anything's better than wondering.'

'OK. This is it – all of it. Michael was found in a small flat – a bed-sit, really – in Kennerley Street—'

'I know. Whose flat?' Claire couldn't resist the interruption.

'It was his . . . well, he rented it. It appears he lived there some of the time . . . at least, he had things there . . . razors, shirts—'

'He lived here,' Claire said wonderingly. 'He can't have lived anywhere else. He lived here with me.'

'I know, darling . . . I know it doesn't make sense. That's why no one wants to discuss it with you, because they could get it wrong. But he was found in bed there and it was obvious he'd been coming and going from the place over quite a long period of time. They have to look into it, even though they're convinced there were no suspicious circumstances. He died of some vascular condition, an aneurysm or a stroke of some sort. They'll know soon.'

'I can't believe this is happening.' Claire heard the edge of uncomfortable laughter in her own voice and tried to suppress it. 'I can't believe any of it.' She made to throw back the duvet but Deborah restrained her.

'Don't get up. Let me make you some lunch. Just something light. Perdy's coming over as soon as she can get away. We'll talk then, the three of us. And Perdy will get something out of them, you know what she's like.'

'Is that man Lambert still here?' Claire had subsided on to the pillow.

'No, he's gone. There's just me. Your parents are on their way, they'll be here soon. And Adam is flying in as soon as he can. I don't know about the others.'

'There's no point in their coming,' Claire said desperately. Her parents and brothers were the last people she wanted to see now, amid all this confusion.

Deborah patted her arm. 'I know,' she said sympathetically. 'But you can't stop them, darling. You'll just have to endure it. If it gets too much, having them here, I'll whisk you to our place and say you need bedrest. Leave it to Perdy and me.'

'What does Perdy think?' Claire said. She saw Deborah's eyes flicker and knew she was right in thinking they'd discussed it. If it had been Hugh, she and Perdy would have wondered, conjectured, come up with possible explanations.

'She's not sure . . . like the rest of us, she's waiting to see.'

'But what does she think?' There was desperation in the question and Debbo responded to it.

'There are two possible explanations, Cleo. A double life – and we can hardly wear that – or that he needed a bolt-hole. Somewhere he could flop. Not talk, not think, even. Hugh does it in the attic – he just shuts off. But this flat doesn't allow that kind of separation. We . . . Perdy and I . . . think that's probably the explanation. He wanted his own space.'

Deborah left her then and went off, returning shortly with an omelette. It was deep and fluffy and seasoned to perfection but the best Claire could do was move it around her mouth, swallowing what she could.

They were clearing the table when the bell went. Deborah opened the door to reveal Claire's parents, immaculate in country tweeds, her father's Guards tie replaced now by sombre black. Her mother's hair looked newly finger-waved, as it always did, and both pairs of brogue shoes were highly polished. There was not a hair out of place anywhere and as her mother bent to brush her daughter's cheek with her lips, Claire found herself wondering just what would ruffle her parents' implacable calm and impeccable grooming. Not even nuclear war?

'This is a bad business.' She had known her father would say that and was glad that his dry peck on her cheek stayed her smile.

'Those people at the door!' Her mother shuddered. 'One of them – a woman . . . a woman – thrust herself at me and screamed questions. You must hold on, Claire. They look for signs of weakness.' She took hold of her daughter's forearms and bent to gaze into her face. 'We're counting on you to be brave, darling. This business will be awful for you . . . and the boys.'

Claire wanted to ask why Michael's death would be 'awful' for her brothers, stationed as they were in British bases hundreds if not thousands of miles away, but she knew what the result of her question would be. Her mother's careful eyebrows would be raised, a small and pitying smile on her lips, and she would say, 'Really, darling!' to emphasise Claire's congenital failure to understand what really mattered.

'Can I offer anyone tea . . . or perhaps a drink?' Debbo enquired. Mrs Halcrow's eyes moved over her sweater and crumpled trousers and then came to rest on her face. Debbo was, after all, married into an old family whose unfortunate Socialist connections were merely a dalliance, rather like the Foots or the Longfords. And her husband was a publisher, which was a noble if somewhat eccentric profession.

'Thank you,' she said sweetly. 'Tea, I think. That would be very nice.'

'We need a list,' her father said, drawing Claire down on to the settee. 'We've come to relieve you of all the arrangements. Let me know who needs informing. I'll need your address book, and Michael's — Adam will be here soon—'

Claire was shrinking under the weight of familial reassurance when another visitor arrived. Stephanie Routh was Michael's Labour pair, a tall, rather abrupt young woman whom Claire knew only slightly. She came into the room in her usual hurried fashion, flashing a half-smile around her without making eye contact, in proper politician's style, eventually fixing her gaze on Claire. 'I'm sorry,' she said. 'That's all I've come to say, that I really am most terribly sorry about Michael. We got on well, all things considered and . . . well, I wanted you to know that. If I can help in any way just say. I spoke to Tony Blair before I left the House; he'll be in touch more formally but he wanted me to pass on his condolences.'

At the mention of the Labour leader's name Colonel Halcrow's brow had darkened. Again Claire felt the threatening smile as she sensed her mother withdrawing

the hem of her garment from someone who knew Social-
ists. 'Thank you, Stephanie. You're very kind. May I
introduce my parents, Stephen and Philippa Halcrow.
Stephanie Routh, Michael's pair in the House.'

Stephanie would need a new pair, now that Michael
was dead. There were holes appearing all over the
fabric of life because one man had died. 'And it all
came tumbling down,' she thought, not realising she
had spoken aloud until she saw everyone's shocked
expression.

'I have to go at once, I'm afraid,' Stephanie said,
breaking the silence. 'I'm due at a meeting . . . it's awful
to dash in and out like this but I had to come.' Suddenly
she held out her arms and enfolded Claire in a hug.
It was a scented embrace, some subtle and expensive
fragrance that was definitely not what Claire would
have thought of as left-wing, and once more she felt
a crazy desire to grin. She managed to turn it into
a grateful smile as Stephanie gave one last apologetic
beam and exited.

'That was nice,' her mother said carefully as the door
closed. 'One doesn't expect that level of kindness from
a political opponent.' She meant 'dangerous left-wing
agitator' but forbore to say so.

'It's a courtesy, I expect,' her father said glumly. 'The
done thing. Still, it's better to observe the decencies.'
The embrace hadn't felt like a decency, Claire thought.
It had felt warm and well-intentioned and unbelievably
comforting. Arpège or Ysatis. That's what it had been.
She had a whole new perspective on Stephanie, anyway,

she thought, remembering the way her crumpled blouse had fallen from the ruddy V at her throat to reveal white skin over rounded breasts.

'I am going mad,' Claire thought. 'I never notice things like that, never think like that. Why now?'

It was a relief when Perdy arrived, depositing her coat and briefcase in one smooth move before advancing on Claire's parents with hand outstretched, smiling reassurance at Claire as she did so. 'I'm here now,' the smile said. 'They can't touch you.'

'It was good of you to get here so soon,' she said to the Halcrows, when they had shaken hands. The words were grateful, but the tone commanding. Claire saw her father's brows twitch a little, but then he smiled. People always smiled at Perdy, as though it was her due. She was in charge, whether or not her father knew it.

Perdy kept conversation flowing, asking about Claire's brothers, their wives and families, giving brief details of her own activities, until Deborah appeared with a loaded tray. Claire felt a slight lessening of tension. Her friends were here; perhaps, with their support, she would be able to cope after all.

They drank their tea and nibbled politely at biscuits no one really wanted and then Claire's father dabbed at his moustache with his napkin. He was clearly going to get down to details now, turn Michael's death into a military operation, and Claire was not sure she could bear it. But her father had hardly uttered a preliminary 'Ahem' before the doorbell rang and Gavin Lambert returned.

There was something different about him now, a weary set to his mouth, deeper furrows between his brows. 'How are you?' he asked, but they were token words.

'He's come here to tell me something,' Claire thought and was suddenly desperately anxious to hear what he had to say in private, away from her parents' disapproving ears. She flashed a glance at Perdy and saw an imperceptible nod of the head, a keen awareness in her eyes.

'I expect you'd like to talk to Claire in private,' Perdy said smoothly, rising to her feet with one of her graceful swoops, taking Claire's arm and propelling her and Lambert towards the bedroom door before anyone could argue. 'Just call if you need anything,' she said sweetly, tongue in cheek in a gesture that said, 'Leave the parents to me.' Claire tried to smile gratefully but her legs were threatening to give way and she was suddenly aware that the crumpled handkerchief she was clutching was sodden and useless.

'Please sit down,' she said, indicating the wing chair by the cheval mirror. As she opened her dressing-table drawer to get a clean hanky the photographs under the plate glass smiled up at her. 'Michael, Michael . . .' she thought. 'What has happened to us?'

She took her time shaking out the handkerchief and blowing her nose, before turning to face Lambert, feeling her way on to the dressing-table stool as she did so. 'I think you've come to tell me something,' she said and saw his relief that he did not need to beat about the bush.

'I'm sorry,' he said. 'I'm truly sorry. If I thought there was the least chance of keeping this quiet I wouldn't tell you, but—' He was licking his lower lip and she wanted to scream at him to hurry. 'It seems that your husband kept . . . shared . . . well, there was a woman who was at the flat frequently. The old lady who lives on the ground floor thought they were husband and wife. She didn't recognise Michael; they gave her some story about living in the Home Counties and needing a *pied-à-terre* in town.' He waited for her to comment but she was silent. Inside her head was an image of a carousel: 'Round and round for ever and ever.' She was going mad . . . or else Lambert was.

He spoke again. 'We don't know who she was. There's a vague description; it could fit anyone. They avoided contact as much as they could, but the flat was obviously used by two people . . .'

She heard her own voice, high but unbelievably calm. 'Was my husband in bed when they found him?' And knew from the way Lambert's gaze dropped that he had been. She almost began to laugh then, all the unbearable tension of the last thirty-six hours bubbling up until she could hardly contain herself. She had heard of it before, lovers betrayed by a heart that gave out at the height of passion – everyone had a story about it. 'Michael, Michael.' She thought of the times he had kissed her perfunctorily at bedtime before turning his back; she thought of their love-making, never orgiastic, at least not for a long time. And now Michael had died for love of another woman.

'Was she a prostitute?'

Gavin Lambert leant forward, his face anxious. 'I don't know. You realise how important it is to keep this quiet. I'm sorry, but we've had so many . . . there's been too much——' He was seeking a euphemism for sleaze and they both knew it. 'If we can keep this as low-profile as possible. I know we can count on you — your part is crucial now.' Laughter gurgled in her throat. They wanted her to make an appearance as a loyal wife. Like all the other wronged political wives she must stand by her man for the sake of the party.

'I think I'd like to lie down for a while,' she said out loud. 'Perdy will see you out.' She held out her hand in a gesture of dismissal and turned her face to the window as he left the room.

At half-past-ten Claire swallowed the two sleeping tablets prescribed by the doctor and went dutifully to her lonely bed.

She had refused her friends' offers to stay with her overnight, knowing that each of them had responsibilities at home — Debbo to her family and Perdy to her work. 'No, I've got my parents. I'm not on my own. I'll be OK.' She had smiled to show how grateful she was and how great her need of them was. 'Not that I won't be glad to see you whenever you can make it—'

Perdy had nodded understanding and Deborah had given her a bear-hug and whispered, 'Round first thing, Cleo. You can count on it.'

Sleep must have come instantly for she could scarcely remember climbing under the duvet when she awoke, dry-mouthed, in the early hours — her heart thudding in her chest, aware that something terrible had happened because the light was on, but unable to remember what it was until her hand strayed to the cold, unoccupied side of the bed. She cried then, turning her face into the pillow, wiping her nose on the back of her hand until it became a struggle to breathe through choked nostrils and she was forced to sit up and ferret for tissues on the bedside table.

It was then that she encountered the card the journalist had given her yesterday. She had thrown it down without looking at it when she took off her coat. Now she read it, remembering the bulky figure, the rather squashed face that had not been eager and vicious like the others but kinder and even slightly embarrassed by the furore. His name was Jake Dennehy and he worked for the *Globe*. There was a telephone and fax number on the card but she would never use them. She dropped the card into the waste-paper basket and lay down again.

For the next few hours she dozed and cried alternately, falling deeply asleep again only when daylight streamed through the curtains and life started up in the street outside. She was woken by her father tapping on her door, a cup of tea in his hand. As usual, he looked immaculate, his pyjama collar tucked neatly into the neck of his Liberty dressing-gown.

Claire struggled up in bed, trying to sound grateful, thinking as she did so, how sweet oblivion had been. 'Have the papers come?' She reached for a bed-jacket, feeling a sudden chill in the air, anxious to see if there were any details on the mystery woman.

'Sing out if you want another cup.' He was turning to leave, ignoring her question about the papers.

'I want the papers, Daddy. I'll come and get them.'
She was half out of bed when he spoke.

'I wish you wouldn't, Claire. It's all cheap stuff. I
don't know why you order tabloids. They shouldn't be
encouraged.'

Michael had had all the papers delivered so that
he could scour them for political comment. Normally
Claire skimmed through one or two of them. Today
she worked her way through four tabloids and two
broadsheets as well as the *Guardian*. There were
discreet items in the weightier papers: 'MP's death under
investigation', or 'Speculation mounts'. The tabloids had
a field day. Michael's life was there in fine detail, including childhood photographs she had never seen. There
was a picture of him laughing with fellow students
in his Cambridge days, fighting his first unsuccessful
by-election, and caught at a party with a pretty girl
called Karen Bensen, whose name Claire had never
heard before. As she looked at the picture she heard
the front doorbell ring and the slip-slop of her father's
leather slippers as he crossed the hall to answer it. She
read on: tales of other untimely parliamentary deaths,
speculation about possible candidates to fill the vacancy
caused by Michael's death, a suggestion in the *Mirror*
that MI5 were looking into the case. Most hurtful of
all, a description of herself as a 'low-profile wife who
played little or no part in constituency affairs'.

There were veiled suggestions of sexual impropriety
in the newspapers, and mention of his 'close friendship'
with Gavin Close, 'the property speculator who shared

45

his digs in Cambridge'. As far as Claire knew there had been little or no contact with Gavin for the last two years . . . or more . . . ever since the bottom had dropped out of the property market, really. They were on a wild-goose chase if they wanted to accuse Michael of a homosexual relationship with Gavin, who had had a string of live-in girlfriends throughout the time Claire had known him. She turned the page to see her own face staring out at her, in an unflattering picture which showed her looking glum and unresponsive at a charity affair at the Barbican. There was a brief description of her childhood and mention of her 'military background'. She sighed, thinking of her mother's reaction. Last night she had patted Claire on the arm and urged her to be strong. 'It's unfortunate,' she'd said, 'but we must make the best of it——'

Claire picked up another paper. 'MP in love-nest riddle' ran the headline. How did you make the best of that?

The bell rang again in the hall and she strained her ears. It might be Debbo or better still, Perdy; she loved her friends equally but Perdy was more of a protector. This time she heard her mother's footsteps in the hall, a brief conversation and then the door closing and her mother receding towards the kitchen.

The bell rang three times while she bathed and dressed and when at last she emerged it was to find the house full of flowers. 'I've put all the cards on Michael's desk,' her father said, 'and they're listed here.' He tapped a small, hardbacked notebook. So there was a dossier, one of her father's meticulous briefs, to be pored over and ticked off, phase by phase. 'I've listed condolences by post separately. The telephone calls are separate too. A printed card will do for most of them but some will require a letter. No hurry just yet.' He was trying to be gentle but she knew the score. He would draw up plans: Phase one, Phase two, with an ETC (estimated time of completion) for each one. He had done it for her twenty-first and for her wedding. Now he was doing it for her widowhood and she would be chivvied and pushed until he could draw a neat line underneath a completed operation.

'Perhaps you should look at some of them now,' her mother said. Outside the sun was shining and Claire longed to be out in the park, scuffing leaves under her feet, enjoying the crisp autumn colours of the trees, feeling fresh, clean air on her cheeks. Instead, she was a prisoner.

The bell rang again. 'That will be Adam,' her father said, but it was Deborah who came in, her face flushed above her polo-necked sweater, odd tendrils of hair escaping from her cottage loaf. Claire felt relieved at the sight of her. Dearest untidy Debbo, she would take care of things.

It was Deborah who eased the meeting with Adam, drawing him over the threshold and beaming all round as she did so. Claire had never felt close to the eldest of her brothers and since he had gone to France to take up his post as military attaché at the Embassy in Paris they had exchanged nothing but the statutory cards at

Christmas and on birthdays. 'Well,' he said when they had shared a brief embrace, 'this is a bad business, old girl.'

'It's good of you to come.'

'Not at all. Least I could do. I spoke to the others last night. They send all their love and that sort of thing. Peter can't get away and Gerald couldn't get here in time for the funeral but Ian hopes to be here if he can once we know the day.' He glanced at his father. 'Any nearer a definite arrangement?' They looked at one another but no answer was given or demanded.

Debbo appeared with tea and as she was pouring it the Golds arrived, Sorrel leading the way in a shocking-pink suede coat that must have cost thousands but which caused Mrs Halcrow's eyebrows to disappear into the careful waves of her coiffure.

'Good girl,' Sammy said as he hugged her. 'Good girl.' His voice was thick with emotion and Claire could see he was genuinely upset for her.

'Listen,' Sorrel said, kissing Claire and then holding her at arm's length. 'You're not to worry about the collection. We can work to your schedule, when you're ready.' Claire heard her mother's faint gasp of disapproval, and felt rather than saw her father's frown. They were wondering how the Golds could speak of work at such a time but she understood. Few people knew how to deal with death, except to mutter 'Sorry' or 'I know how you feel.' And some people could not even manage that, so they talked of anything and everything, as long as it was not death itself.

Debbo handed out cups and Sammy tried hard to make conversation with Claire's parents but it was an uphill struggle. They were using their Wimbledon technique, patting each conversational ball back but serving no balls of their own. Adam sat silently in a chair by the window, feet neatly together, hands resting on the arms of his chair.

'When you feel like it,' Sammy said at last, 'come and stay. We could go somewhere even . . . Sorrel loves a break.' Claire smiled and nodded. He meant to be kind but she could not see a time when she would ever be able to relax, to have a break. All she could see ahead was further bleakness. 'I don't understand,' she thought. 'This is happening to someone else . . . not to me.'

Sorrel was glancing at her Gucci wristwatch when Chief Inspector Maynard arrived. The Golds stood up, speaking in unison as they often did. 'We must go. But remember, Claire, remember what we said. You've got our number.' She embraced them both and walked with them to the door.

'I have to be brave,' she thought, knowing that when she turned back into the room her family would close in, anxious to hear every word the Inspector said. Across the room Debbo hovered, anxious, but she did not have Perdy's panache when it came to manipulating people. 'I have to do it myself,' Claire thought and lifted her chin.

'Would you come into my bedroom, Inspector? I'd like to hear what you've discovered.' Adam was rising to his feet, moving forward as she had known he would.

'It's all right, Adam,' she said. 'I'll be perfectly OK on my own. In fact I'd prefer it.' She saw her brother's expression harden, sensed her mother's little moue of disapproval, and then she was in her bedroom and the Inspector was moving to the chair he had occupied yesterday. Claire sat down on the dressing-table stool and gave him her full attention. The sooner it was over, the better.

'We have the post-mortem results,' he said. 'It's as we expected . . . a cerebral aneurysm. They say it could have happened at any time. It's a tragic thing but not as uncommon as you might believe — if it's any consolation, the pathologist thinks that if your husband had survived there would have been severe disability. As your husband wasn't under the care of a doctor — he hadn't visited his GP for some time apparently — I'm afraid there must be an inquest but it will be a mere formality. There's no need for you to attend, unless you wish to be there, of course.' His tone implied that no one in their right mind would wish to attend an inquest unless forced to do so but Claire had made up her mind.

'I want to be there. I want to hear for myself.' She half turned to look at the photos on the surface of her dressing-table. Michael smiling, Michael squinting into the sun, Michael reflective, thinking he was unobserved. And at least one of them must be of Michael lying through his teeth. How long had he lied to her? And why?

She turned back to the Inspector. 'Had my husband

had sex prior to his death, Inspector? I believe they can tell these things.' She saw the shock on his face, shock and distaste in equal measure. Nice women were not supposed to be up-front about matters like these.

'Yes,' he said slowly. 'There was evidence of recent sexual intercourse.'

'Was the woman there when he died?'

'We'll never know that, Mrs Griffin. Unless she comes forward, of course. Perhaps she was there and took fright when she saw it was serious. Perhaps she'd left before he became ill.'

'Was she the woman who called in?'

'I think so. But again we can't be sure. I don't suppose you have any idea of the woman's identity?' Claire shook her head. 'No,' he said, 'I didn't think you would.'

He stood up, turning his braided cap round and round in his hands. 'If I may give you some advice, I'd try not to think too much about it. It doesn't do in my experience.' He cleared his throat. 'I'm going to have a word with the Press boys as I go out. I'll see if I can get rid of them for you. In the meantime, take it easy. I'll ring you as soon as we have a date and time for the inquest.'

'Thank you.' She walked with him to the front door, sensing the tension in the room. They would have to know sometime – it might as well be now. Closing the door she walked to the sideboard. 'Time for a drink, I think.' She poured whisky for the men and for herself, sherry for her mother and gin and tonic for Deborah, proud of her steady hand.

'I expect you'd like to know about the post-mortem. It was a cerebral aneurysm: a congenital weakness in an artery in the brain. It was probably best he didn't survive. There was a woman there with him . . . probably until he took ill.'

'I hope it's not going to be sordid.' Her mother spoke absently, almost to herself. Someone was laughing – she could hear them quite distinctly from the other side of the room.

But it was *her* face that Adam hit clinically and with little force. 'Now, now, Claire,' he said mildly. 'That'll be enough of that.'

They sipped their drinks for a little while, some of them, including Claire, accepting the refills Debbo pressed on them. As she filled Claire's glass she bent to whisper, 'Perdy's coming at twelve-thirty. Keep your pecker up till then.'

In fact Perdy arrived at twelve-fifteen and before leaving for chambers again she managed to ease the Halcrow family out to a taxi to buy Claire a suitable hat for the funeral and have a few hours of freedom. 'Debbo and I will hold the fort,' she said reassuringly. 'Cleo will be fine with us.'

When the three of them were alone she topped up their glasses and listened, arms round her knees, as Claire repeated the Inspector's news. 'Will the woman's name come out?' she asked, when she was finished.

'I think so,' Perdy said. 'They'll have to say how they found Michael, what the state of the flat was, that sort of thing. And as it wasn't his principal residence there'll be evidence of how long he occupied it, who else was there. They'll try to find the woman; they'll need her evidence, if possible. You can imagine how it'll be — but I'll be there, Cleo, whenever it is. That's a promise.'

'So will Hugh and I — he's coming round later,' Debbo grinned. 'He's always had a soft spot for you, Cleo. He'd've come before now but we knew it would be hectic. Now, let me get rid of all this.' She began to gather up the cups and glasses and convey them to the kitchen, waving aside their offers of help.

'I've got to go, Cleo darling.' Perdy was shrugging back into her coat. 'I've got a GBH at Bow Street tomorrow and I've got to do some prep. What would you like to do tonight . . . what will the family be doing?'

They agreed that she would ring at five-thirty and they'd make arrangements then. 'Stick it out,' Perdy said as she let herself out of the front door. 'And don't try to make sense of it, Cleo. Not yet. There's no sense to be had.'

Claire went into the kitchen, anxious to help, but Debbo was up to her elbows in suds, the radio burbling on the window-sill beside her. 'I don't need help. Honestly, almost done. Why don't you go and have a long, lazy bath?'

But it was to the bedroom Claire went, shutting the door behind her with relief that she was at last alone, free even of Deborah. She opened the wardrobe door and began to flick through the clothes hanging there. She would need something subdued for the inquest, even more subdued for the funeral. She picked out a charcoal wool suit and a navy coat-dress. Her mother was buying her a hat but it would probably be black. Her only black suit had braid trimming and huge gold buttons. Michael had bought it for her in Nice, in a boutique behind the Promenade des Anglais. He had hated the careful country clothes her mother had picked out for her trousseau and the Ungaro suit had been a protest. She had worn it at the Negresco that night, her hair piled on top of her head, gold studs in her ears and ridiculously high-heeled black strappy sandals on her feet. She had walked through the salon with its glittering sofas, feeling grown-up for the first time in her life, and they had drunk champagne and emerged to see the moon reflecting on the water like a pathway to heaven. Or Africa, whichever you preferred.

Now she held the black crêpe suit at arm's length, wondering if she could wear it to the funeral of the man who had picked it out for her and died in the arms of another woman. 'I am doubly bereft,' she thought. For betrayal was another kind of death. She put the suit back in the wardrobe and walked to the window. There was only one man opposite, lounging against a wall, a camera slung over his shoulder, and two women who huddled together beside a car. Soon there would be no one. Someone else's tragedy would hold centre stage. She let the curtain fall back into place and went to lie down on her bed, hoping to find some ease for eyes that still burnt in their sockets like twin coals.

5

Claire had avoided pills for the last two nights, preferring a sleepless night to the muzziness that came out of a bottle, so she was awake when daylight infiltrated the curtains and the World Service gave way to national news. She listened to bulletin after bulletin, half fearing mention of the inquest on Michael, half affronted that something so traumatic did not merit inclusion. For the last two days she had received an endless stream of condolences, in person or by phone. Today she hoped to be left alone.

At six-thirty she crossed to the window and peeped behind the curtain. There were three of them there already, or perhaps they had been there all night. The woman was huddled into her long, hooded coat and looked the picture of misery and Claire felt a small stab of satisfaction. They deserved to suffer. She remembered the journalist with the kind face, the one who had pressed his card into her hand as she came back from the police mortuary. He had not reappeared.

Perhaps he had lost interest, or perhaps he was relying on her turning to him. If so, he would wait a long time, a hell of a long time.

She realised that her fingers had curled into her palms so tightly that relaxing them was painful. She tried to remember far-off Yoga lessons . . . what did you do to relax? In the end she screwed up her shoulders and then let them go, doing it several times without any noticeable effect. 'I want to walk in the park,' she thought. 'I want to walk on and on and on and leave all this behind me.' But when she had suggested going out yesterday her mother had said, 'I don't think so, dear. Not just yet.'

She turned back into the room, feeling like a prisoner whose only escape would be to be conveyed swiftly to an inquest courtroom. After that, back to seclusion. She put her hand to her mouth, suddenly aware that it wouldn't end with the inquest nor even with the funeral. It would go on for ever, the whole of the rest of her life.

It was too much. She knew she ought to go to the kitchen, make tea, eat a slice of toast to quell the rumbling of her stomach . . . but the urge to get out of the house overcame her. She scrabbled through drawers and wardrobes, looking for anything behind which she could hide. In the end she used Michael's track suit, hauling up the bottoms and taking in the slack at her waist with a leather belt. She put on several sweaters to bulk out the top and crammed a striped woollen ski-hat on to her head. When her hair was tucked up inside and a muffler crammed into the track-suit neck she looked asexual and unrecognisable.

She practised walking in front of the cheval mirror, imitating the style of boxers she had seen on TV, bandy-legged and ducking and weaving. When she was satisfied she could carry it off, she picked up her keys, thrust her hands into the slanting pockets of the track-suit top and let herself quietly on to the communal landing. There was a side door to the flats but the caretaker had the only key. She would have to use the front door, but if she was quick enough, and kept up the pose of the dedicated runner, she would probably be round the corner and out of sight before the watchers were fully aware of her. And if it came to the worst and they spotted her, none of them looked up to a chase.

She gave thanks for her own fitness regime, infrequent but thorough, as she pattered down the stairs and drew back the bolt. The next moment she was out on the steps and sprinting for the corner and Kensington Church Street. She dared not look back but there was no shout of recognition and no sound of pursuit. She was out! She raised her face to the weak early-morning sunshine and made for Holland Park.

She ran for half an hour, sometimes pausing to catch her breath, sometimes letting out a sob about nothing in particular and everything in general. At the beginning she looked over her shoulder frequently, half expecting to see the pack in full pursuit. There was no one except for solitary men on their way to a day's work or the odd runner, head down, breathing according to age and fitness. One man, who looked at least seventy, passed her, elbows tucked in, his walk the waddle of the seasoned marathon runner. 'We must be mad,' he said cheerfully and she smiled, thinking his words deliciously funny because they had nothing to do with death.

In the end, though, she had to turn for home, keys at the ready so that she wouldn't be trapped on the steps with the Press at her heels. She had almost reached the last corner before her own street when she saw a man standing under a plane tree, hands in his pockets, almost as if he was expecting her. It was the journalist from the day of her return from the mortuary. What was his name? Dennehy, Jake Dennehy.

For a second she hesitated, wondering if she should turn on her heel and jog away. But he looked wide awake and fit and she had no energy left for a chase. The belt at her waist had slackened and the track-suit bottoms were creeping down over her trainers. Besides, why should she run away from him? She thought of his effrontery the day he had followed her up the steps of her own house and mouthed 'When you're ready' at her, as though confiding in him was a foregone conclusion. She avoided his eye and kept on going but when she drew abreast of him he fell into step beside her.

'How are you, Mrs Griffin?' She ignored him but he went on as though he'd received a courteous reply. 'I hope you will contact me, when you're ready. I'm

Dennehy and I'm with the *Globe*. You've got my card.
I don't distort, I don't sensationalise. And I can keep the
rest of them off your back — remember that.' Without
waiting for a reply he slowed his pace and let her pull
ahead. She was glad of an excuse to feel angry, clenching
her teeth, her mind seething with resentment. But when
she had braved the larger crowd around the steps and
was safely back in her bedroom she took out a pen and
wrote down his name and the name of his paper, just in
case she forgot it.

She could hear someone in the other bathroom, Adam
probably. She cast off the track suit and assorted
sweaters and went to run her own bath, glad that the
flat boasted two bathrooms, one of them safely inside
her own bedroom.

She lay in the scented water for as long as she could,
willing it not to grow cold and force her out to face the
day. The inquest was timed for eleven-thirty and her
father and Adam had insisted on accompanying her.
She closed her eyes, picturing them both immaculate
in their British warms, black ties and shoes the colour
of burnished chestnuts. Both faces would be impassive,
the slightest switch of a muscle instantly repressed. Her
mother would see them off looking equally immaculate
in twin-set and pearls or perhaps a neat Peter Pan collar,
her hands lightly folded and tremorless. 'I am flesh
of their flesh,' she thought, 'but we have nothing in
common, nothing in common at all.'

As she reached for the soap and began to scrub she
acknowledged the fact that her family belonged to a

distant past, a Raj that had no place in the 1990s. The Halcrow men had been in the Army for five generations and had mostly married daughters of other soldiers. But the way things were going there would be no certain military future for the next generation. 'What will they do?' she thought with wry amusement. 'What on earth will they do then?'

They were there when she emerged from her room, dressed as she had imagined, even to the British warms folded over a chair.

'Have you had breakfast?' her mother enquired and Claire lied cheerfully.

'Hours ago. Did you find everything you needed?' Her mother's resigned smile implied all kinds of unfilled needs but Claire was past caring. Besides, Adam was clearing his throat so something ominous was due.

'We thought it best to engage a solicitor, Claire. In the circumstances. Father spoke to Angus Harper . . . he recommended a London firm. They're thoroughly reliable. It's a Keith James . . . he'll meet us at the court.'

'I wish you'd asked me.' As she heard her own words she despised herself for their weakness. 'How bloody dare you?' was what she wanted to say. 'Butt out of my life . . . Sod off . . . Get a life.' And all she could say was 'I wish you'd asked me.'

'You must be guided by the men,' her mother reproved her. 'Now that Michael——' Her words trailed away.

'I've got Perdy. She's a barrister. And why do

I need anyone else? It's an inquest, mother. Not a trial.'

'That remains to be seen.' Her father's voice was gruff but when she turned to face him he looked away. It was her mother who spoke.

'Your father and Adam . . . and I agree with them . . . we are afraid that things will be said, damaging things. This James man will keep a watching brief. We thought you'd be grateful. I hope you're not going to be difficult.'

There it was, the anthem of her childhood. 'Don't be difficult.' She had felt herself to be a problem child, for incipient 'difficulty' had lurked at every corner. She felt the old familiar desire to shrink away, to remove herself so that she presented a difficulty to no one, but it was not so easy in her own home. She was trying to decide what to say when the bell rang. 'I'll go.' It was a relief to beat them to the door and let in a welcome outsider.

Gavin Lambert was soberly dressed as usual but this time he carried a document case. 'All right?' he asked, sounding genuinely caring. Their eyes met and she saw concern there but the next moment he was advancing into the room and greeting the others. 'Have you told her?' His words were addressed to Adam and uttered *sotto voce* but she heard just the same.

'Told me what?'

Her father crossed to the wing chair and motioned to her mother to sit down. Adam took up a stance with one arm on the mantelpiece, one immaculately shod foot crossed over the other. They were arranging themselves for conference and Claire bowed to it, feeling for a chair and sinking into it. Eyes met around the room and then, as if by unspoken agreement, Lambert spoke.

'It's nothing important . . . well, not momentous. We, that is Central Office, feel there should be a statement after the inquest. It's in your interest; if we give them something they may go away. I've prepared a short piece—' He reached for the document case with one hand, pulling reading glasses from an inner pocket with the other.

'How can you have prepared something? We don't know what the inquest will uncover?' She sounded braver than she felt.

'Michael's death was due to natural causes, Mrs Griffin. The verdict will be just that.' He paused. 'The various other matters — what may be discussed during the proceedings — all that will be irrelevant to the verdict.' He produced a single sheet and began to read aloud.

'Mrs Griffin and her family wish—'

'Do you want me to sign that?' This time her voice was harsh. 'Because I won't . . . not till I've heard what they have to say.'

'There's no need for you to sign anything. It's not a legal document, Mrs . . . Claire. We thought, that is, I would be grateful if you would be there when I give this to the Press. We won't ask anything of you except that. It would make a difference if you were seen to be—' He hesitated.

'Bearing up?' She was smiling now but not amused. 'That's the tradition, isn't it? Loyal wife smiling bravely. Now is the time for all brave women to come to the aid of the party? What would *The Times* do without us?'

'Now you're being foolish, Claire.' Her mother placed her hands on the arms of her chair, as though ready to lever herself to her feet. 'Everyone is being so supportive. Surely you could do one small thing in return.'

She felt the weight of their disapproval, four pairs of eyes united in distaste. She wanted to argue but it was too much. She stood up and turned to the side table. 'I'm going to have a drink. If anyone else wants one, help yourselves.'

The unaccustomed whisky was still fiery on her tongue when Perdy arrived with Deborah in tow. Claire felt an overwhelming sense of relief at their appearance, especially when Perdy took in the tense atmosphere and flashed a smile around the room. 'I want to talk to Claire for a little while. I'm sure you'll understand. It's marvellous that you're all here for her but I do want her to know that Deborah and I are behind her . . . we won't be more than a few moments.'

The next moment she had whisked Claire into the bedroom and was pulling the door to behind her. 'What's up? You look like a terrified rabbit, Cleo. Are they giving you a hard time?'

'They want to put out a statement. All of them, not just the man from Central Office.'

'And they want you to substantiate it?' Perdy grimaced. 'I thought they'd do this; they've got to keep the lid on, Cleo, and it's not in your best interests for it to become a running story. I don't fancy their chances of damping it down, not unless there's something else – a fresh hare. All the same, unless they want you to back up a deliberate untruth, I'd do it.'

Debbo appeared in the doorway, a glass in each hand. 'Do you want a refill, Cleo darling?'

Claire shook her head. 'I'm OK.'

'Sherry,' Debbo said, handing Perdy a glass. 'Is that OK?' Perdy nodded absently.

'They are going to put out a statement.' She was obviously confirming something she had suggested to Debbo earlier. 'And Cleo has to back it up.'

'Well,' Debbo sounded placatory. 'If it puts an end to all the Press fever I suppose it's worth it. What do they want you to do?'

'Put a brave face on it,' Claire said. 'But on what? They don't seem to want to know what happened.'

'They do know, darling.' Debbo sighed and made a glum face. 'It's awful but it's pretty straightforward. It's just unfortunate that something that would have happened sooner or later happened in, well, unfortunate circumstances. It's hell for you, but it's no big deal, is it?'

'Come on, Debbo.' Perdy was scornful. 'It's not Joe Bloggs we're talking about. It's the PPS to the Minister of Agriculture, Fisheries and Food. On the Richter scale it's not Profumo but it's not inconsequential.' She put an index finger to her mouth and pushed against her white teeth.

'The thing is, will Cleo appearing calm things down or excite them?' She smiled ruefully at her friend. 'You make a lovely victim, darling, all eyes and wistfulness. On the whole, I think it's better you show — if they think you're going under they'll press you deliberately. A second victim makes a better story. Come on, where's your blusher; we'll be there and it'll only take a minute. I'll go out there now — Debs will stay with you — and make sure they keep it brief. And don't be downtrodden with your folks. I know they're intimidating but they'll be out of here soon.'

'I've said you're coming to me after the funeral.' Debbo reached out a comforting hand. 'They were discussing whether they should stay or you should go back with them so I jumped in. I hope it's OK with you.'

'Thank you.' Claire's words were heartfelt. 'It'll only be for a day or two . . . I'll be all right on my own—'

'Well, we'll see. Now, where's this make-up?' As Debbo began to rummage on the dressing-table Perdy quit the bedroom and Claire felt a glow of comfort. If she had her friends she could make it through the next few days.

Her new-found confidence evaporated as the inquest unfolded. She allowed herself to be ushered to a seat, shook the solicitor's limp hand and listened intently as the witnesses came forward. The bulk of the evidence came from Chief Inspector Maynard. He told of an early-morning call to the Police Emergency line. The caller, a woman, had not been traced but the information given had been acted upon and found to be correct.

The body of the deceased had been found unclothed in a bed in the flat in Kennerley Street. The state of the bed suggested there had been another occupant and traces of semen had been found upon the body and the sheets. The body had been discovered at seven-fifteen and the medical examiner believed the death to have taken place at least ten hours before.

'In other words,' Claire thought, 'Michael died before I expected him home.' She listened numbly as the Inspector told of her identification of the body and of his subsequent enquiries at Kennerley Street. Neighbours had told of a woman who frequented the flat but descriptions were vague and enquiries as to her identity had so far been fruitless. 'Did they really look?' Claire wondered. 'Or are they quite happy to let it go?' After all, it wasn't murder. It wasn't even a crime.

The pathologist gave evidence then, talking at length of congenital defects.

'So the deceased could have died at any time?' the coroner enquired.

'Yes.' The pathologist was Asian and earnest. 'He was, so to speak, under sentence of death.'

'He might have died in my arms,' Claire thought, but when she tried to remember their love-making the image failed to materialise. Had they ever been real lovers? Had she ever really known the man who had been her husband for eight years?

As the voices droned on, she tried to visualise him. She had loved him most in the mornings, when his hair was rumpled, his chin stubbled and he had begged for soldiers to dunk in his three-minute egg. And she had loved to listen to him when he became impassioned about a cause or a political argument . . . except that sometimes he had chided her for not joining in, counter-arguing, playing devil's advocate.

'Don't just sit there,' he had said once, when she refused to come down on one side or the other. And yet he had chosen her because of her gravity; he had told her that on their wedding night. 'I saw you there, like a quiet little sister of charity, and I knew I had to have you, there and then.' She realised she was smiling at the memory and hastily schooled her face before anyone could see and misconstrue.

When a verdict of death by natural causes was brought in she accepted the whispered condolences and painful arm-squeezes of those around her and followed Gavin Lambert out into the sunlight, to stand by while he expressed sorrow at her loss, gratitude to those who had helped to bring matters to a conclusion and a heartfelt plea for the widow to be left in peace.

A forest of arms protected her as she stepped into the car Lambert had provided, Debbo and Perdy squeezing in either side of her, sitting forward so that she was partially screened from prying eyes.

It took only a few hours for an early copy of the

Standard to blaze the trail. 'Who is mystery woman?' the headline blared. 'MP dies in bed with mystery companion. Widow bemused by inquest shock. Turn to page seven.' There was a blurred picture of her, looking doe-eyed and startled, turning to look over her shoulder as though desperate for support.

6

At the funeral Claire felt suddenly tranquil. It was almost over, the arranging, the decision-making, the endless detail, the speculation. The wondering would always be there, the curiosity about the woman who had shared Michael's bed on the last day of his life, but the need to manage would be over. She let her eyelids droop as the vicar droned on about achievement and public service. Closed, her eyes felt hot and dry but the pain was more bearable than watching sun stream through stained glass, red and blue and gold. She pictured the pews, filled mostly with acquaintances or colleagues, mourners out of duty rather than from choice — and not even many of them. Most people would wait for the memorial service, when the notoriety had evaporated. The Minister had swept in with his entourage, all of them murmuring soothing nothings, each with an eye on his or her watch.

On her right sat her family and Michael's cousins; on her left Perdy, Debbo and Hugh. Behind them were the Golds, looking less confident than usual in an alien church. It was Hugh who had held her elbow as she made her way into the church and his whispered 'All right, old thing?' had been a comfort.

Before they left the flat her mother had said, 'Be brave, dear,' in brisk tones and her father had added, 'Soon be over.'

Adam had let the curtain fall back into place and turned back into the room. 'Watch for them, Claire. Don't give them a inch. Keep your chin up – you know how they twist things.'

So she had composed her face, allowing no emotion to show, and in the end the Press had parted to let her through, as though the wearing of widow's weeds was an 'open sesame'.

They had their plans laid for the aftermath of the funeral. Last night Perdy had carried in an empty suitcase and left with it full. Clothes and toilet articles were waiting in Debbo's guest-room, to which Claire would escape as soon as she decently could.

She tried to picture the scene back at the flat. Who would come home with her for the smoked salmon, the canapés, the excellent wine arranged by Adam? The feast that uniformed caterers were even now arranging? Her friends would be there to back her up; Stephanie Routh probably, although she wouldn't stay; Gavin Lambert and at least two of the Conservative group; Pamela Corby probably – tall, elegant now in grey; and Sir Harry Cox, whose constituency adjoined Michael's. Their neighbours from the mansion block would be there, the representatives of the Constituency Party and of course her family. About twenty in all, twenty hands to shake, at least ten cheeks to kiss, ten voices to murmur, 'Anything we can do . . . you only have to ask.' It had gone on for six days, only a few more hours to go now.

In the event, in addition to her family and close friends, six people returned to the flat. Stephanie Routh was there, looking unusually well-groomed and rather beautiful, but she kept one eye on the clock all the while. She stood uneasily alongside Pamela Corby, the most glamorous of the Conservative women Members, elegant today in black barathea with a white lace stock at the neck.

Maeve, Michael's secretary, moved around the room, her eyes occasionally misty as she tried to do her last duty for her dead employer.

'Sit down,' Claire told her. 'There are people to see to things. Relax . . . the last few days must have been hard on you.' Maeve smiled gratefully but kept on her peregrination as Claire chatted to Madelena Dimambro, her neighbour from the floor above. She was unusually fair for an Italian, with an attractive broken accent and today she was full of sympathy for Claire.

'You are so . . .' she breathed in and rolled her eyes. '. . . so brave. Good girl – and this will pass. Everything passes.' Her eyes rolled heavenwards and Claire knew she was referring to her own divorce.

'I know,' she said. 'I know.' She had used that

71

phrase a dozen times today. It seemed to cover every eventuality.

Alison Morris, who had succeeded Claire's father as Constituency Chairperson, was deep in conversation with Gavin Lambert, no doubt discussing Michael's successor. Claire was glad she did not have to cosset a woman she had always disliked. 'I don't have to keep her sweet any longer,' she thought. That was a tiny bonus but a bonus nevertheless.

Alison was doing most of the talking and Gavin Lambert had the slightly punch-drunk air of a man under too much pressure. That was hardly surprising. There had not been a day since Michael's death when the papers had not been full of scandal or the rumour of more sleaze. Two government ministers had quit, one almost as soon as the 'cash for questions' row had erupted, another, Neil Hamilton, only today. Details of a £3,300 bill at the Ritz in Paris had been disclosed and Mohamed Al Fayed had threatened to name a Tory Minister who had taken a £500,000 bribe. The whole unsavoury matter had completely overshadowed the Prime Minister's efforts to start a peace dialogue in Northern Ireland, coming as it did in the wake of the doings of Mellor and Milligan and Norris and their ilk. And yet there was idealism in the House. Claire had seen it sometimes in Michael, when he spoke of equality of opportunity and the right to freedom from fear of old age and infirmity.

She smiled when Alison Morris took her leave. She would most probably never see the woman again so she could afford to be civilised. As if Alison had given the lead, the others made their excuses and departed. Gavin Lambert took her on one side before he left. 'You can leave all the practicalities to me. I've taken Michael's address book, your brother gave it to me . . . if I need anything else, I'll let you know.' Brief fury seized Claire. How dare Adam hand over something that now belonged to her? But her anger subsided almost immediately. What did it matter, after all?

Lambert cleared his throat. 'I've left a small parcel in the study, Michael's personal possessions . . . the things he had with him the day he died. There are only small things, his keys, some petty cash, that sort of thing. Maynard gave them to me yesterday.' He took her hand. 'You know where I am if you need me. Let me know where you can be contacted.' A moment later he was gone.

At last, only her parents, Adam, Perdy and Debbo were left. 'Come on then, Cleo,' Perdy said at last. 'Let's get you out of here.' It had all been agreed but still a glance flashed between Adam and her mother.

'Are you sure about this, Claire?' Her mother's voice was cool and she avoided looking at her daughter's friends. 'Surely you'd be better off coming home. Is it fair to Deborah? She has a husband and children to think of, you know.'

'Insensitive bitch.' Claire heard her voice and was seized with terror that she had spoken aloud. But it was all right, no one's eyes had flared alarm, no lips had tightened in disapproval. And mercy of mercies, Debbo was answering the question for her.

'We think the Press would follow her to Yorkshire, Mrs Halcrow, and that would be so awful for you. If she comes to Hugh and me, especially if we can get her there on the QT, well, it'll be easier all round. Just for a few days, until the excitement dies down.' Was that relief in Adam's eye?

'Well,' her father said. 'For a day or two . . . we can review the situation then.'

She changed out of her charcoal suit, hanging it neatly in the wardrobe, knowing she would never, ever wear it again. They had agreed that she should use the jogging device once more but this time Hugh would be waiting in his car outside the park, ready to whisk her away. She found herself giggling at the thought of a James Bond-type chase and tried to subdue the laughter, knowing it would end in tears, but it was too late. She stood there in her ivory slip, holding herself tightly, arms to chest, and let the tears flow. 'What am I crying for?' she thought. 'For the death of a husband, or the betrayal of my trust? For fear of the future, or the memory of the past?' She was making vain efforts to wipe her eyes and make her mind up at the same time when there was a discreet knock and Perdy stepped into the room.

'OK? No, don't apologise. I don't know how you've borne up . . . still, we'll get you to Deb's and if the kiddy-winkies get on your wick, you can come to me. I'd say come now but Debbo's clucking like a mother hen at the thought of cosseting you. I couldn't bear to deprive her. Now, where's this jogging suit?'

She had confessed her early-morning exploit to Deborah and Perdy and they had backed her when Adam pronounced her escape plan 'infantile'. Now, when she was ready, hair tucked out of sight, shoulders hunched, Perdy let out a whistle of approval. 'I wouldn't've believed it, Cleo, you look like a boxer in training. I think you just might get away with it, especially if we arrange a diversion. I've booked a cab for one-thirty, to go to King's Cross. The news-hounds will have a contact in the cab firm . . . if not they'll nobble the driver. We'll keep it ticking over at the kerb and then I'll go out with a suitcase and put it in the cab. I'll turn back as though I'm going to get you and while I'm doing all this you'll come out and jog off up the street. After a little while your parents will come out and get into the cab. With a bit of luck, they'll think you're still in the flat. By the time they twig that you've gone . . . well, it could take two days before they realise you're not here, especially if Debs and I pay the odd visit.'

'Isn't all this a dreadful fag for you?' Claire knew she sounded feeble rather than grateful and Perdy's reaction was swift.

'Horrendous, but I'm loving every minute of it.' She smiled, wrinkling up her eyes. 'You are a clot, Cleo. Firstly, I'd cut off an arm for you, and secondly, it's appealing to my devious side. I love plotting. Now, come and say your goodbyes to the parents. The cab'll be here any moment.'

Her mother tut-tutted at her appearance but no one said anything discouraging. 'Keep in touch,' her father said gruffly. Her mother kissed her cheek and Adam held out his hand.

'We'll all be in touch, Claire. Peter and Rachael want you in Cyprus as soon as you feel up to it.' Claire smiled dutifully at the prospect of a sojourn with her brother and sister-in-law and thanked Adam for coming to lend his support.

'Not at all, least one could do in the circum-stances.' There was a world of meaning in the last three words.

And then Perdy was grasping one of her mother's suitcases and Debbo was leading her out to the landing. 'As soon as I'm through the front door, come down,' Perdy said. 'And don't look at them, just move.' A moment later Debbo was urging her down the stairs and she was out in the street, head down, resisting the impulse to look towards Perdy and the taxi and trying to emulate the loping trot she had used so successfully the last time. There was no furore behind her, no snapping of camera-shutters. She kept on running until she had rounded the corner and crossed the road and could see the red Audi waiting by the kerb, Hugh's eyes looking anxious in the wing mirror as she drew level and reached for the door handle.

'Good girl!' He had started the engine before she drew the door shut behind her and sank into the seat.

It took fifteen minutes to negotiate the traffic and reach the leafy Hampstead street where Hugh and Debbo resided. Hugh drew up at the kerb and switched off the engine.

'There now, let's get you in and put the kettle on. Nothing like a good cup of Darjeeling in a crisis. Not that this is a crisis, not now.' He helped her out of the car and kept hold of her hand. 'It's over now, Claire, the worst part, at least. Time to get your breath. We want you to stay here as long as you choose, and that's not just Debbo's invitation. I want you here — remember that.' She looked up into his nice, freckled face with its slightly crooked nose and kindly eyes.

'Thank you,' she said and let him lead her into the house.

It was pleasant to sit in Debbo's huge, untidy kitchen. It was a long, raftered room, lined with cupboards, china winking behind their leaded-glass fronts. On one wall there was a huge pegboard aflutter with cuttings and memos and children's pictures of 'Mummy and Daddy' and every possible kind of animal.

Hugh had installed Claire on a long, velveteen *chaise longue*, which occupied one wall of the eating section. A brown-and-white spaniel lumbered up to settle at, or rather on, her feet and a white cat wove in and out of the furniture until it deigned to rest on the velvet arm of a chair, from which it could gaze down at her from blue and inscrutable eyes.

'Tea,' Hugh said, shedding his jacket and scarf. 'I shouldn't think Debs will be long.' He chuckled.

'It's rather fun, this cloak-and-dagger stuff. I was all prepared for a car chase. I had my get-away planned – still, more tranquil for you that we weren't pursued and that's the important thing.'

Claire watched him as he got the tea together. 'How nice he is,' she thought. 'How normal and how nice. Deborah is lucky.' Somewhere far off she could hear children's voices so Daniel must be home from school. He was almost nine, Fiona was five and Emlyn two. Deborah was lucky indeed.

They were drinking hot, strong tea when Debbo arrived. 'It went like a charm,' she said gleefully. 'Your Ma and Pa went off in the taxi and the news-hounds looked a little disappointed but they don't suspect a thing. They're still there, glued to the door. Of course Perdy had to ice the cake . . . you know what she's like. "Why don't you leave her alone?" she said as we left and glanced back at the windows of the flat, as though we'd just left you there.'

She set her cup back on the saucer and leant towards Claire, who was trying to smile at her friend's enthusiasm. 'Are you OK, Cleo? I'm rattling on as though it was one huge game but it isn't fun for you.'

'No,' Hugh said. 'And I've set you down in all this chaos. Let's move into the living-room.'

'No,' Claire said. 'Please, it's lovely here.' It was pleasant to sit in a room redolent with the odours of spices, drying herbs strung from a beam, fruit and vegetables glowing in corners, in other words a picture of plenty, and above all of normal living.

'All right,' Deborah said soothingly. 'We'll go up and sort out your room when we've had this tea and then you shall sit here while I make dinner. And don't get uptight about eating. Just take what you want . . . we'll be too busy pigging it to notice what you eat.' She looked down at her waistline. 'I must do something about a diet soon, but not now. Food's so gorgeous at this time of year. All that autumn abundance; I love it.'

The children came in then, Emlyn in his nanny's arms, Daniel and Fiona tumbling over one another in their eagerness to greet their guest. Before long Emlyn was cuddled in to Claire's side and Daniel was confiding his pride in his gerbil who had just produced a litter of seven. Claire looked at their eager, enthusiastic faces and felt tears prick her eyes. If she had had a child there would have been reason for living. An hour or so ago she had heard her mother confiding in a fellow mourner how relieved the family were that she was unencumbered by a family. 'At least she can make a new life. She's still young.' She had listened impassively but inside her there had been such a fierce anger that it had threatened to choke her.

By seven o'clock the two youngest children had been bathed and Emlyn was carried in, rosy in his dressing-gown, to be kissed good-night. Half an hour later Claire was allowed to lead Fiona up the wide staircase to a bedroom furnished in polka-dot drapes and crammed with dolls and furry creatures.

'Good-night, Aunt Claire.' The rosy face was held up, mouth pursed for a kiss. Claire bent to oblige, blinking fiercely to discourage tears. 'I'm awfully sad about Uncle Michael.' Fiona was speaking in what she obviously believed was a grown-up way. 'He's with Jesus now so I expect he's all right but I've put him in my prayers.'

'That's nice,' Claire said and smoothed the sheets as the small figure snuggled down.

She grinned up at her aunt. 'Mummy says it's all right to pray in bed. She says God's too sensible to want you to catch a chill on a cold floor.' Her grin displayed both relief and disbelief and Claire found herself smiling back.

'I'm sure your Mummy's right,' she said. 'She usually is.' She switched on the bedside lamp so that she could put off the main light at the door. 'Now, go to sleep. I'll need you to wake me up in the morning.'

On the landing Daniel was lurking. 'Good-night, Aunt Claire. I'm going to read for a while so I'm going to bed now.' He was anxious she should realise that his status as oldest child carried privileges with it and he could stay up if he chose, so Claire nodded.

'Sensible,' she said. 'I'm not going to be late myself. See you in the morning.' As she walked downstairs she felt the strangest mixture of emotions: joy in her friend's possession of such a lovely family, despair that her own life, by comparison, was such a wasteland. 'Today I buried my husband,' she thought and could find no reality in the statement.

They ate in the oak-panelled dining-room, lobster bisque and casseroled lamb followed by redcurrant tart and cream. 'All from the freezer,' Debbo said when Claire expressed amazement. 'I have huge cooking splurges but it comes in handy when I'm short of time. God bless whoever invented refrigeration.'

Hugh brought in coffee and almond biscuits when the meal was over. The dishes were pushed aside and while Hugh popped the tiny sweetmeats into his mouth one after the other, Debbo put her elbows on the table and regarded her friend.

'Well,' she said. 'Do you want to talk or shall we put on some Mozart?'

'Don't let her stampede you,' Hugh said. 'She's bursting with ideas about taking you out of yourself but I've told her you need space.'

Claire smiled at him. 'It's not so much that I need space as that I don't have the faintest idea of what to do next.' She paused. 'I'd like to know more about Michael's death . . . but I don't expect I ever shall.'

'It's best to let it go, Cleo.' Debbo's brow had clouded. 'Why don't you go off somewhere for a while? I know you're not keen on Cyprus but there are lots of people from our year who'd love you to visit. What about Margaret McEnemy? She's in Barbados and she'd smother you with hospitality.'

Claire grimaced. 'I can just imagine. I would like to get away but I don't much want to visit anyone. I've thought about going to the cottage for a while—'

'Not Cumbria in winter.' Hugh and Deborah spoke together. 'And it will be winter by the time you get there,' Hugh continued. 'Far better to go somewhere hot. You could take a villa somewhere — Tuscany, the Algarve — and come to us for Christmas.' His wife frowned at the mention of Christmas.

'Don't wish the year away, darling. Do you want to get right away, Claire? Away from familiar places, I mean?'

Claire nodded. She began to trace a pattern on the polished table, seeing the wood steam over at the trace of her fingertip. 'I'd like to bury myself somewhere . . . the heart of a city maybe, somewhere where I know nobody and no one knows me. I could finish the collection, and by the time I came back everyone would have lost interest. I could make decisions then, about where I'm going to live. What's certain is that I don't need a London flat, a four-bedroomed house in Yorkshire and a cottage in Cumbria. A bed-sit would do me.'

'So you want to disappear for a while,' Debbo said. She pushed up the sleeves of her sweater and sank her chin into her cupped hands. 'I just might have an idea. You might hate it but it's at least worth suggesting.'

'Come on then,' Hugh said impatiently. 'What is it?' Both he and Claire leant forward, pushing cups aside as they did so, fixing their eyes on Debbo's face.

'Well,' she said, enjoying the fact that she was commanding their full attention. 'Remember when I went to that seminar in Leeds and met that nice history don, Celia Davy? She loaned me a paper on Elizabethan attitudes to women when I was writing *Airs and Graces*. Anyway, yesterday I was talking to

her at another seminar, and she told me of a Durham historian who's off to the States this weekend for a lecture
tour and he still hasn't found anyone to sit his animals.'

'In Durham?' Hugh enquired.

'On Palace Green . . . well, almost. Apparently he's
dotty about his dog and cat — well, it may be dogs and
cats — and he's taking a sabbatical to do some lecturing
in the US but he won't put his beloved animals into
kennels. She said he was frantic. He's bound to have
a nice place, you know how these academics live. And
no one would look for you there . . . not in Durham. It
would see you through to Christmas.'

'I don't like animals,' Claire said, but there was a
waver in her voice that spoke of indecision. Before she
mounted the stairs for bed she had agreed that at least
Debbo should find out whether or not there was still
an opening.

In bed, with London quietening down outside her
window, she thought of Durham. There would be
misty lamplight on Palace Green and young voices
and laughter from groups making their way back to
the colleges or to shared flats. The life of the city
would ebb and flow, uncaring of scandal or politicians,
there would be fruit and freshly plucked fowl in the
indoor market and Londonderry on his tongueless horse
presiding over the Market Place. 'I was happy there,'
she thought before she turned on her side and began to
count sheep leaping in a Durham meadow.

7

B y the following morning, everything was arranged.
'He's going tonight,' Deborah said when she came
back from making the call. 'He almost wept with relief
when I told him you'd come. He was ready to call the
whole thing off because he couldn't get someone he
trusted. He's leaving today. I said you'd been brought
up with animals and were almost a veterinarian . . .
that's what clinched it.'

'I can't stand dogs.' Claire said, suddenly dismayed.
'I wouldn't hurt them but I really don't like them, and
as for knowing how to care for them—'

'Never mind,' Deborah said firmly. 'Ring Hugh if you
get stuck. He knows everything, and if he doesn't know
he'll have a book on it. Apparently there's a char, a
treasure . . . but she has a family so she couldn't look
after them and he wouldn't put them in kennels. There
are two dogs and a cat.'

'They're not Great Danes, are they?' Claire asked
weakly.

'Eat your egg,' Deborah said. 'One's a boxer and the other's a Heinz. The cat's Burmese. But the house . . . it's in North Bailey so it will be gorgeous. God, I envy you – Durham in the autumn with the trees turning on Palace Green and leaves underfoot on the river bank. I'd come with you for two pins. Still, must get back to my manuscript or I'll have to give back the advance.'

'You've been wonderful,' Claire said contritely. 'I hope I haven't caused any problems for you . . . or Perdy.'

'*You* haven't caused anything, darling.' Deborah reached for Claire's face and squeezed it between her palms. 'You are not to blame for any of this, no one is, it's life. Now dip those soldiers and then we'll make plans. We've got to get you there in secret, remember, but Perdy has all that under control. She and Hugh talked on the phone for an hour before breakfast . . . well, twenty minutes anyway. She's coming over this afternoon, to bring some more of your things. In the meantime borrow anything of mine that you won't drown in.'

Claire played with Emlyn before lunch, staying in the garden just in case, although there was no sign of the Press in Deborah's leafy street. In the afternoon Perdy arrived with two cases. 'If I missed anything just say. I rather like slipping in and out of that place as though you were still incarcerated. I turn on the steps and wave back at you – it's enough to bring a tear to the eye.'

They all fell silent then, suddenly realising the

incongruity of making a jape out of the aftermath of tragedy. Even Perdy looked a little abashed but she eventually broke the silence. 'Seen this morning's paper? Another Ritz bill has surfaced. Jonathan Aitken's this time.'

'That's old news.' Deborah made frantic attempts to tuck in a stray bit of hair as she spoke. 'I must get this damned hair sorted, it's driving me mad. The Aitken thing was ages ago. I can remember Hugh mentioning it at the time. Still, I never mind seeing the Conservative Party in shtuck.' She grimaced. 'Sorry, I didn't mean——'

'It's OK.' Claire managed a grin. 'We can't all watch what we say all the time . . . and I don't see Michael's death as part of the sleaze thing. It was a private matter, quite separate from the "questions" row.'

They fell into a discussion then, arguing whether or not a politician was entitled to a private life. It was difficult at first but then her friends' old love of argument surfaced and Claire felt the tension ease.

At last Perdy pushed back her chair. 'Well, enough of Lloyd George, fascinating though he is. I've got to leave at one and we have a lot to do. This may come as a shock to you, Cleo, but you are about to metamorphose.'

'I am?' Claire looked from one to the other for explanation.

'We think you need to change your appearance,' Debbo said. 'Nothing drastic . . . just your hair, and perhaps some specs.' A few moments later they had repaired to Deborah's huge, Gothic bathroom, where

Perdy cut and tinted Claire's long, dark hair. The result was astonishing. When the towel was removed an ash blonde with short, tousled hair looked back at her.

'You'll need to change your make-up shades,' Perdy said. 'I bought a rag-bag of my stuff to experiment with. Actually, I meant you to pass in a crowd but you look quite stunning. I hope it doesn't get you into trouble.'

In the mirror her dark eyes looked back at her from under a fringe of blond hair. 'I look a different person,' Claire thought and wondered why this thought should give her such pleasure.

She kept most of the plan from her parents when she rang them, saying only that she was going to stay with some friends of Debbo. 'I'll ring as often as I can,' she told her mother and there was such relief in her mother's voice at the news that Claire was dodging the spotlight that nothing else seemed to matter.

'Give me the address,' her mother said eventually. 'I've got a pen here. Daddy has made some notes for you and we've ordered some cards for the formal acknowledgements. We'll send it all first-class.' Her voice softened from its usual brusqueness. 'This has been difficult for you, Claire. We do realise that . . . and you've been brave. We're all proud of you. After a while, when it's all died down . . . you can pick up the threads again. We'll all help. Daddy has plans already but it's best to let things lie for a while.'

'I'm in purdah,' Claire thought when she'd put down the phone, 'or limbo, or whatever they call the region widows inhabit.' Suddenly she remembered ancient gravestones glimpsed in childhood. 'Sarah, relict of Samuel.' That's what they had called them. Relicts!

'Cheer up,' Deborah said. 'You shouldn't let them get you down.'

'It's not that,' Claire said, sitting down because suddenly her legs felt weak. 'Mum was quite sweet, actually – she meant well, anyway. It's just that it keeps coming home to me, quite suddenly, that everything has changed. It's not just that Michael is gone. It's my whole life – the whole framework of my life has shifted.'

Deborah's rosy face seemed to pale. 'Poor Cleo,' she said, putting aside the small dungarees she was repairing, as she rose to her feet. Her arms, when she wound them round Claire, were infinitely comforting. Claire did not cry but she stayed there, safe in her friend's arms until the sound of Emlyn's tricycle in the hall let them break away without embarrassment.

The following morning Claire got behind the wheel of a hired Ford Fiesta and took the AI north.

It was a relief when Yorkshire was behind her and she could feel free of Michael's constituency. She had half expected the car to leave the AI of its own accord and turn towards Devening but it kept on going north and soon she could see the distant outlines of the Cleveland Hills on the right, a sign that Durham was not far away.

Although she had been driving for more than four hours she still glanced frequently into the driving mirror, shocked at what she saw, marvelling at how quickly the whole thing had been arranged. It was only two days since Michael's funeral and in that time Perdy and Deborah had arranged a miracle.

On the seat beside her the morning papers were folded. She had read them in a lay-by south of Newark, seeing that already the column inches allotted to Michael were shrinking. In a week or two it would be over. In the meantime she would lie low in Durham, using her middle name, Louise, and her mother's maiden name, Cantrell.

To her left, the Pennines were petering out and soon after she saw the square tower of Durham Cathedral on the skyline. People had sought sanctuary in Durham since the time of St Cuthbert. Now she, too, felt an easing of tension. If it was a pleasant house, if there were books to read and familiar places to rediscover, the time would pass. She could finish the designs she knew the Golds were waiting for anxiously, although they were too concerned about her to say so. Above all, she could begin to put the past behind her and make plans for the future. And it had been a relief to get away from Debbo's because, welcome though they had made her, she could see that her presence was inhibiting the displays of affection that were so much a part of Hugh and Debbo's life together. 'They're sorry for me because I have no man,' she thought. 'I have become an embarrassment even to my best friends.'

Memories came crowding back as she made her way into the city. She had come here first in 1982, clutching her shoulder bag, anxious to make a good impression.

She hadn't known either Perdy or Debs then and now they were as vital to her well-being as her very breath. 'Let them come to see me soon,' she prayed, as she negotiated Saddler Street and saw the Cathedral looming above her in all its glory.

The house in North Bailey was tall and narrow, its door painted yellow, its windows discreetly lace-curtained. The woman who opened the door was fortyish and looked flustered. 'Mrs Cantrell? Come away in, I've got the kettle on. You've driven from London . . . You must be worn out.'

Claire let herself be drawn over the threshold, leaving the unloading of the car until later. The living-room led off the hall, its leaded windows giving on to the street. A fire sparked in the large fireplace, its glow reflected in brass fittings and gleaming William Morris tiles. There was a big, grey corduroy sofa next to squashy chairs in well-washed chintz but the focal point of the room was a hearthrug obscured by a large boxer and a slightly smaller, black-and-white dog, whose stout barrel-shaped body sat oddly on stumpy legs. The boxer stayed supine but the mongrel sat up, its head on one side, one ear drooping, the other erect in enquiry.

'That's Max,' the charwoman said. 'The boxer's called Brutus. The cat's Calliope: she's around somewhere but she keeps herself to herself. My name's Freda Barnes by the way — sit down and I'll fetch a cuppa. What have you had to eat? Not that motorway food, I hope. It's all plastic.' She paused for breath and then continued. 'I'm that glad to see you, not that I'd've seen him stuck – Dr Gaunt, I mean – but dashing back and forth, well, my man works shifts so the day's all to pot. Anyway, you're here now. Now, where's that tea-caddy?'

Over tea Freda explained the routine, her salt and pepper head nodding to emphasise her words. 'I come in every weekday, nine to eleven. I do a supermarket shop once a week, for Dr Gaunt. He's paid me to stay on while he's away so let me know how you want things done. I do him veg for the weekend on a Friday. The heating comes on twice a day and there's constant hot water. I'll show you where everything is when we've had this tea.' She put a hand to the breast of her flowered overall. 'By, I'm glad to see you and no mistake.'

'Is there anything I should know about the animals?' Claire asked tremulously. At close quarters the dogs seemed unbelievably daunting. What would she do if they disobeyed?

'He's left you a list, well, its more like a saga . . . there's two pages. He's got them ruined; I wouldn't pay too much attention. Then there's his birds—'

'Birds?' A cockatoo would be the last straw!

'He's got everything out there . . . woodpeckers, chaffinches – I don't know what half of them are but he puts nuts out regular as clockwork.'

When they'd finished their tea they toured the house. It was a place of nooks and crannies, of shabby but magnificent furniture, of faded chintzes and plant pots trailing greenery in unexpected places.

'Nice, isn't it?' Freda said. 'Shabby but homely.' The Wellington chest she was looking at was probably worth a thousand or so, but Claire nodded agreement.

'It's lovely. Now, where's this list?'

There were two closely written pages in a neat but somewhat flamboyant script.

Everything was itemised, down to the precise amount of birdfood to be put into each container. Claire looked through the window to the tree where a collection of containers hung. There were birds feeding there even now, hanging upside down to peck viciously at the containers. 'What are they?' she asked.

Freda shook her head. 'Search me. But there's a shelf-ful of books in the study if you've got the time.' She twitched aside the curtains. 'There're his binoculars, if you want a closer look. They won't all be there . . . some of them go as soon as the nights cut in. You don't see them again till the spring. Do you want a look?'

'I'll leave it until tomorrow.' Claire studied the list. 'He doesn't leave much to chance, does he? This looks like a full day's work.'

'He's a bit fussy about things like that,' Freda said. 'But he's a nice chap. Too clever, if you want my opinion. They say it addles them, all that brain power.'

She was still talking when Claire eased her over the doorstep and waved her down the path. Alone at last, she leant her forehead briefly against the closed front door and then straightened up. It was six o' clock. According to the list she should walk the dogs at six-fifteen. Tonight she would be walking on territory she'd not seen for years, so the sooner she started the better.

The city was already lamplit and the Rose Window of the Cathedral glowed like a huge jewel, lit from within. She walked up North Bailey, towards the Heritage Centre, remembering with each step her student days. How carefree they seemed in retrospect. She turned into Bow Lane, heading towards the river and Kingsgate Bridge, built on the site of an old ford, below the city gate that gave it its name.

According to legend the King had been William I, who had passed through it in haste, conscience-stricken at his attempt to open the coffin of St Cuthbert. But there was nothing ancient about the bridge itself, built in 1963 and designed by Ove Arup who was said to prize it above some of his better-known masterpieces. It was as slim and lofty and elegant as she remembered and she paused there in admiration for a moment before seeking the path into a wooded area running behind the houses, which Stephen Gaunt had recommended.

She had no need to look for it. The dogs, once free of their leads, led the way although she paused, once she was out of range of the lamplight, and let them explore on their own. The treed area was dark and threatening, the leaves that occasionally drifted past her face like ghostly fingers in the dusk.

She felt better when she was safe back in the house, the bolts shot home and lights on everywhere. Freda had left a chicken casserole in the kitchen and she spooned some of it on to a plate and put it in the microwave. As she turned back she saw both dogs were in the doorway, regarding her reproachfully. 'Off you go,' she said as firmly as she could. Neither of them budged. 'Shoo!' She waved an imperious arm. No reaction. 'Come on,' she said, trying to manoeuvre past them and lead them back to the sitting-room.

They remained as still as Buddhas and suddenly she realised their eyes were fixed on one of the wall cupboards. 'Food? Is it food you want.' A globule of saliva gathered in the boxer's jowl and hung trembling. Claire retrieved the list and checked. 'Feed dogs six-forty-five,' it said. It was six-fifty-two. Already she was falling down on the job.

She was spooning food into bowls in the proportions dictated in the list when there was a yowl and a blue cat sprang from nowhere on to the kitchen bench. It began to purr, weaving in and out of her arms as she chopped and stirred.

'All right, all right . . . you want feeding too.' For the first time today she felt the frightening impulse to laugh although nothing was funny. Surrounded as she was by salivating animals, Debbo's miraculous idea was looking less attractive by the minute. 'I'm here in a strange house, under an assumed name, not even my hair colour is my own—'

She thought of that night, little more than ten days ago, when she had set a romantic table and showered in anticipation of love. Now Michael was dead, of love for a stranger rather than her, and the world had turned around on its axis.

For a moment she wallowed in self-pity but then she pulled herself together. There was one thing she could do as soon as the feeding ritual was over, get aquainted with the strange house that was to be her home for the next few weeks.

She left the dogs gobbling their food, the cat nibbling delicately, and moved from room to room, half determined, half ashamed of prying. Somehow this was different from the guided tour Freda had given her. She could take her time, peer closely at things of special interest, even open the cover of a book or lift the lid of a jar.

The study walls were covered with photographs. She moved from side to side, seeing that two men recurred in the photographs, one fair and muscular, one dark and more intense. They were pictured in a canoe, grinning up at the camera, squinting into the sun on a ski-slope, arms round one another's shoulders in the aftermath of some sort of team sport, clowning around in grass skirts at what was obviously a beach party. She had imagined Stephen Gaunt to be old, or at least middle-aged, but if he was one of the men in the photographs he couldn't be more than in his middle thirties, judging by his clothing.

She was about to explore the master bedroom which adjoined the room she had chosen for herself, when the phone rang. She moved to the extension at the bedside and picked it up somewhat timorously.

'It's us . . . well, me, Perdy. Debbo's here beside me. How's it going?'

Claire sank on to the bed. 'It's lovely to hear from you. It's fine here — very nice, really — but strange.'

'Strange unfamiliar or strange horrid?'

'Unfamiliar . . . it's not horrid — anything but. The animals are huge, though. I wouldn't like to cross them, and apparently their owner has ruined them. They actually told me they wanted feeding . . . I couldn't budge them.'

'Talking dogs! You'd better send for Esther Rantzen.' Perdy was attempting light relief and it worked.

'Anything but Esther, I'm not up to it. I walked over Kingsgate just now . . . and the Rose Window is right outside my door. You should see it.'

'You're making me nostalgic. I'm glad you're on the Peninsula. It makes me feel you're sort of safe. Hold on, Debbo's desperate to get in here.'

'Claire . . . it's my phone and she won't let me near it. Are you OK?'

'I'm fine. The house is lovely. Quite grand but very, very comfortable. I'm going to love it.' She was not yet sure of this but it was the least she could say when they had made such an effort.

'Well,' Debbo said, 'that's a relief. If it had been awful I'd have felt responsible. What are the dogs like?'

They talked for a while and then Deborah announced she had good news to impart. 'We're coming up to stay with you next weekend. How about that?'

The euphoria caused by her friends' phone call lasted through the next hour. Perdy and Debbo were coming and it would be just as it had been before, the three of them together, laughing, talking, sharing intimacies, putting the world to rights. But as the night drew on her depression returned. It was ten-thirty. Almost twelve hours before she had another human being to whom she could talk. She could die here in this strange house and no one would know.

Since Michael's death, thoughts of her own mortality had surfaced often. You could die in the flick of a finger. One minute fully alive, the next a statistic in a coroner's notebook.

When fear threatened to overcome her she decided to unpack. Freda had helped her unload the car and her bags were piled in the hall. She carried them upstairs, two by two, at first watched by two alert dogs, later unobserved when both dogs grew bored and went back to the fire.

When everything was upstairs she began to empty the cases and put away her belongings. She was half-way through the second suitcase when she came across the newspaper cuttings. 'Inquest hears of mystery woman.' 'MP dies in lover's arms.' They had exercised their imagination to the full. There were several pictures of her and Michael together, others of her alone, one showing her desolate outside the coroner's court, eyes flaring with alarm as they caught the photo-flash. 'Wife betrayed', the sub-title read.

She sat down on the bed, the strips of newsprint

falling from her suddenly lifeless hand, and wished she hadn't brought them. She felt suddenly overcome by anxiety, a terrible fizzing restlessness that made her want to get out of the house, to run hither and thither, anywhere she could escape from thoughts that tormented.

In the end she stayed put but the sobs came, racking her chest, making her nose run, twin rivers of mucus and misery, tears scalding her painful eyelids until even blinking was agony. She was crying steadily when she felt something cold and wet against her knee. The black-and-white mongrel was nuzzling her hand, where it lay in her lap, its warm tongue lapping her fingers endlessly in a way that should have revolted her, but instead was comforting. The nose was cold and questing, the warm tongue a panacea for woe. She stood up, fondling the bulky head. 'Come on then,' she said. 'Let's cheer up and go downstairs.'

She had washed her face and put on the kettle for a nightcap when the phone rang but even as she moved to answer, the ringing ceased. There was a sudden burr and then the familiar sound of a fax machine. She tracked it down to the study and read the fax as it peeled off the block. It came from San Francisco and the heading was '*Nota Bene*'. It went on to give extra instructions for the dogs and the birds. It explained where there were signed cheques to pay for supplies and amplified all the previous instructions. Whatever Stephen Gaunt was doing in San Francisco it wasn't occupying him sufficiently if he could nit-pick like this. She turned to the dogs. Brutus's nose had sunk upon his paws. Max opened his mouth in a huge, silent yawn. 'He is the giddy limit, this master of yours,' she said and was rewarded with a yowl of agreement from the invisible Burmese cat.

It was a relief to have the animals to talk to. She bid them a fond good-night eventually and mounted the stairs on weary legs. When she had put out the light she felt suddenly panicky. What if she couldn't sleep? But Perdy's words came into her mind then: 'I'm glad you're on the Peninsula.' Inside her head an aerial picture of Durham appeared. She was indeed on the Peninsula, held in the comforting arms of the river, for the Castle and Cathedral and their environs had been built on a horseshoe loop of land which had the River Wear on both sides. And within the arms of the river she was safe.

At first she started at unaccustomed noises, a bark somewhere or laughter in the street. She had forgotten students were nocturnal and she half smiled in the dark at the memory. She started to count bridges then . . . Kingsgate, Old Elvet, New Elvet, Prebends, Framwelgate, Milburngate . . . she was circuiting for the second time when sleep came, Ove Arup's bridge fading gently into oblivion.

8

Claire slept soundly in the strange bed, but it was not the alarm, set for seven-forty-five, that woke her. It was the ringing of the phone and then the clatter of the fax machine in the study that had her sitting upright, heart pounding.

She went downstairs shrugging into her robe, barefoot, convinced that a seven a.m. fax must be of momentous importance.

There was only one sheet and the message was brief and handwritten. 'I forgot to put Max's arthritis drops on the list. He gets them last thing, three drops on his tongue – he doesn't mind. There are treats by the drops. Give him two after the drops. You will find them on the shelf beside my—' The 'my' was crossed out and 'the wing chair' substituted.

She knew which chair he meant. She had seen it last night and known it was the chair he sat in because the Indian carpet was worn in front of it, worn by the feet of someone who habitually sat there. She was suddenly touched by the image of the lonely academic sitting in his chair each night to administer medicine to a well-loved pet. All the same — she calculated the time difference — it must have been ten or eleven at night when he sent the fax. He should have known it would wake her. So the good doctor cared about animals but not too much for house-sitters. She screwed up the fax and put it in the waste-paper basket before she went to let out the animals and put on the percolator.

There were papers and letters in the front lobby. *The Times*, the *Independent* and *Gardener's World*. Yet another unexpected side to the doctor. She put the letters and the magazine on the desk in the study and carried the papers through to the kitchen. The dogs rose from their baskets, stretching and yawning but pleased to see her. The mongrel's body twisted hither and thither, the boxer thrust its head into her hand, seeking a caress. She opened the door to the garden and let them file past her, followed by the cat, which had appeared from nowhere and was not in the mood to greet anyone.

It was a sunny morning but it had rained in the night. It glistened on petals and leaves and dripped, crystal-like, from the gutters. She moved further out, suddenly enchanted by the scene before her. It was not a large garden but there were flowers and shrubs of every description planted higgledy-piggledy all over it. The walls were faded old brick, where they peeped between climbing plants, and there seemed to be no ordered plots or planning, only a central path and what had been a riot of colour, dying now with the approach of winter.

There was a small patio edged with grass and then the flowers began, ragged asters in shades of mauve and pink, gladioli, orange and scarlet and white, showering fuchsias side-by-side with hydrangeas, still beautiful although they had lost their colour. She saw Rose of Sharon, past its flowering, and Solomon's Seal and hostas tinted by autumn. An odd, browning rose showed here and there and there were dahlias and hollyhocks against the walls but most of the flowers were annuals which must have been planted that year. So he made use of his *Gardener's World*!

She bent to squeeze an antirrhinum, as she had done in childhood, seeing its mouth gape open and snap shut under the pressure of her fingers. They had lived in seventeen houses during her childhood and adolescence, everywhere from München barracks to Nato headquarters at Fontainebleau so she had seen many gardens but never one which, in summer, would be as crammed and colourful as this. It was the work of a genius or a fanatic, she was not sure which.

In the end she had to tear herself away after she had fed the birds, returning to the kitchen to make coffee and see what the morning papers had to say. The papers were not tabloids and neither of them mentioned Michael. She let her breath out in a small puff of relief and put two slices of wholemeal bread in the toaster, before rescuing the crumpled fax and putting it on one side to read again later.

She had bathed and dressed and given the animals their specified early-morning snacks by the time Freda arrived. 'I usually have a cup of tea before I start,' the char said firmly. It was obviously an accepted practice and she wanted to make that clear.

'Please,' Claire said. 'I don't want my being here to interfere with anything. Just go on as though I wasn't here.' Freda was still looking doubtful so Claire decided to confide, just a little. 'I've been ill . . . glandular fever. My husband died a while ago . . . it happened after that.' She felt a tear course surprisingly down her cheek. How could she lie so easily? And cry to order, except that she hadn't done it deliberately!

Freda nodded eagerly. 'I could see you looked peaky last night.'

'I was working abroad when it happened so I didn't have anywhere over here to convalesce. A friend heard about Dr Gaunt needing a house-sitter so it was a godsend. But I'll be leaving here in a few weeks. Heaven forbid I should get in the way of your routine.'

Freda was mollified by the thought of Claire being a bereaved and helpless invalid. 'Poor thing. Don't you have any family? It's hard being under the weather when you're on your own.'

'I've got cousins,' Claire said, improvising rapidly. 'But we're not close. I do have good friends but they're mostly married so they have commitments . . . you know what it's like.'

'Of course I do.' The older woman had folded her hands over her midriff, clasped in satisfaction at having found a soulmate. 'Not that I've ever been in that position but I can use my imagination. That's why I favour Dr Gaunt. He's a lonely soul.' She closed one eye in a wink. 'Not that the ladies don't flock round — bees to a honeypot, I can tell you. "Say I'm out, Freda," he says more times than not. There was one once, she was a sociology lecturer, bonny girl but it came to nothing in the end. He's not like his brother; three times married and this latest one won't last. Now, where's that caddy . . . and you sit still while I make you a nice cuppa.'

It seemed diplomatic to accept a cup of tea and a little more gossip. She learned that Dr Gaunt's Christian names were Stephen Charles, that he was thirty-eight years old, limped slightly from a knee injury received playing tennis, was fond of music and no trouble at all to look after. 'A proper gentleman . . . never raises his voice.' Freda warmed to her theme. 'Not that he doesn't like things nice: coal tar soap upstairs and down, best-quality towels, if he says three-forty-five he means it, not three-forty-four.'

'Pernickety,' Claire thought but forbore to say so. If Freda wanted to think her employer a saint, fair enough. Claire was less sure. He seemed like someone with a large ego who had built a rather self-indulgent routine for himself. What would the next fax be about? The way the bath towels should be folded?

As she laid out her drawing-board and pencils she realised that it was rather nice to look down on Stephen Gaunt, just as it had been nice to be angry with Adam. Anger kept other emotions at bay, grief and fear and above all puzzlement. Why hadn't she realised there was another woman? Other women, for all she knew. Had she been complacent? Had she simply not cared enough?

She picked up a piece of fabric; its rough texture was pleasant to touch. No, not pleasant . . . intriguing. 'Perhaps I bored Michael?' She said it aloud and as she spoke her eyes met the reflected stare of her own image in the mirror above the mantelpiece. She lifted the fabric to her cheek, rubbing gently, all the while holding her own eye. She had thought she was safe in a good – if barren – marriage. But it had all been an illusion. She had not been safe at all. She put a hand behind her to feel the chair and sank into it slowly, able to stop staring only when her reflection vanished beneath the mirror's edge.

Useless to try to draw now. Her fingers felt lifeless, her mind resisting the very idea of work. 'I want to think,' she decided. 'I want to make sense of it.' How had she used to assemble information for an essay? Chronologically was easiest. Begin at the beginning.

She had met Michael at a Conservative function her mother had forced her to attend. What had happened then? He had moved across to greet her father and then held out a firm hand – a warm, dry hand. Suddenly she remembered the way he had held her hand; on Cumbrian walks, on London streets, in Nice, when she had teetered in her black patent heels until he had insisted she take them off and they had run, laughing, from the Negresco to the waiting car. She mustn't cry, not now with Freda lurking nearby.

On their first date he had taken her to the cinema in Leeds. She couldn't remember the name of the film but Faye Dunaway had been the star. He had poked gentle fun at her; about studying anthropology, about her reticence, about his own need to impress the daughter of his future Constituency Chairman. She had countered that Alison Morris was Chair in all but name and that was where he should direct his attention and he had shaken his head and smiled at her and she had known that she would go to bed with him before too long. 'He did love me.' It came almost as a revelation after all the uncertainty of the last few days. She felt comforted enough to take up her pencils until she remembered that, whether or not he had loved her then, he had transferred his affection elsewhere later on.

She went to the kitchen in search of coffee and found Freda sitting at the kitchen table stringing beans. 'Ready for coffee? Dr Gaunt has his about now when he's here.'

Claire pulled out a chair and sat opposite. 'Can I help?' Freda was standing up, rinsing her hands under the tap. They were strong hands with square but well-kept nails. Only the parched skin showed them to be the hands of a worker. She dried them carefully on a tea-towel.

'You relax. You've been working. I know book-work

wears you out as much as real work.' She grinned suddenly. 'Well, you know what I mean. I saw all your portfolios and things.'

'I'm a fashion designer.' Claire could never say that without feeling self-conscious about her lack of formal qualifications but Freda seemed to accept it easily enough. 'My designs are in quite a few of the mail-order catalogues,' Claire added.

'Fancy that,' Freda said, holding the kettle spout under the tap to catch the gushing water. 'That won't take long. I'm doing french beans for your dinner; they were going off. There's potatoes in the pan, which only need salting. I haven't done anything about meat but the freezer's full. He mostly buys chops and steaks. Can't cook a joint for one, he says. So you won't go short.'

They drank their coffee from mugs, sitting either side of the table, gradually warming to one another as facts emerged. Freda was a mother of two and a recent grandmother. Her husband, Jack, was a janitor at Shoichi, one of the halls for Japanese students at the University of Teikyo.

'A Japanese university?' Claire was surprised. Here was something she hadn't expected.

Freda was warming to her theme. 'He went there in 1990, when it opened. There's a hundred students – lovely manners, Jack says, really polite. They're only here for a year.'

As Claire listened she grew more amazed. Teikyo was part of an international education organisation, providing accommodation for students from Japan, who spent a year developing their knowledge of English language and culture.

'Do they socialise with the other students?' Claire asked as Freda paused for breath.

'Oh yes . . . they have meals in the other colleges and they play a lot of sport. And sometimes they swap rooms with the other colleges, but they have their own ways. You should get Jack on about the Tea Ceremony. That'd set you thinking.'

'I'll bet,' Claire said faintly. Japanese Tea Ceremonies in the sober haunts of Durham! She had come back expecting everything to be the same but it wasn't. It was more exciting.

'There's a lot of Jap money in the North-East now,' Freda said. She drained her cup and wiped the corners of her mouth with a delicate forefinger. 'Not just Nissan, although that's the one they all talk about. There's plenty of other companies . . . my nephew works in one at Peterlee — works alongside the Japs. He likes them; they're very hospitable, he says — and they know how to work. Some people don't like it but I say you can't bear grudges for ever.'

'No,' Claire said, not thinking about the nation of Japan. 'No. I suppose you have to forgive in the end.'

'Anyway,' Freda said, rising to her feet to signal the end of leisure-time, 'there's a lot going on here. I could get you some brochures, if you like. Jack's got loads. You might as well get up to date about the place. It's a hot-house, according to Fred: Chinese, Japanese . . . you can learn them all. Yes, it's a hot-house, all right.'

Claire decided 'hot-house' meant 'power-house' but forbore to say so. You should never contradict an expert.

'We'll need to talk about shopping,' Freda said at last. Claire promised to confer tomorrow and they washed up the coffee things side-by-side at the sink, Freda washing and Claire drying.

As she waved Freda off, wondering what on earth she could cook to go with potatoes and french beans, she postponed the decision by telephoning her parents.

'It's nice that you found a refuge,' her mother said when they had exchanged greetings. Claire knew what she meant. It was not so much a refuge as a place of quarantine, where lepers could be confined and hidden from sight until they were cleansed.

'I've brought shame on the family,' she thought ruefully. 'Guilt by association.'

She would have to stay away from her family long enough for feelings to cool, memories to fade. Above all, until there was no need for anyone to get emotional about the situation. That had been the unwritten sin throughout her childhood, to display the tiniest sign of emotion. When she had cried at the death of Adam's white mouse her father had reproved her. 'No need to get hysterical.' Her mother had stayed her tears with a look of astonishment that anyone could make such a fuss about nothing.

Now, when her mother had told her that her brothers had written and the letters were redirected and in the post, and they had bid one another goodbye,

Claire thought once more of her buttoned-up childhood. Was that why she had failed Michael? Perhaps there was not enough emotion in her because it had been stemmed at source? Was that why he had needed to find release elsewhere? And the fact that the woman was probably a tart and any emotion she displayed was spurious was hardly relevant to her own feelings of ineptitude.

She thought of going out into the garden but it had started to rain. She looked at the clock. Twelve-thirty. The day stretched ahead of her, a wasteland defying her to fill it. She was half-way to the kitchen in search of lunch, not out of hunger but for want of something to do, when she was struck by the silence of the house. She opened up the stereo unit and picked a tape at random, a blank tape that had obviously been filled by Stephen Gaunt. His spidery writing was on the container. 'My top ten,' it said. She slid it into the cassette player and turned up the volume before she went back to the kitchen.

The first track was one of the 'Songs from the Auvergne'. She couldn't be sure which, but the hauntingly beautiful voice was unmistakably that of Victoria de los Angeles. The second track started as she unearthed a spring roll from the freezer and put it into the microwave. She took out a lamb chop for the evening and left it on a plate to defrost. She would have to go shopping soon, to get supplies of her own and replace anything of Stephen Gaunt's she had taken. 'A Whiter Shade of Pale' by Procol Harum washed over her. That had been a hit in the late '60s. She had been four or five then and they were living in Germany but her British nanny had been besotted with the tune, playing it over and over.

Claire was biting into the spring roll when the Bob Dylan song started up. 'Lay Lady Lay', the first truly erotic record she had ever heard. It had aroused her as a teenager and played backdrop to her first painful experience of sex. Now it worked its magic again. She stood in the neat kitchen feeling a stirring in her pelvic region, a sudden yearning to be held, touched until she grew moist with desire. 'I will never have sex again,' she thought and was suddenly desolate. She cupped her breasts in her hands, feeling her nipples harden, knowing that this was senseless, an arousal that was doomed to disappointment, trying to remember Michael's face as the face of a lover, struggling to remember his lips, his touch, seeing only the dead face in the mortuary. But it had been good in the beginning, when they had laughed together as well as loved.

Once more it was the mongrel that summoned her back to the real world, a world that was cold enough but not as frightening as fantasy. She put the spring roll in the bin, no longer hungry, and went through to the study to get down to work. That was the best remedy for foolishness.

It was hard at first to fix her mind on the designs but gradually the release of thinking about fashion rather than people took over and she worked solidly for two hours, pausing only to get coffee and a piece of bread and cheese from the kitchen. Last year had been her most successful so far; she didn't want to lose ground now.

She was beginning to feel a tension in her shoulders and contemplate giving up for the day when the phone rang but before she could answer it the fax machine began to whir once more. She held the paper at arm's length to read the scrawled writing. 'Hope you have settled in. I would like to emphasise that the birds have been trained to expect feeding. They will not seek food sources elsewhere and so the food for them is vital.' It was signed S.G.

It was too much! Claire reached for a sheet of paper. It was two-thirty here in Britain and six or seven a.m. in San Francisco so he must have leapt out of bed to hound her. She scribbled her reply.

'Surprisingly, you are not the only wild-life enthusiast in Britain. The birds were fed at seven-fifteen.' She signed it L. Cantrell. When she'd slid the paper into the machine and transmitted it she regretted her impulse but by then it was too late.

Debbo rang an hour later. 'How's it going?'

'Fine,' Claire said and was glad that it was probably true. 'I mean that, Debs. Full marks for finding this place. The house is lovely, the char's friendly, the animals are docile, except the cat which I seldom see. On the whole I feel fine. It's so good to be away from—' She hesitated, looking for a word somewhere between tragedy and mess. 'Well . . . you know. Anyway, I'm fine, apart from Dr Gaunt, who keeps sending me faxes. About nothing. He left a list as long as a roll of loo paper but he faxed last night, and again this morning.'

They were discussing her knee-jerk response and whether it would elicit an instant eviction notice when she heard the machine springing to life in the study once more. 'Hold on,' she said. 'He's at it again.'

This time the fax held only one word. 'Sorry,' it said. She went back to the phone and relayed the news. 'What a poppet,' Debbo said. 'At least he's got the grace to apologise.'

The loneliness returned once Debbo's call was over. If every day dragged like this she would go mad. She tried to remember what it had been like to be incarcerated in the London flat, the Press in hot pursuit. Freda's face had not even flickered when they met. No one here knew she was Michael's widow, or would care if they did. All the same, she was alone in a strange house in a city she had loved once, in another lifetime. Could she be happy here again? It was all very well to say 'fine' to questioners but did she mean it?

The dogs were alert at the appointed time, eyes on the hook where their leads hung. 'Come on,' she said and went to get her coat. At first she had been afraid, unsure of her ability to keep hold of the dogs if they took it into their heads to run away or behave badly. But gradually she was beginning to feel more sure of herself, even to enjoy the company of the animals. Tonight she walked them down South Bailey to Watergate and Prebends Bridge. Above her the sky was clear and cold, stars partly obscured by feathery clouds. As a child she had loved the night sky, seeing in it islands and lagoons and castles high on nimbus peaks, but this sky was somehow bleak. She tried to think of her friends' coming visit and how nice it would be to have the house full but she found she was shivering, whether with anticipation or fear she could not be sure. Back in the house she gave Max his drops and then administered treats all round. She had put out the cat's food earlier but only now did it appear and eat, leaping to the top of the microwave when it was done, to lick its whiskers and let out the occasional yowl of approval.

Claire went upstairs to shower and change into a warm robe but instead she found herself pushing open the door of the master bedroom. Somehow the single-word fax had brought Stephen Gaunt into focus. She had been foolish to lash back when he was only double-checking that the birds were being cared for. 'You were a bitch,' she told herself. And now she was invading his bedroom. She hesitated, consumed with guilt, and then became defiant. If she was a bitch she might as well go the whole hog. She advanced on the wardrobe and opened the doors, seeing a neat row of tweed jackets, formal suits, two dinner jackets – the wardrobe of a gentleman.

Suddenly, for no reason, she bent to put her face against the rough fabric of the jackets, feeling the tweed prickle against her face, sniffing for some subtle male odour, remembering how Michael had smelt and how she had once exulted in those secret places of a man's body. Why had she let that slip away . . . not even noticed it was gone? She closed the doors, a sudden chill upon her, and moved to the dressing-table, fingering a stud box, a pin tray, an array of bottles that let out sharp, exotic fragrances when she uncorked them.

They had spent the first week of their honeymoon in a villa in hills above Eze, looking down on Cap Ferrat and the huge turquoise-blue sea. They had done things there that she had never done before . . . walking naked to look down on the moonlit panorama below . . . and once, daringly naked in daylight, Michael teasing her about her fear of being seen, laughing away her inhibitions. He had not been her first lover but he had been the best. He had been the best . . . or had it been the moon's path on the water or her delight at getting away from home? The uninhibited sex had vanished when they came back to London — or at least been reserved for special occasions. In Eze they had made love morning, noon and night; afterwards it was reserved for bedtime, but she had never felt safe in Michael's love. The revelation was so astonishing that she sat down on the bed in the strange room, her legs suddenly weak. On the surface his affection had been there but underneath . . . ? And then there had been the night they went to Monte Carlo.

They had dressed up to the nines and climbed into the hire-car to wend their way along the Grande Corniche to Monaco. She had sensed the wildness in him as he sped the car too fast along the winding road but somehow she could not voice her fear. He had taken her into the magnificent Casino, striding through the ranks of elegant men and women to try his luck at chemin de fer and baccarat before settling to play American roulette. She had watched him gamble, knowing he had changed all the money they possessed for chips, seeing the light in his eye as he dared and lost and dared and won and won and won again, taking risks, never flinching at the losses, until at last he had accumulated a small fortune.

They had drunk champagne and then driven too fast back to Eze so that he could decant his winnings on to their bed and sift the notes with taloned fingers. He had looked up at her at last and when he spoke it was quietly. 'I am an MP now, a politician, therefore I can never, ever do that again. But by God it was wonderful!'

The love-making that followed had been as abandoned as the gambling that had preceded it. When the booking on the villa was up they had moved to the Negresco, the grandest hotel in Nice. She remembered evenings on the terrace there, moonlight through trees, siestas in shuttered rooms, waking to make love and bathe and go down to La Rotonde, to sit in a pink and perfect booth and be served by waiters who loved their jobs. There had been prancing fairground horses there and an automaton which sprang to life to play the barrel-organ. And it had all been expensive. By the time they left for England the small fortune was no more.

She found she was crying at the memory, or rather at

the fact that she had half forgotten such a momentous night. Where had it all gone, the excitement, the wonder? Or had that need for thrills remained in Michael, satisfied only by sordid encounters in a rented flat?

When at last she slept it was a fitful, dream-laden sleep from which she woke at dead of night crying, '*Au secours, au secours,*' a cry for help in a foreign tongue.

9

The letters from Claire's brothers, forwarded by her mother, arrived by the first post and she read them at the breakfast table. 'Dear Claire,' Peter wrote, 'Rachael and I are so very sorry we couldn't be with you. Michael's death is a sad loss to us all. He had great promise as a politician.' The letter continued in the same stilted vein. In the end she let it fall to the table, remembering the brother who had shown her no affection in childhood and now was writing to her as though they had once, briefly, been next-door neighbours.

The letter from Ian was a little warmer. 'It's too bad this happened, old thing, but at least you're young and can make a new life. Anything yours truly can do to help will be done pronto. You could come out here when you're ready. German hotels are first-class and we'd be able to see quite a lot of one another. There are some good chaps in the Mess.' He wants me married off, Claire thought, and was able to smile at her brother's idea of a neat ending.

The morning papers were still obsessed with sleaze. Neil Hamilton's father was reported to be bitter about his son's loss of position, accusing John Major of sacrificing him. Jonathan Aitken's Ritz bill had been explained away and David Mellor was expressing disapproval of 'tabloid TV'.

Claire tried to equate all this dizzy talk of sojourns at the Ritz with her own experience of political life. Michael had never taken her further than the constituency unless in a private capacity. They had had good holidays, it was true, but they had been paid for out of their joint earnings. Memories of hotels in sunny climes threatened to intrude and she turned swiftly to another page. She was tired of having a nose permanently stuffy from weeping.

There was a large picture of the Prince of Wales: 'His Royal Petulance', as Michael had once christened him. The Dimbleby biography was due out in a few days' time but judging from the speculation and leaking there would be little left to surprise anyone who bought it. She thought of the Princess of Wales, suddenly struck by fellow-feeling. She too was a betrayed wife and not allowed privacy to lick her wounds. 'I never sympathised before,' Claire thought ruefully. She had always thought the Princess lucky. She was young and rich and beautiful; her problems had appeared quite bearable. Now Claire knew better.

She turned to the back page for the astrology section.

Today, as a Gemini, she was to 'let go of an old problem and see her way to a new and more fulfilling existence'. She looked at the astrologer's picture, smiling from the top of the column. 'From your lips to God's ear,' she said aloud and went upstairs to shower.

By the time Freda let herself in, Claire was dressed and had walked the dogs and put a load of washing into the machine.

With Freda's help she drew up a shopping list, locations where the best value was available printed alongside each item. She began in the Market Square. The indoor market was a revelation, spice and antiques stalls, handbags and fruit and shoes and books all mixed up together. 'I had forgotten how nice it is,' she thought, emerging at last into the sunlight to sit by Londonderry's statue and look around her.

On a seat opposite, an elderly woman sat nursing an oiled canvas bag. Beside her sat a younger woman with remarkably similar features and between them sat a child – a girl of about five – her legs in their long, white ribbed stockings sticking straight out from the seat, ending in bright red boots. The older woman reached into the bag and produced a white paper parcel oozing with grease. It contained two large and overflowing pork sandwiches. She handed one to the other woman and retained one for herself. Each woman then broke off a portion of their sandwich, biting at the pork where it refused to give way, until each had a sizeable piece to give the child. It was obviously a familiar ritual. The three generations munched with every appearance of satisfaction and Claire felt suddenly envious. How wonderful to sit in the autumn sunshine and share a pork sandwich with flesh of your flesh.

'God, I hate doing this,' Michael had muttered each time he had had to produce sperm at the clinic and she had shrunk in her seat and wondered why she was a failure even at that most universal of functions: reproduction.

'I can't understand it,' her mother had said when at last she and Michael had agreed to give up. 'You were such a healthy little girl.'

Now Claire stood up and moved towards the pub. But even as she walked her feet turned to lead. 'I want a drink,' she told herself. 'I have a right.' But nice women didn't frequent pubs unaccompanied and if she was nothing else, she was nice. She could hear her mother's voice now. 'People of our sort don't do things like that.' 'People of our sort' were never infertile and above all did not carelessly lose husbands in inauspicious circumstances. The full realisation of her own shortcomings was a spur. She reached the door of the pub, pushed it open and entered the musty fug of the bar.

To her relief there was another solitary female figure at the bar. She turned at Claire's entrance and studied her from head to foot before turning back to her half of lager. 'A dry white wine, please,' Claire said firmly and hoisted herself on to a tall stool.

The wine was surprisingly cool and pleasant and she relished the first mouthful. 'Local?' The question was a surprise and she turned to the woman who had voiced it. She had a round, rosy face and a mouth of enormous sweetness but her eyes were small and cold and her glance flickered as rapidly as a lizard's tongue. 'Local?' she asked again but this time she smiled, her perfect Cupid's bow lips revealing small pointed yellow teeth.

Claire shook her head. 'No. I'm just here for a few weeks.'

This time the smile was triumphant. 'Thought so.' The woman moved closer. 'I can always tell a stranger. But at least you're one of us.' Claire felt a giggle threaten to rise. She couldn't escape from that paralysing phrase, 'one of us', no matter where she went. What was she expected to say? She contented herself with a knowing smile and it didn't seem to matter because the woman was now in full flow.

'They come in off the plane and they're in our houses, our jobs. Our sort has to wait but not them. They'll swamp this place . . . I can see it. I've written off to London but they take no notice.'

Claire looked desperately for help but the bar was almost empty and the barmaid was polishing glasses as though her life depended on it.

'Yes,' Claire said as non-committally as she could, hating herself for appearing to agree with such loathsome sentiments.

'They've dragged this country right down.' The barmaid's eyes met Claire's gaze as she raised her shoulders infinitesimally in a gesture of resignation.

'Yes,' Claire said. She had wanted to savour the

wine, make it last, perhaps even have a second glass, but now it was spoilt. She drained her glass, smiled desperately at the barmaid, bobbed her head to her fellow-drinker and went out into the sunlight once more. 'I am not one of you,' she thought. 'Or if I am, I choose not to be.'

As she walked up Owengate to Palace Green she glanced at her watch. Only eleven-thirty. What was she going to do with the day? She wanted to save working for tonight, when it was dark outside and she needed something pleasant to occupy her mind. On an impulse she turned and made her way to North Road. It was still there, the hairdresser's they had all patronised in the first weeks of term, when their allowance looked as though it would last for ever. She pushed open the door and went in, the bag containing her purchases banging against her thigh.

It was all right while she was being shampooed, the warm water cascading over her head like a benediction. The trouble began when she had to look at herself in the mirror and accept that the gaunt and shadowed features looking back at her from under the unfamiliar fair thatch were her own. Behind her the young stylist kept up an endless banter about holidays past and Christmas to come. Christmas! Where would she spend Christmas? 'God save me from Christmas,' she thought and felt the treacherous tears break through the dam of her self-control.

Her mumbled excuses of colds and allergies fooled no one. The assistants exchanged meaningful glances, reflected in the mirrored walls, and as if by magic a junior appeared with a cup of tea.

It was a relief when at last she was out in the street and hurrying home. It was noticeably colder and when she reached the house and switched on the radio they were warning of frost to come in the night. She thought of the asters, waving their plumed heads so bravely in the garden. Tomorrow, if the frost was as severe as they were predicting, they would be grey and lifeless like her. On an impulse she took scissors from the drawer and went out to cut armfuls of the exotic plumes, so many that in the end she had to use milk bottles and jugs and whatever came to hand to contain them.

Stephen Gaunt possessed only two vases, both small and ornamental rather than functional. 'I'll buy him a decent vase before I go,' Claire thought and was filled with sudden terror at the thought of leaving her bolt-hole until she began to do her sums. She could stay till mid-December. Six weeks, forty-two days, 1,008 hours . . . or was it 1,080? She gave up then, satisfied that it was a big enough number to defy mental arithmetic.

She had just settled to her work when the phone rang. It was Sorrel Gold, Sammy talking in the background every few sentences, much to his wife's annoyance. They were ringing to enquire about her welfare but she could tell they were relieved to hear she was working again.

'I'll deliver on time,' she promised. 'There's nothing to distract me here.' There was nothing to distract her anywhere now. When she put down the phone she went to the sideboard and poured herself a large sherry.

'I must stop this,' she said aloud. Glass in hand she wandered from room to room, trying to imagine Stephen Gaunt's life in this house. He was alone. He managed. He was even content, according to Freda. 'So will I be,' she promised herself but even as she did so she acknowledged that she could never be truly content again with so many questions left unanswered.

After another drink she took a grip of herself. So her husband had had recourse to prostitutes? Lots of men did that. Women's magazines were full of letters from women whose husbands masturbated in the middle of a thriving sex life or read pornography, and the agony aunts all had the same answer. 'Accept!' 'It isn't important.' 'Look at the whole picture.' Or, if they were of the militant variety, 'Tell him to get the hell out of it.' But they all agreed it was not the wife's fault. 'It was not my fault,' she said aloud. 'I was not to blame.'

She was drinking herself into a maudlin state when the phone rang again. It was Perdy and she took in the situation from Claire's first slurred word of greeting. 'Hang in there, Cleo. The cavalry will be with you at the weekend.' They were coming on Friday night and would stay till Sunday. When Claire put down the phone it was to cry afresh but this time they were tears of relief.

She had walked the dogs and was safely in bed when she realised there had been no fax that day. Perhaps she had choked Stephen Gaunt off? Which was all to the good, so why did she feel a twinge of regret?

Freda's eyes widened at the sight of the cut asters. 'Who cut them?' she said, a statement rather than a question as the glance she directed at Claire was one of pure reproach.

'I did,' Claire said sheepishly. 'I thought there was going to be a frost . . . it seemed a pity to let them die.' Through the window the asters remaining in the garden bobbed a healthy denial of her words. Freda sniffed.

'He never cuts his flowers.' A heavy sigh escaped her. 'Still, what the eye doesn't see the heart doesn't grieve over.' Claire felt an apology trembling on her lips and bit it back. She liked the house full of flowers. It was one of the best things she had done for ages, gathering the shaggy, vivid flowers and massing them into vases and jugs. It was November now. Soon there would be no more garden flowers.

She escaped Freda's further disapproval by pretending urgent business elsewhere. She had meant to ask Freda if there were any bowls in the house for the hyacinth bulbs she had bought in the market, but now didn't seem the best time. She tried the study first, sliding open the wall-cupboards gently, hoping to see the gleam of china, finding only masses of paper and cardboard folders. She straightened up and looked around her. If he had such things, where would they be? In her own home they were kept in the cupboard under the sink but Freda reigned in the kitchen for the moment.

She began to study the photographs which lined the walls, trying to pick out her landlord in childhood, in adolescence, in youth. She could date one photo because there was a cinema poster in the background for *Goodbye Again*, one of her favourite Ingrid Bergman films which she knew had been released in 1961. He must have been four or five in '61, if he was thirty-eight now. The other man she'd seen in the canoe picture cropped up in the childhood pictures too. A brother? Cousin? Neighbour's child? Was he the brother with the multiple marriages? He looked the womanising type. Whatever the relationship they were obviously firm friends.

She looked into the bespectacled face of the man she now believed to be Stephen Gaunt. So he never cut his asters, did he? 'Sod him,' she thought, with a high degree of satisfaction, and went in search of bowls.

She managed to assemble a motley collection of containers, discarding anything that looked in the least like an heirloom, settling in the end mostly for plastic cartons. It would be shameful to have to leave a note saying, 'Sorry I cracked the Ming.' She started to chuckle until she remembered that his homecoming would mean her own return to London. Or somewhere else? 'Where do I belong now?' she wondered. 'Where do I want to go?' There was always this torment in her head now, questions, wondering . . . the total absence of any kind of certainty.

She banished uncomfortable questions and began to fill the bowls with bulb fibre, pressing her fingers into the cool black compost like a child with plasticine. It was satisfying to make a hollow and pop in the fat, reddish hyacinth bulbs, leaving only the tip to show. It was late to plant them but they would flower eventually. She would take the plastic cartons with her and leave Stephen the two pottery bowls. She grinned, wondering what would happen if she plundered his garden and left him a vase of something cut as well. She felt suddenly optimistic, partly because of the bulbs, mainly because Perdy and Debs would be there in seven or eight hours.

She went out to buy food mid-morning, ignoring the dogs' pleas to accompany her. 'You've been out once. Later on . . . if you're good.' She would walk them on the river bank after lunch, to fill in time until her friends arrived. After that, the evening would be bathed in a rosy glow . . . and then there were two more days of pleasure to follow.

She bought the familiar food and drink from their student days: pasta, vegetables and red wine. There were some decent-looking bottles in the rack in the study but she had tampered with them enough. She bought a bottle of Fino to replace the one she had taken days ago and carried her purchases home in triumph.

Freda had coffee with her before she left, promising to have 'a nice weekend'. Freda was thawing slightly, the rape of Dr Gaunt's garden forgiven. 'You looked peaky when you landed here. You need a few good meals to put some colour in your cheeks. And a good night out. It's a good thing your friends are coming.'

Claire promised to enjoy her weekend and then sat down at the kitchen table to draw breath before she prepared for her guests. It was nine years since their student days. Nine years in which all their lives had changed and only Perdy had really fulfilled her intentions. Deborah was happy and her life was full but she had meant to have a career before she became embroiled in motherhood. She had achieved publication but the books had created scarcely a ripple in the field of scholarship, other than the odd good review. 'As for me . . .' Claire thought.

She tried to remember the course of her life. It had been the summer of her second year when she met Michael. After that first date her mother had taken charge and she had allowed herself to be hurled at Michael's head. Had she loved him at first sight? Difficult to remember now. All she could remember was the excellence of his tailoring, the pristine shirt-cuff projecting the precisely correct length beyond his sleeve, the hands, well-shaped and brown with hairs on the backs of the fingers. His face she could not conjure up at all.

He had smelt right, that she did recall. A faint, very clean, masculine odour . . . and when he had put his arm around her there had been steel under the broadcloth and she had felt very safe. A sudden, vivid picture came into her mind: Michael grinning in triumph whenever he finished *The Times* crossword. He had liked to win.

She stood up and threw the remains of her coffee into the sink before filling the kettle for a refill. Last night her mother had said, 'You can be proud of him; he would have gone a long way.' Claire had understood the coded message. 'Can' meant 'must'. 'You *must* be proud of him.' That was to be the family line, an edict that made a three-line whip look puny.

As she sat down again she tried to picture her wedding day. If she could remember Michael doing the crossword, surely she could summon up the face of him as her bridegroom? But it was useless: she could remember only the horse-drawn carriage that had taken them to the lych-gate of St Andrews, and the forest of top-hats, swept off as the guests entered the flower-strewn marquee for the reception.

Michael had proposed at Christmas, five months after their first meeting, producing the solitaire ring that lay now in the dressing-table drawer upstairs. She smiled, remembering the feverish excitement of it all. She had loved him then, loved him in the Moorish house above Eze, loved him when the honeymoon was over and until the cold finger of infertility touched their lives. But who had she loved? A man who had looked her in the eye and lived a lie? Once more the shadows; the man she had not known completely, the woman she did not know at all, loomed up to terrify. She carried her still steaming cup to the draining board and went in search of the dog leads.

There were students on Kingsgate Bridge, holding hands or chatting animatedly as they hurried to their next tutorial. For a moment, nostalgia threatened to overwhelm her. If only you could turn back the clock . . . but if you did that you would be robbed of hindsight and without hindsight you would probably make the same mistakes again. She would still drive to the church in a horse-drawn carriage and honeymoon on the Riviera and wait each month for a sign of pregnancy. Round and round for ever and ever, like Debbo's Daniel's gerbil on its wheel.

She tried to lose herself in the damp splendour of the woods but nostalgia would not leave her so she turned her thoughts to happier times, before loving Michael had changed the course of her life. She had chosen a women's college deliberately as a refuge from her male-dominated home and never regretted it. The college occupied a pleasant site opposite the Cathedral; the river between them, St Aidan's and Trevelyan close by, the University Library an easy walk away. From the window of her room, in those first few months, she had been able to see the Cathedral tower above trees which turned with autumn as she settled into the life of the college; the comradeship of the Junior Common Room, the debates in the Union Society, the special-occasion candlelit dinners and the joy of always having someone within earshot who shared your problems and your dreams. They had followed the tradition of wearing gowns for two formal meals a week but they too had been relaxed and joyful. As a graduate she still had dining rights but she couldn't possibly exercise them now. 'Remember me? I'm Claire Griffin – Claire Halcrow that was – you must have seen me in the newspapers. I'm famous, or notorious . . . not for anything I've done; by association.'

In any event, it was probably unwise to go back. Nothing was ever as wonderful as you remembered. Once she had revisited a house she had thought very grand in childhood and found it to be a tiny box of a place, devoid of splendour. Her visit to St Mary's might have the same effect. Better to remember it as a place of grace and halcyon days.

The others arrived at five-thirty, hurling themselves from Perdy's MG with cries of delight. 'The house is a dream,' Perdy said, moving over the threshold and gazing round. 'Nooks and crannies and wide window-sills. Heaven! I don't care for his colour-schemes but otherwise it's brill.'

Debbo popped her head round the kitchen door and pronounced it 'very adequate', high praise indeed.

They moved into the study, where the newcomers peered at the photographs with all the curiosity Claire had shown. 'He's the one in specs,' Deborah pronounced.

Perdy shook her head. 'That's stereotyping. He's an academic therefore he must look studious. Rubbish. I bet he's the hunk in the canoe. What did you say he was . . . a history don? He can have my life history any time.'

'A quid you're wrong!' Debbo said.

'A quid? And you married to money! I'll bet you a tenner I'm right.'

'Done!' They slapped palms on the bet and Claire felt her face crease into a huge and foolish grin. It was balm to have them there, making jokes, making light of everything. Even the dogs had perked up at their advent. 'It's going to be all right,' Claire thought. 'I can be happy again. Perhaps one day I will.'

'I thought you said there was a cat?' Perdy asked.

'I only see it at mealtimes,' Claire said. 'I think it's a ghost.'

They went upstairs then, the newcomers aghast to find Claire was not occupying the master bedroom. 'You're mad, it's got a view of the river,' Perdy said. 'I'll sleep here.'

'And I'll sleep with Cleo . . . if that's all right?' Debbo had slipped her arm through Claire's.

Claire looked at Perdy, wondering if she would prefer company, but Perdy was nodding. 'Good. I like sleeping alone . . . I'm like a cat in that respect.' She sounded sincere, as though she thoroughly enjoyed her single state, but with Perdy you could never be sure that it was not pride speaking. She did not like to appear vulnerable.

134

'Speaking of cats—' Debbo had moved a damask curtain that covered an alcove on the landing and the cat, curled on a pile of folded linen, was regarding her with eyes that glittered dislike. 'Excuse me!' she said and let the curtain fall into place. 'You didn't say it was a puma, Cleo! Now, where's the kettle? I'm desperate for some char.'

They went to the pub for a pre-dinner drink, relishing the student atmosphere.

'It hasn't changed,' Perdy said, her voice thick with nostalgia. Around them the bar heaved with laughter and exuberance, shouts of 'Watch out,' when drinks were in danger of being spilt, here and there a couple so wrapped up in one another that no one else existed.

'It has changed,' Deborah said ruefully. 'We were never as liberated . . . look at the body language. "Women rule," it says.'

'Surface show.' Perdy was definite. 'We appear to be in control but underneath the water we're still paddling like hell.'

'How can you say that?' Debbo pushed up her spectacles and settled them on the bridge of her nose. 'You've never had an unliberated moment in your whole life. I bet you had the midwife intimid-ated.'

'I wish!' For some reason Perdy didn't want to continue the argument. Hard to imagine Perdy dis-comfited but then how sure could you be of anyone's inner thoughts?

'Well, some things have changed,' Claire said. 'Wait

till you see the up-to-date bumf on our old Alma Mater. You're in for a shock.'

They went home then. 'Only a Marks & Sparks lasagne tonight,' Claire apologised. 'But we've got lots of wine.'

'Let's not wash up,' Perdy said, when the meal was over. 'We never did in the old days and sometimes I lust after being a slob again. Since I had the kitchen done I've become too pernickety. I can't bear a blemish on my Italian tiles.' They pushed the dishes aside and leant their elbows on the table to reminisce.

'Do you remember Ewart McCall?' Debbo asked. 'He was a Castleman and thought he was God's gift.' Claire and Perdy nodded in unison, remembering the arrogant young man in the red blazer, proud of belonging to University College and residing in the Castle. 'I saw him the other day,' Deborah continued. 'He was on a traffic island in the middle of Ken High.'

'Did he speak?' Perdy asked.

'He didn't see me. He looked really faded. Nothing like I expected . . . but it was definitely him.'

'I was keen on him,' Perdy said, a little shamefacedly. 'Not for long, but I did fancy him. He was so tall he had to stoop to get into the bar at Mary's, remember? I thought he'd be at least PM one day . . . What did he do?'

'I don't know,' Debbo said, 'but when I saw him he looked like a piano-tuner.'

Claire laughed aloud. 'What does a piano-tuner look like?'

'You know . . . seedy, furtive——'

'If he looked seedy and furtive he's probably a journo,' Perdy pronounced. 'Male journos are always seedy and furtive, and Ken High is swarming with them.' She turned to Claire. 'Speaking of journalists, Cleo . . . I asked around about that Dennehy character who forced his card on you. Apparently he specialises in political hoo-ha, so I'd watch him. No one bad-mouthed him but they say he's wily, so be warned.'

Claire nodded but she was determined not to discuss her problems. Not tonight, when there was an opportunity to think and talk about other things. 'Are you going to visit Mary's while you're here? I'd like to, but I can't, really — though that needn't stop you two. And we must visit the old haunts; I've only dipped my toe in so far so it's all to explore.'

She had done it; they were back in the safe world of reminiscence with wine to lubricate the wheels when they slowed.

At midnight they put the dogs on leads and went out into the street. 'Up to Palace Green or down to the river?' Debbo asked. They turned towards the river bank and walked arm in arm, setting the dogs free when they reached Kingsgate Bridge.

'This is still our island,' Perdy said, looking back at the Peninsula.

The Castle and Cathedral loomed above, floodlit now on their rocky outcrop. 'It feels safe, doesn't it?' Debbo said. 'Once you're over Milburngate — well, any of the bridges really, depending where you're coming from — you feel you're on an island.'

'It's a place for pedestrians,' Perdy offered. 'I mean, cars are really an encumbrance here. You can see why the monks chose it for Cuthbert's resting place . . . for a sanctuary.' They were silent for a moment, thinking of all the tales of sanctuary obtained by touching the grotesque mediaeval knocker on the door of the Cathedral.

'Do you think they were true, those stories of people just making it to the door ahead of their pursuers?' Deborah asked.

It was Claire who answered. 'Oh yes,' she said. 'I'm sure people found sanctuary here. They still do.'

They stayed on the bridge, arms on the parapet, looking down towards Elvet Bridge, breathing in the damp night air, enjoying one another's company. 'Let's do this again,' Perdy said as they turned at last. 'We should've done it before now — come back to the wellspring. It's a pity one of us had to be so hurt before we realised it.'

They called up the dogs from among the trees and turned for home. 'Can we have cocoa?' Debbo asked eagerly as Claire put the key in the lock.

'You do *have* cocoa, I hope?' Perdy queried. It was bliss to produce the drinking chocolate they had used in the old days and see them beam with pleasure.

'Even the same brand,' Debbo said. 'Clever girl.'

Claire felt really good about the day as she mounted the

stairs. She had done everything correctly and they had not asked if she was all right because she demonstrably was all right. But when she and Debbo were in bed and the lamp was out she felt Debbo's arm come round her, soft and heavy and comforting. 'It's going to be all right, Cleo. Just you wait and see.'

'So I didn't fool them after all,' Claire thought wryly and fell asleep almost immediately.

Claire must have slept soundly for she did not feel Deborah slip from the bed and go downstairs. She was woken by light flooding in as the curtains were drawn back and the smell of freshly brewed coffee enveloped her. 'Coffee, eggs and toast,' Debbo said, holding the tray aloft while Claire shuffled up on the pillows. 'The dogs have been out in the garden and everything's under control so you lie back and enjoy. Perdy's seeing to the birds — she seems to know what she's doing . . . I'll find something she hasn't fathomed one day. Do you want a bed-jacket?'

Claire stammered her thanks but Debbo was already half-way down the stairs so there was nothing to do but fork up the delicious scrambled egg and bite into toast done to a perfect golden-brown. For a few minutes she felt like a child again, spending a day in the school san after some not very debilitating illness, knowing that someone was in charge and she was safe in an island of pillows and blankets until it was time to put foot to floor and re-enter the fray.

When she had eaten she lay back, holding her cup in both hands, enjoying the warmth that flowed from it, thinking of the day ahead. Trying not to think of how empty the house would seem once they had gone. She was still lying there when she heard the sound of the fax machine. A few moments later Perdy came through the bedroom door bearing two flimsy sheets. 'It's from your landlord,' she said and Claire felt an unexpected surge of pleasure that Stephen Gaunt was still making contact.

She poured herself another cup of coffee before she read it. 'Dear Mrs Cantrell,' it read. 'I hope I'm forgiven for my fussiness — my former fussiness, I hasten to add. I have mended my ways.' She found she was smiling foolishly and composed her face before she read on. 'This is not in any way an instruction, rather a supplication. As the days shorten I usually supplement the birds' feed with rather disgusting balls of fat and seed which I buy in the indoor market. If you could possibly do this I would be grateful. I meant to put it in my original . . .' there was a long dash here and an exclamation mark and then he resumed '. . . suggestions but forgot. I'm quite sure that you are ahead of me on this and only paranoia forces me to mention it. Please use the cheques I left; fax if they run out. I hope you are enjoying Durham. I miss it and envy you. Stephen.'

Claire showered and dressed quickly and then faxed her reply. 'Birds disgustingly obese already but will obey. Paranoia is hard to bear.' She signed it 'Mother Nature' and chuckled her way into the kitchen although she did make a mental note to be gone before he came home. Fencing with faxes was one thing, face to face would be quite another.

Debs and Perdy came with her when she walked the dogs. 'This has been an amazing autumn,' Debbo said as they crossed the cobbles of South Bailey. Everywhere trees were turning, shedding leaves that glowed like ripe fruit until they dried and curled and were swept into piles. They passed through Watergate and on to Prebends Bridge, pausing to gaze down on the river and look towards the weir and the bridge beyond.

'It hasn't changed a scrap,' Perdy said. 'Thank God for something that isn't biodegradable.'

The dogs ran hither and thither on the Elvet banks while the three women stood silent, each content with her own thoughts. Perdy was the first to glance at her watch. 'If we're going to do everything we planned—' she said.

It was enough to make them turn for home but not before Deborah had looked towards the Castle and Cathedral once more. 'They cared more for spiritual things in those days, didn't they? The Cathedral dwarfs the Castle so you can see where they put their effort.'

'Don't be fooled.' Perdy was attaching Max's lead for the journey home. 'That castle was the only northern fortress the Scots couldn't conquer, however hard they tried. If we had time I wouldn't mind a trip round it for old times' sake.'

'If not this time, next time,' Debbo said comfortingly. 'We'll come again, Cleo, I promise you. Won't we, Perdy?'

'Definitely. Now, what's the plan?' An hour later they were piling into the car, but not before the garden had been inspected and admired. 'It's not much bigger than a London garden,' Debbo said, 'but he's used every inch, the clever devil.'

'That robin came almost to my hand when I fed them this morning.' Perdy puffed out her cheeks. 'I looked right into his beady little eye and he puffed himself out just like a Christmas card.'

'Christmas,' Claire thought. 'Let's not talk about Christmas.' The asters and gladioli had given up the ghost but the bronze chrysanthemums were still rampantly alive and there were primulas coming out here and there, violet and crimson and yellow.

'He knows his garden.' Perdy voiced Claire's thoughts. 'There's something for every season here.' But as Claire looked around she could see beads of moisture hanging everywhere, giving the foliage a sad air. The hydrangeas' leaves were now more colourful than the faded flower-heads and everywhere green was giving way to gold, gold to brown, brown to black. The Michaelmas daisies were wizened and only the odd brave rose clung to its leafless stem. Claire felt sad until she remembered the primulas.

'Yes,' she said. 'He's clever. Thank God you found this place, Debs.'

They piled into Perdy's car when they had settled the

dogs. 'Where to?' Perdy said, as she let in the clutch.

'Just drive,' they said in unison but she drove in the direction they had both desired, down through the Market Place and via New Elvet Bridge to Quarry Heads Lane and their old college. They parked in front of the classical building, the towers of the Cathedral ahead in the distance.

'I wish we had time to dine in,' Debbo said wistfully. 'You don't realise how much it means till you see it again. Still, there'll be other times.' She looked at Claire. 'And times for you too, Cleo, when you can come and be recognised and take your rightful place.'

Claire smiled and nodded but it was hard to envisage a time when she could walk into the Senior Common Room and be proud to be acknowledged. 'Which is very unfair,' she thought. For she was a victim, not a malefactor.

'Imagine this when it was parkland,' Perdy said. 'All the way down to the river . . . greensward and trees and grazing deer, probably. And all eyes fixed on the Cathedral.'

They argued for a little while then on the merits and demerits of building in the classic style in the 1950s. 'Thank God they did,' Perdy said. 'It would have been prefabricated concrete if they'd been contemporary.' Before they drove away they got out of the car and gazed at the place that had played such a crucial role in their lives. 'We were lucky,' Perdy said at last. 'Or good pickers. Whichever, I'm grateful.'

'Remember the conversation . . . I think that was the best bit,' Cleo said. 'You could float an idea in the bar or at mealtimes and there was always someone to run with it.'

'Or squash it,' Debbo said practically.

Perdy pursed her lips. 'I wonder if we'd've been — well, what we are — without Mary's. I mean, we ran everything without any men around to defer to. That stood me in good stead later on — and, God, I needed it when I was in pupillage.'

'We still had good mixed events though.' Debbo was smiling reflectively. 'Weren't some of the men gorgeous?'

'You're married,' Perdy said. 'Stop wallowing in nostalgia. Or fantasy. Blokes are blokes. Now, are we going in or are we going places?'

'We can't go in.' Debbo flashed a glance at Cleo. 'Not today . . . but we will next time. We'll have to come back in '99. It'll be the centenary year. The first residence for women in the University of Durham — there'll be a huge shindig. We'll have to keep an eye on the newsletter.'

'I'd've liked to have been here when it was on the Peninsula, near to the Cathedral,' Perdy said. The building in front of them had been built in 1952 but its mellow walls and Georgian windows had the air of a much older establishment.

'Remember how peaceful life was then?' Debbo said. 'Life's so hectic now. Then we had all the time in the world—'

146

'Balls!' Perdy said. 'We were always running some-where, losing books, doing essays at two a.m., pissed out of our tiny minds . . . don't wince, Cleo. You were reasonably sober but Debs and I were wild children. Peaceful! Get in the car, Debs, before nostalgia carries you away.'

They drove west then, deep into the land of the Prince Bishops. 'God, I'd forgotten how beautiful it is,' Perdy said, halting the car on a rise above the Wear, seeing the river meandering below, the Pennines low and dark in the distance. 'If this was summer we could pick wildflowers . . . remember when we found the spring gentian?'

'Easter '85,' Debbo said. 'We talked of nothing else for a week.' There was a pause and then she said, 'Were we nicer then?'

'Greener,' Claire offered. 'We're still nice.' But she knew what Deborah meant. There had been a trust in them then, at twenty, that was gone. They were mostly silent on the way home, except when someone pointed out something well-remembered or something which had not been there before.

'I can't believe the pits are gone,' Perdy said. 'When we were here before the whole place revolved around coal. Where do they work now?'

'They don't,' Claire said, remembering Freda's tales of out-of-work relatives and neighbours. 'There's mas-sive unemployment . . . they're offered training schemes but if you are a highly trained manual worker, how do you turn into a shop assistant or a manicurist?'

'Marks & Spencer's managers,' Perdy said as she changed gear. 'That's what Thatcher wanted everyone to be.'

'Don't start about politics.' Deborah groaned as she spoke. They were on the outskirts of the city now and the splendour of the towers and the keep reared up against the darkening sky.

'Well . . .' Perdy said, pursing her lips. 'As none of us seems able to talk about the one thing that's at the forefront of all our minds, why not politics?'

For a moment Claire felt a sense of outrage but it quickly dissolved in a huge feeling of relief. It was out, no need to smile and pretend all was well unless she wanted to do so.

'I don't think this is a good idea . . .' Debbo said but she sounded uncertain. 'Sometimes, Perd, you're—'

'For God's sake, Debbo, her husband died three weeks ago, and she found out things she didn't like — we can't pretend we came here for an old girls' bash. She needs to talk.'

'It's OK,' Claire said. 'I think I'd like to talk but let's get home and put the kettle on.'

They made tea in a big, brown earthenware teapot and carried it through to the living-room 'Who'll start then?' Deborah said as she poured. 'If you're both determined—'

'I ought to.' Claire tucked back her hair and tried to collect her thoughts. 'I haven't grieved . . . cried, that sort of thing . . . as much as I expected. I do cry, but only now and then. What I mainly feel is confusion . . .

and that's difficult because I'm too confused to work out what to do about it. Does that make sense?'

'Eminent sense.' Now that Debbo had got over her initial reluctance she was giving it her full attention. 'You're confused because the situation *is* confusing. Your life suddenly disintegrated but it wasn't the life you thought it so what have you lost?'

'I was happy,' Claire said. 'I believed I was happy.'

'I think, therefore I am,' Perdy said. 'Have you thought that this thing . . . this relationship . . . might have been a one-off thing? Upsetting but utterly irrelevant to the total picture of Michael's life with you?'

'But why the flat?' Claire said. 'If he'd been in some bordello, a working girl's flat, I could've said it was an instant's aberration − but he leased that flat. He owned property and I didn't know, and that bugs me; that he could deceive me, day in, day out . . . We discussed other places, we bought the cottage . . . why didn't he discuss that place with me?' Her voice broke then and Deborah moved to put an arm round her.

'I said this would end in tears . . . still, have a good cry, darling. It'll do you good.'

But even as she stemmed her tears and blew her nose, Claire was answering her own question. He couldn't tell her of another place in London because there was no rhyme or reason for a second London place unless to conceal something from her.

They took turns to shower and change then, intending to go out for a meal, but when they reconvened in the living-room Deborah proposed a change of plan. 'I've looked in the kitchen,' she said. 'That man's got a good spice cupboard and every pasta known to science. How's about we go to the pub and then I'll make one of my old pastas?'

'Yes, please.' The others spoke in unison and it was done. They linked arms for the walk to the smoky, noisy fug of the pub and ordered halves of lager and lime, as though the last ten years had never happened and their tastes and their purses remained unchanged.

They had to stand near the bar for a while, clutching their glasses, until a booth became vacant. 'Get in quick,' Debbo said, and then, when they were safely in the corner, backs to the wall, 'Isn't this nice?'

'Is it me,' Perdy said, looking out at the throng, 'or do they look fresh out of infant school?'

'I bet they know more than we did at that age.' Debbo propped her chin on her cupped hands as she spoke. 'Do you remember that piece I did for *Palatinate* about "Woman Emerging"? This lot've emerged all right. I'm envious.'

'Things have certainly changed,' Claire said. 'According to my Freda there are more than 6,000 students now, pretty evenly split between the sexes.'

Deborah whistled softly. 'Six thou . . . that's about half as much again as in our day.'

Claire nodded. 'And only Mary's is single-sex. It used to be Trev's and Mary's for women and Chad's and Hatfield and Castle men only but of course they've all mixed now. So we're taking over . . . or at least infiltrating.'

'I'm sorry for women today,' Perdy said with such vehemence that both Claire and Deborah stared at her. 'Too many choices, too many pressures . . . and although we appear to have a fair degree of equality, underneath not that much has changed.'

'What d'you mean?' They said it together and laughed.

'Well,' Perdy said, taking a drink and licking the lager froth from her lip. 'In theory I can work or be kept, have or not have children, farm them out if I do . . . even become Lord Chief Justice, my lifelong ambition. The reality is that although they daren't stop me they don't actually give me a fair shake. If I get angry, I'm pre-menstrual; if I change my mind, it's hormonal. In a few years' time they'll say I'm menopausal—'

'More than a few years,' Deborah said mildly.

'Well, you know what I mean. Don't nit-pick. We're victims of our sexuality. Most men still think a woman's place is on her back.'

'Perdy—' Debbo was looking warily at Claire but Perdy was not to be gainsaid.

'Men still think women who agree with them are angels and women who stand up to them are whores.'

'Men like whores,' Claire said suddenly and then, seeing their startled faces, 'Well, don't they?'

'That's as may be,' Debbo said, 'but we should be on to our second half now. Let's have your glasses.'

They talked about work after that; Claire's collection, Perdy's latest case, Deborah's new book which was really to make its mark. They were in a mellow mood as they walked back to the Bailey and set their appointed tasks, Debbo to cook, Claire to lay the table and Perdy to open the wine.

The pasta was served in a huge willow-pattern tureen, the sauce deposited in wonderfully gooey globs straight from the pan.

'Oh God, that's beautiful.' Perdy threw back her head to breathe in like a Bisto kid.

'I've improved, haven't I.' It was a statement, not a question, and Debbo beamed at them.

'I've enjoyed today,' Claire said as she licked in a stray curl of pasta. 'And it was good just to let out how I feel. Thank you.'

'Do you want to talk some more?' Perdy offered.

'No.' Claire sounded and felt certain. 'You moved me on. I can't work out exactly where to − not yet − but I'll work it through. And I'm grateful. Now, I'm not changing the subject, I'm just—'

'Changing the subject,' Debbo said. 'Good.' Claire saw a tiny frown cross Perdy's brow and wondered if she was mirroring Claire's own thought, that it wasn't like Debs to want to sweep things under the carpet.

'I've got a lot of bumf Freda brought me. Up-to-date stuff on Durham now . . . the new colleges. Everything. It's quite impressive.'

'We were so lucky to get here,' Perdy said, as they settled around the sofa, the pamphlets spread out around them. She sounded wistful, for a second not the rising young barrister but someone as uncertain about her future as Claire felt about her own.

'I wonder,' Claire thought. 'Would she tell us if she were hurting?' She never had before but everyone had a breaking point. And then they were absorbing the new facts and Perdy was her usual, animated self.

'We really were lucky to wind up here. I keep saying it but it's true.'

'They've just won a Queen's Prize,' Claire said. 'I saw it in the paper and kept it for you.' She fetched the cutting from the study. 'It's for a University-led scheme involving engineering students with the outside world — schools as well as companies — to give kids some interesting technological opportunities.'

'We never realised the effect our presence had on the community,' Perdy mused. 'Remember how we used to walk the streets, quite oblivious of the life of the city? If it wasn't happening in Cuth's or Trev's or Mary's it wasn't happening at all. But it's different now. There isn't room for ivory towers. It says here the annual budget is eighty million. Ye gods!' She was silent for a moment, devouring facts and figures, and then she looked up. 'They're moving with the times — computer literacy, communication skills, European languages for all students — there was none of that in our day! No wonder Durham's near the top of the graduate employment league table.'

'I hope at least one of mine will come here,' Debbo said. 'They must choose for themselves but I shall lobby for it, if only because Durham's completion rates are so high.'

'We only lost one,' Claire said. 'Stuart Pringle. Remember? He dropped out and went to India, didn't he?' They fell to reminiscing then, growing misty-eyed with nostalgia and alcohol.

It was two a.m. when Claire fell into bed, unsure that she would hit the pillow before exhaustion and red wine overtook her. But two hours later she was still wide awake, the World Service murmuring softly away on the bedside table so as not to wake Debbo. She was listening as a news reader told of ex-President Reagan's announcement that he had Altzheimer's disease. His 'Spitting Image' puppet came into her mind, amiable and vacuous and cruel. How awful to be senile, but at least he had Nancy. Who would she have when her time came to rage against the dying of the light? She turned on her face then and wept.

There was nothing about Michael in the morning papers. To the tabloids, he was old news now that David Mellor was back in the spotlight, pledging to stand by Lady Cobham. Once more, Judith Mellor was being the loyal wife. The broadsheets seemed preoccupied with the hammering Bill Clinton was sure to take in the mid-term election. Why did anyone choose politics? You lost the right to a private life and could be cast aside without a moment's regret. You were flavour of the month one day and crap the next. And yet Michael had never loved her as he had loved the Palace of Westminster.

The house seemed empty now that Perdy and Debs had gone back to London and Claire moved from room to room, anxious for the sound of Freda's key in the lock so that she could have a conversation. As though the dogs sensed her loneliness, they moved in on her, with warm tongues, cold noses, nuzzling heads. Nowadays, to her surprise, she found herself welcoming their attentions.

She had been determined to endure them, now she was almost fond of them.

Both Perdy and Debs had promised to come again as soon as they could but reason told Claire they couldn't put their lives on hold too often, especially Deborah. Hugh was close to an angel but even he would have a breaking point. It was less than six weeks to Christmas, six weeks to be filled somehow. She rubbed Max's head. 'You're all I've got, old thing. Let's go walkies!' By the time she came back, Freda would be there, bustling about with spray and duster, giving the house a sense of normality once more.

She walked on the river bank, shivering a little in the east wind. Winter was setting in now and she would have to wear a warmer coat. This morning it had been painful to see the death throes of the garden. The odd dahlia still bloomed but the leaves of the iris were threadbare and gaunt and the antirrhinums had given up the ghost. Even the chrysanthemums looked wet and beaten to the ground. But if the blooms had faded their leaves were still battling on. The hydrangeas were a red and gold blaze and the cotoneaster leaves flamed red and orange, but when she looked beyond the garden wall she saw that the trees were turning to bare Chinese works of art before her eyes.

Now, as she turned for home, she tried to remember if she had been as aware of nature before Michael's death. She had always liked flowers, had her own small plot as a child, but this autumn she seemed alert to every nuance of the changing season.

156

She was almost back at North Bailey when she saw a man in the distance, walking towards her front door. As she drew closer she realised it was the big, bulky journalist she had seen on the day of Michael's death and again when she was out running. How had he found her here? And more important, what did he want?

For a moment she contemplated turning on her heel and going back to the river but it would have been useless. There was something about him, about his slightly hunched shoulders and unsmiling face, that denoted determination. If he had come all this way to see her, he wouldn't give up lightly.

It was hard to meet his eye as she neared the door. Should she speak first or try to push past him? In the end, it was he who took the initiative. 'Mrs Griffin, I haven't come to hound you.' His voice was deep and slightly accented, Scottish or Northern Irish. She waited for him to speak again before she could decide.

'What do you want? I haven't anything more to add to my statement so you're wasting your time.' She put a hand to the door as she spoke.

'I've come to tell you something. Could we talk inside? I want to help, if I can.'

She hesitated on the step. Could she trust him? Was it a ruse to get inside the house? Could she afford to tell him to go to hell? What if he brought the rest of the pack down on her?

She went into the hall and turned to face him. 'You'd better come inside but only for a moment.' She moved into the kitchen, unwilling to afford him the courtesy of the living-room. 'Well?' she said, sitting down at the kitchen table.

He pulled out a chair and sat opposite her, finding it difficult to accommodate his long legs. 'May I?' he asked.

'You already have! Now, please get a move on.' She was dying for a coffee and apprehensive about Freda, who could be heard hoovering upstairs. 'I have to go out in a moment so I haven't much time.' He was built like a barn door and his face had a slightly battered look but his eyes were kind. She felt her guard drop a little . . . perhaps she could offer him a coffee . . . but while she was still deliberating his first question took her by surprise.

'Were you in South America in May, Mrs Griffin?'

'No. Why do you ask?' He didn't speak and after a moment she continued. 'Michael went on a fact-finding mission. He was there for five days, but—'

As her voice died away he pulled out a small notepad and read from it. 'On the 9th of May, 1994, Mr & Mrs Michael Griffin booked into the Excelsior Hotel in Rio. They occupied a double room on the fourth floor. They checked out on the 10th and moved to a guest-house inland. They were there for three days and flew home via New York.'

Suddenly the fax machine sprang to life in the study and Claire was glad of the interruption. 'Do you want to get that?' the journalist asked.

Claire shook her head, her mind working furiously.

'What did you say your name was?' she asked. 'I know you gave me a card but I've lost it.'

'Dennehy. Jake Dennehy. I'm with the *Globe*.'

'It can't have been Michael,' Claire said automatically. 'He was there but he went with other Members. You've made a mistake.'

It was his turn to shake his head. 'No mistake, Mrs Griffin. We checked it out. We weren't the people to uncover it . . . I came to tell you it's coming out on Sunday in the "News of the Screws."' He saw her look of puzzlement. 'The *News of the World*. And there's more. They've signed up one of the neighbours from Kennerley Street. As far as I can gather there's not much substance to the story . . . a lot of comings and goings, probably a fair bit of invention—'

One side of Claire's brain had succeeded in pinning down his accent; Northern Irish Protestant. The other half of her mind was scrabbling for a way to escape. She was going to open a paper and find out what had been going on in her own life. Not speculation, not insinuation – the truth. Papers didn't publish unless they had some fact. There was a law, she was sure there was a law.

'Mrs Griffin?' He was expecting a response of some sort. She cleared her throat.

'How do you know all this? It's not your paper.' He smiled, looking suddenly human and rather like a rugged American film star who usually played policemen and whose name she couldn't remember.

'Believe me, Fleet Street has no secrets, not among

159

its own. I know they have facts and figures from the Rio trip — including a photostat of the hotel register. Now, if you weren't there, it was someone else. The round-the-doors stuff doesn't amount to much. It seldom does. Give a house celebrity or notoriety . . . half the neighbourhood wants to sell you their story. But who was in Rio?'

She had to ask the question although she feared the answer. 'The woman in the flat?'

He nodded. 'I think so. Unless your husband was an unaccountable womaniser I think it's safe to assume there was only one woman . . . at a time, that is . . .' He was suddenly embarrassed. 'I mean, well—'

She decided to rescue him. 'In addition to me, you mean?' He nodded, relieved. 'Why are you telling me?' she asked.

He leant closer, anxious to convince her. 'I meant what I said that day, outside your door. I want to help. Oh, I want a story all right, but I don't like seeing an innocent person victimised. In my book you aren't to blame for anything. I can keep the worst of them off you and if you give your reactions through one outlet it cuts the feet from under the fantasy-merchants . . . because you're saying it as it is in my paper so no one pays attention to what they *say* you're thinking or feeling in theirs. Get it?'

She was far from convinced. He wanted her to commit to him but why should she trust him? Why should she ever trust anyone again after Michael?

'You mean I'd talk to you and no one else?' Upstairs

the hoover had ceased. Freda would come downstairs at any moment.

'Yes. But we'd give you safeguards. We wouldn't pad or tamper with what you said — and once you were tied in with us the others would back off. Why publicise *our* story? I promise you that's how it works.'

'Why should I trust you?' she asked as defiantly as she could.

'You can't. But I mean what I say.' His gaze was steady when it met her own.

Claire thought for a moment. 'I'm not sure. I'd have to talk to someone . . . a friend who's a barrister—'

'Perdita Lawrence?' He was grinning. 'I saw her with you at the inquest and at your place. She knows what it's about all right. Yes, talk to her. She'll confirm what I'm saying, I'm pretty sure. Give her a ring.'

Claire went through to the study to make the call. While Perdy's number rang out she reached for the fax. As she expected, it came from Stephen, and she put it aside to read later.

Perdy's phone was still ringing, not even her answering machine switching on. Claire replaced the receiver briefly and then dialled Debbo's number. It was answered almost at once by a Deborah sounding slightly out of breath.

'992 0476'

'Debs? It's me, Claire.'

'Darling . . . are you OK?' At once, Deborah was alarmed by the tone of Claire's voice.

'I'm fine. Well, I'm OK but I need some advice. I've got someone here from a newspaper——'

Before she could continue Debbo interjected. 'Which one?'

'The *Globe*.'

'Don't say anything, Cleo. Just "No comment" and nothing more.'

'It's not that like that . . . well, not exactly.'

'Cleo, for God's sake, don't tell me he's got nice eyes and he means to be kind, that's their stock-in-trade. Get him out of the house and bolt the door.'

'Look,' Claire said desperately. 'There's something coming out on Sunday in another paper. He knows all about it. Something about Michael being in Rio with a woman . . .'

There was silence at the other end of the line until Debbo sighed. 'Oh Cleo, how awful for you. It's probably not true but if they will cook things up——'

'Michael was in Rio. In May. He went with some other Members. At least, that's what he told me. Apparently he was with a woman: they have details and documentation. I expect it is true — they must've checked it out. Anyway, this man . . . his name is Dennehy . . . wants me to give my version — well, I think that's what he wants — but I don't know if I should commit myself.'

'Hugh!' Debbo was calling her husband to the phone. 'I don't think you should do it, Cleo. Stay away from them.' She turned from the phone to carry on a breathless conversation with Hugh. Claire could hear his deeper tones, questioning, suggesting, and then Debbo returned to the phone. 'Hugh says you should ring Perdy and get her to deal with it. But above all, he says don't sign anything.

When Claire emerged from the study Freda was coming down the stairs, holding the hoover in one hand, a duster in the other. 'That's upstairs done. I'm off now if there's nothing else.' She looked towards the kitchen. 'Company?'

'Just an old friend,' Claire said. Freda's coat and bag were in the kitchen. What if Dennehy gave himself away? But he handled the meeting admirably, bowing courteously to Freda when Claire flustered an introduction, then turning back to the window while Claire made her goodbyes and saw Freda to the door.

When Claire went back to the kitchen he was still staring out of the window. He turned back at the sound of her entrance. 'Did you get Miss Lawrence?'

'She's not in, but I spoke to other friends. They say I shouldn't do anything until I've spoken to Perdy.'

He held up his hand, palms outward. 'Fine! The last thing I want to do is hassle you. I'm staying at the Ramside for a day or two.' Again he held up his hands. 'I'm not nosing around up here. Well, not about you anyway; your story's down south. You can ring me at the Ramside up to Friday morning. I'm back to the smoke then. But don't leave it too late. There's another Mellor-induced feeding frenzy at the moment but when it's over they'll come back to you. I'll give you another card.'

He handed her the card with blunt, square-tipped fingers. He saw her looking at their somewhat roughened state and grinned again and in spite of herself Claire's own mouth turned up in response.

'Shocking, aren't they? Not a pen-pusher's hands. I fish whenever I've got the chance. I'm going up Weardale tomorrow. And I've got a garden . . . just a plot in North London but it's green.'

'Fishing and gardening? It doesn't sound much like the street of shame,' Claire said.

His face creased with amusement. 'You should smile more, Mrs Griffin. It suits you.'

He had gone too far with the blarney. She felt her face harden. 'Tell me, how did you find me?'

Again the gesture with the hands. 'I plead diplomatic immunity on that one. But I'm the only person who knows where you are . . . well, the only journo, anyway. And as far as I'm concerned it'll stay like that.'

For no sensible reason she believed him, holding out her hand at the door to shake farewell.

'One question,' he said, 'and then I'll leave you in peace. Before all this happened, did you have any inkling — not just of another woman but of anything untoward?'

'No,' Claire said resolutely. 'I'm almost ashamed to say it because it makes me seem a complacent idiot, but until that night when Michael didn't come home, until then I had no idea that anything . . . that everything wasn't as it seemed.'

But after he had gone she thought again. There

had always been another side to Michael. She had just chosen not to acknowledge it.

Throughout the rest of the day she tried Perdy's number intermittently but at some stage she missed her friend's return home for when she rang again at eight p.m. the answering machine was on. She left a message, asking Perdy to ring her when she could but added, 'It's not urgent,' in case Perdy brought someone back with her. Perdy had been quiet about her love-life lately but someone so attractive must have someone somewhere. She couldn't interrupt a *tête-à-tête* with more of her own miseries.

It was growing dark when she remembered the fax. She took it up from the table where she had left it and read it through. In her last reply she had accused him of overfeeding the birds. Now he was retaliating.

'If you consider feathered obesity a problem please diet accordingly. I trust your judgement. If you look in the right-hand bottom corner of the garden you will find some hellebores. Not the common one, *Helleborus niger*, but *Helleborus foetidus*, which has a head of green bells trimmed with red. I hope they bloom for you before you leave. Not entirely unselfish on my part, I want them there, open in welcome, when I get back. Flowers here are mostly huge and lurid – spectacular, but too Disney-like for my taste. Give me an English garden any time.' It was signed with a flourish and he had added a PS: 'I offer no suggestions for the garden as no doubt you are an FRHS in addition to being a FZS. PPS: I hope you are enjoying your stay.' She looked the initials up in a dictionary to check what she thought them to be: Fellowships of the Royal Horticulture Society and Zoological Society respectively.

Ever since Dennehy's visit, the new and unwelcome information had lain over her like a cloud. Now, suddenly, she felt in the mood to do something silly. She found a torch in a drawer in the kitchen and went out into the gloom of the garden at dusk to locate the Christmas roses. They were there, nestling close to the ground – two clumps of dark-green foliage with one or two incipient buds just showing in the depths of the stems.

She was smiling as she sat down to write her reply.

'Hellebores on course for home-coming. Birds banting, dogs adorable, cat aloof. Yours, *in locum tenens*, Louise Cantrell. PS: As a gardener you are *nem. con.*'

Let him look that up if he didn't know it stood for *nemine contradicente*, 'without opposition'. But as a historian he probably would know and also know she'd declined it improperly or some such other solecism. She scribbled through the postscript until it was indecipherable before she fed the paper into the machine.

When she had sent the fax she felt suddenly deflated. She was not over the worst of Michael's death, however much she might try to push it to the back of her mind. The worst, in terms of notoriety, was obviously still to come.

The phone rang again as she was preparing the dogs'

food. It was Gavin Lambert, apologising for ringing her in the evening.

'It's all right,' she said. 'I'm not in the middle of dinner or anything.'

'Did you get my letter?'

'No,' Claire said.

'No matter.' He sounded nonchalant. 'There was nothing of urgency. A few details and a note on the Kennerley Street premises. I think we can get rid of them . . . I expect that's what you'd prefer?'

Claire drew breath. 'I don't want to let go of the flat yet. Soon . . . but I'd like to leave it for a week or two.'

'Is it that you want it cleared? I could arrange that.'

'That's kind of you. And perhaps I will ask you . . . eventually. But for now I'd like it left just as it is.' To her own ears she sounded amazingly decisive and Lambert must have agreed for he let the matter go.

In reality, she didn't know why she had spoken as she did. Did she want to see the flat? Surely not!

'I'm arranging the service for December 12th. I hope that's agreeable?'

Claire indicated approval and he continued, 'Pamela Corby, you remember her — the member for Barminster — is helping me . . . she's proving invaluable. But of course we'll defer to your wishes on anything: you only have to let me know.' She promised to let him have details and was about to put down the phone when she remembered the exposé. If he had prior warning he could do some damage limitation, if such a thing were possible.

'There was one other thing, Mr Lambert.'

'Do call me Gavin.' It was said smoothly in the perfect PR way and she almost smiled at the thought of the bombshell she was about to drop.

'You probably know already, Gavin – I know you have your sources – there's something about Michael coming out in the *News of the World* on Sunday.'

There was silence at the other end and then a groan. 'Are you sure?'

'Pretty sure. It was a journalist who told me.'

'You haven't said anything?' He almost gasped out his words.

'No. They've got nothing from me. Apparently they have details of Michael's trip to Rio: he didn't go alone. And one of the neighbours in Kennerley Street has sold them a story.' If she was going to tell him she was going to the flat, this was the moment! Instead she listened to him moan about trying to cope with a rising tide of rumour and innuendo, and thought of the moment when she could settle down with cocoa and think about something nicer than tabloid journalism.

Before she went upstairs that night she reread the fax. 'I hope you are enjoying your stay.' Stephen Gaunt was a strange man: fair-haired hunk or bespectacled academic, whichever he was. Before she climbed into bed she was suddenly drawn to the master bedroom, to the wardrobe that held his clothes, and she stroked the rough tweeds, the smooth gaberdines, the woollen

168

sweaters on the shelf above, half smiling at the thought that there was almost a masculine presence in her life. Somehow the clothes made her feel safer . . . which was ridiculous!

But once in bed, with the light out, she did not feel safe at all. Usually she enjoyed the Sunday papers: now she was dreading them — all of them, for the other papers would try to trump the *News of the World*, passing comment on its story as though they had known about it all along. And if she did talk to Dennehy, what would she say? What could she say? That she had been no more than a smokescreen in Michael's life? That he had married her because she was the perfect Tory wife; virginal — or almost — good background, well-spoken, well-mannered and above all, pliable? Whatever she said, or did not say, she would be exposed for the fool she undoubtedly was.

She lay there, trying to sort out her jumbled thoughts. Should she let the Kennerley Street flat go, unseen? Or go there and face it? Perhaps even form a picture of the other woman . . . There must be some trace of her there? But even thinking about it was terrifying.

She turned on her side, feeling her legs draw up into the foetal position, hugging herself, suddenly cold so that the bed seemed not a refuge but an ice-chamber. She lay there, tormented and shivering, until she could stand it no more. She leapt from the bed and ran across the moonlit landing to snatch a woollen sweater from Stephen's wardrobe. It fell to her knees and covered her hands and that made it even more blissful. She was back in her own bed and sinking into sleep before she questioned why she had not chosen a warm garment of her own but by then she was too tired for speculation.

13

There were three letters for her landlord on the mat when Claire came downstairs, and one for her. One of Stephen's letters was personal, one was a circular from a shirt company, the other marked Royal Bank of Scotland. So that was where he kept his money. She dutifully re-addressed them and put them ready to post before carrying her own letter through to the kitchen. She opened it while the kettle was boiling and read it standing with her back to the cooker. The letter was the expected missive from Gavin Lambert and came on Central Office notepaper.

He hoped she was well and bearing up in exile and detailed some minor matters he had dealt with on her behalf. It was the final paragraph that mattered. It stated that he had managed to renegotiate the lease on the Kennerley Street flat. It would shortly be offered for rent and as soon as another tenant had been secured would cease to be a drain on Michael's estate. He was sure this would be to her satisfaction and with her permission he would arrange for the flat to be cleared ready for viewing by prospective tenants.

For some reason the letter filled her with apprehension, as though it heralded the irrevocable closing of a door. While she drank her tea she tried to tell herself that it was closing on all the bad things of the last few weeks, that while the scene of Michael's death remained frozen, Miss Haversham-like, as it had been on the day of Michael's death, there could be no going forward. It was useless. She was filled with terror at the mere idea of its being swept away, and the fact that she had forbidden Lambert to get rid of it seemed small comfort.

As Freda arrived she was bundling the dogs into the car, desperate to get away from her fears. But driving out of the city and into open countryside she felt no better. She drove west for a while but then changed her mind and drove south and east towards the coast, pulling up at last in the entrance to a farm track.

She climbed over on to the path that skirted a field, the dogs wriggling under the gate to join her. It was a warm day for November, almost an Indian summer, and the rich, dark Durham earth was already sprouting a winter crop, although the seedlings were too new and fragile to be identified. At the end of the field the ground sloped upward to a scrubby hillside deep in bracken.

She began to climb, the dogs running and sniffing, first behind and then in front, in a frenzy of excitement at each new scent. When she reached the top of the hillock she looked around her, seeing the odd-shaped fields in mulled greens and browns, higgledy-piggledy English hedges, hawthorn and wild rose and dogwood and elder, beginning to lose the reds and golds of autumn now. Over on the right there was a newly tilled field, dark and rich and patterned in fine rows. How wonderful to drive round and round your own field making patterns in the earth.

There were some ruined buildings on her left and a piece of agricultural machinery abandoned in the corner of another field, and a fine, grey cast lay over the whole scene, something she had noticed you only found in the North. No vivid greens, or black, black soils; everything temperate and gentle. She felt her panic gradually subsiding. This scene had probably not changed for a hundred years or more. It made her own situation seem unbelievably transient and therefore less threatening.

She stayed there for a long while, trying not to think about Kennerley Street or anywhere else, trying not to wonder why Perdy had not rung that morning, knowing all the time that sooner or later she must go back and face it all.

Eventually she walked back from the summit and along the field path, passing a sycamore tree, its leaves winnowing gently to the ground. She had almost reached the gate when she saw the tiny blue flower on the path in front of her, just one blossom no bigger than a pea. Her eyes filled suddenly with idiotic tears. She could so easily have crushed it under her heel. She bent down, meaning to grub it out with her fingers and transplant it to a place of safety, but realised that if she did that, it wouldn't stand a chance.

As she walked away she told herself it was a weed, a thing of no consequence, but now the tears were coursing down her face and Max was suddenly aware of her distress and pawing at her jeans.

When the dogs were safely in the car she reversed on to the road and made for the nearest pub. It was eleven-twenty but if it had been seven a.m. she would still have demanded a drink. The pub was dark but as her eyes grew accustomed to the gloom she saw that already there were signs of Christmas everywhere: a trio of snowmen in one corner, complete with scarves and red noses; a poster advertising Christmas lunch in another. Christmas! 'God save me from Christmas,' she thought. Christmas had been the one time she could be sure of having Michael to herself for two whole days, as they both slopped around in track suits, eating the leftovers at any hour they chose, drunk with wine and unaccustomed leisure. Yes, God save her from Christmas.

She was sipping her Amontillado, feeling it warm and comfort her, when the girl came in. She was small and thin and hardly looked old enough to be drinking but her white sweater bulged above jean-clad, pipe-cleaner legs. Her face had the huge-eyed hungry look of the pregnant woman and the older woman who came in behind her hovered anxiously, like a mother hen.

Within minutes Claire's new-found sense of ease had

evaporated. She was back in the days of hope, when every month had begun with at least the chance of conception and ended in disappointment; when every friend had regaled her with stories of people who endured disappointment only miraculously to conceive in the end or adopt children who turned out to be child prodigies and angels to boot.

She had gone on trying, would have gone on for ever if Michael had not called a halt. 'Let's settle for what we've got, Claire. I'm tired of being pawed over, so God knows what it must be like for you.' They had tried everything except IVF. Apart from that there was only adoption and Michael's face had twisted at the mere idea.

She drained her glass and got to her feet, driven out by memories more painful than whatever might await her back at home. As she drove back to the city she debated whether or not to go to London, to Kennerley Street, and lay the ghost. With each mile she changed her mind. She could, she couldn't, she would, she wouldn't. When she reached the house she rang the British Rail information line. She could catch a train to London at nine-twelve and return from King's Cross at five-thirty on the Tyne-Tees Pullman. Ample time in London to see all that Kennerley Street contained.

'I'm going,' she said aloud.

She checked her appearance in the mirror above the telephone table. She would have to tint her roots but the face that looked back at her was not the deathly-looking face that had been pictured in the

175

papers. With luck, she would get away with it. She was still regarding her reflection when the phone rang.

'Cleo? Sorry I couldn't get back to you sooner. What's up?' She told Perdy about the visit of the journalist and waited for a verdict.

'Well,' Perdy said at last, 'I'd like to ask around a bit more first, see if he's kosher. If he is, you might be better off — it all depends what they've got. Leave it with me for a little while. I did enquire about him before but not in depth. This time I'll bottom him.'

She was about to tell Perdy about the letter from Central Office when something stopped her. If she was going to Kennerley Street she wanted to go alone, and neither Perdy nor Debbo would stand for that. She promised not to contact Jake Dennehy until she heard from Perdy and assured her friend that she was feeling positively chipper. 'You don't sound too good,' Perdy said dubiously. 'Still, I'll ring you tomorrow and we'll sort something out. And I'll be up again as soon as I can.'

As though by telepathy, Deborah rang as soon as Perdy went off the line. 'Perdy's the best person to advise you,' she soothed. 'She'll find out if he's a shit and if he is you can tell him to bugger off. Hugh'll do it for you if necessary. You mustn't be intimidated, Cleo. You're too anxious to please; everyone puts on you.'

When she put down the phone, Claire poured herself a large Scotch and went into the study in search of a wildflower reference book. There were three but she could find no trace of the tiny blue flower in any of them, which made its isolation all the more poignant. Tomorrow she would go back and grub it up, no matter what. Was she anxious to please? She had not pleased Michael . . . at least not enough.

From the wall the two men looked at her dubiously. She raised her glass to them and inclined her head slightly. 'I am going mad,' she thought, 'toasting photographs. I'll be talking to them next.' But she longed for someone to talk to, even Dennehy. She could ring his hotel now but even as she thought it she knew it was impossible. She had been vulnerable yesterday, she would be easy meat today.

She left the study clutching a reference book on birds. She fed them every day, she might as well know what they were. For a moment she contemplated sending another fax. It was better than drinking herself senseless. Instead she reread his fax again and again until it had partially restored her faith in human nature.

She put on the kettle for hot chocolate then and while she was waiting for it to boil she riffled through a magazine Freda had left on the bench above the washer. There was a page of horoscopes and she looked up her own sign, Gemini: 'Be suspicious when things seem straightforward,' she read. 'Hidden twists and complications are more than likely while Mars is transitting your sign.' So that was who she could blame, the god Mars. There was a telephone number you could call for a lengthier version and she went through to the study phone and dialled it. 'Hello, Gemini.' The voice on the other end of the line was female and friendly. She listened for several minutes, wincing at the thought of the phone bill but unable to tear herself away from the soothing tones until she remembered that phone bills were itemised nowadays. If Stephen saw the 0891 number and checked it out he would know her for a fool and for some odd reason she didn't want that to happen.

14

While Freda was in the house, humming, hoovering, offering impromptu 'cuppas', Claire was able to work steadily. She knew now that she would be able to deliver her designs on time and was fairly certain the Golds would like them. She had been more imaginative in her choice of fabrics, using satin and hand-painted panne. She was grateful that the era of porridge- and muesli-type colours was over, that she could splash pink and orange and lime together to create a look. Freda appeared to go into raptures each time she passed the drawing-board but Claire could see she thought the drawings bizarre. She thought of telling Freda she had once won a Promising Newcomer award but decided against it. Freda didn't rate the rag trade too highly.

Freda's own preoccupation was with the new National Lottery. 'Someone's got to win,' she said. 'Instant millionaires they say.' She offered to buy a ticket for Claire and spat on the proffered pound coin 'for luck'. 'They're queueing out into the street,' she said but the thought of all the other hopeful punters didn't seem to get her down. 'Someone's got to win' was her mantra and it made Claire change her previous opinion of the lottery as a frivolous exercise. People were buying a pound's worth of hope and each week there would be fresh hope, another chance. Claire smiled as she went back to her sketching, thinking of Freda busily plotting how to spend her first million.

But when Freda had gone and the house grew quiet, unpleasant thoughts begin to crowd in again. Ever since reading Sunday's newspapers Claire had felt wretched. Since Michael's death, she had almost come to terms with the idea of his seeking sex elsewhere. Perhaps he had wanted something she could not or would not have wanted to offer. In those last months they had seldom made love but when they had it had been as fulfilling as ever. Or had it? Had it simply been ordinary? The minute doubt entered, it flourished. They had not laughed in bed for a long time or reached for one another at inappropriate moments. 'Statutory coupling.' The phrase popped into her mind from God knew where but it fitted. 'He was doing his duty,' Claire thought miserably and laid down her pencil to weep.

There had been a lurid account of noisy love-making between Michael and the mystery woman, supposedly overheard by a Kennerley Street neighbour. There had been copious details of Michael's trip to Rio, where he had apparently swum and dined and danced with a woman purporting to be his wife, never taking his eyes from her and constantly caressing her. 'Like newly-weds,' according to the hotel receptionist. There had been a vague description of the woman as unglamorous and wearing dark glasses, which really said nothing at all. At the guest house, in the Brazilian hinterland, they had failed to emerge from their room, except for meals. It was all highly coloured stuff.

Claire herself was depicted as a drab little country mouse whom Michael had married fresh from school and neglected ever since. She was said to be inconsolable and travelling abroad, 'probably in the company of one of her brothers, all high-ranking officers in the British Army'.

The piece had ended with the suggestion that a man who was capable of such deception should not have been privy to Government secrets. 'Where was MI5?' a sub-title demanded above a picture of Michael in his Cambridge days, wearing a harlequin mask and cloak and leering up at the camera, looking for all the world like the Devil incarnate.

Claire had not dared to ask if her parents knew of this latest development but Perdy and Debs had been quick to ring and offer comfort. 'Hugh says there's nothing in it . . . its just a soufflé of misinformation and you shouldn't give it another thought.'

Perdy had been equally definite. 'It could have been much worse, Cleo. Frankly, I'm relieved: there's almost nothing of substance. They're simply beating the air. I think it will all die down now—' She had paused then and Claire knew what was coming. 'That's why I think you probably shouldn't speak to Dennehy. If they get to know you're poking around they'll think there is something to find and they'll go on and on. And if they can't find anything, they'll make it up.'

Claire had not given way. 'We'll see' was all she said but her resolve to discover the identity of the woman in Kennerley Street, the woman who presumably had gone with Michael on the Rio trip, was firmer than ever. If she had not known of the poky little flat, if she had not known about the Rio trip, how much else was hidden?

A bulky letter from her father had arrived that morning, full of neat lists. 'Guests at funeral repast' had been one. 'Mourners at church' another. 'Letters of condolence' ran to three sheets, 'Donations in lieu of flowers' to two. At some stage she would have to think about letters of appreciation but not yet. Not until she knew more of the truth. She dried her tears eventually and went through to the kitchen to make her lunch, the dogs padding behind her, half in sympathy and half in expectation of a tit-bit. Why had she never before realised the comfort dogs could give? She knelt to take Brutus's great head between her hands and gaze into his mournful eyes. He stayed rock-steady while she laid her head against his velvet ear and the warm bulk of him was such balm that she might have stayed there for ever if a lithe, blue-grey body had not insinuated itself between them, arching and pushing its way through. She looked into the cat's gleaming eyes, seeing an almost amused contempt there. 'All right,' she said, getting to her feet, 'I can take a hint.'

She made cheese on toast and coffee and carried them through to the window-seat in the study, from where Stephen Gaunt watched his precious birds. They were there in the trees now, a whir of activity around the seed containers. Claire tried to concentrate on the birds, enjoy their antics and forget the more questionable activities of human beings, but it was useless. The pictures that flashed across her mind's eye were of Michael and the woman he had taken to Rio. Had they met at the airport? Sat side by side in the plane? Had he held her hand during take-off and landing, as he had always done to comfort her? Above all, had they fucked often and savagely, there in a strange land, surrounded by the exotic sights and sounds of Latin America? 'Oh God,' Claire said aloud, shocked at her own choice of words, and leant her forehead against the cold window-pane to try and ease her troubled thoughts.

This was not how she had expected widowhood to be. In the early weeks of her marriage she had often thought how wonderful it was to have Michael; how terrible it would be to lose him. Once or twice she had pictured herself bereft, silent and noble, bringing up Michael's child or children. Wrong on two counts! She was being anything but noble and there were no children on which to dote. But she was learning a valuable lesson. You could never predict behaviour – not even your own – unless you had been in the situation. So you should never sit in judgement on others.

'I want to pick up the pieces,' she thought. 'I want to get it right this time.' In the night she had decided a visit to Kennerley Street would not only be unwise, it would be counter-productive but when at last she pushed aside her untouched plate, she had made up her mind. She could not go to Rio but she could go to Kennerley Street and hopefully she would find something there that would explain, at least in part, why she had not been enough for the man she had married.

She walked the dogs on the river bank behind the houses and then let them back into the house before walking down in to the Market Square in search of a chemist's shop. This morning she had seen the dark roots of her own hair showing stark against the rest. She armed herself with everything she would need to touch them up and carried her purchases back to North Bailey, determined to tackle the task with the panache that Perdy had shown when she did it.

She was half-way through the messy process when she heard the fax machine start up downstairs. She wanted to run down and see what Stephen Gaunt had to say, for it must be from him, but she made herself continue dabbling the dye along one parting after another, as Perdy had instructed and as she had seen others do often enough in hairdressing salons.

There was so much to be done if she was to carry out her plans. She would have to be more systematic, less impulsive. Besides, she wanted to save the fax for the hour before bedtime, when she often felt low. She would read it then and perhaps compose a reply and if she was lucky it would divert her long enough for her eyelids to droop and sleep to overtake her.

She was preparing the dogs' food, Calliope pawing at the upholstered top of the kitchen stool, when the phone rang. This was the time her mother always phoned. Claire put down the cat's bowl, knowing Calliope would give her no peace if she didn't, rinsed her hands under the tap and dried them on a towel as she made her way to the study. It was not her mother on the other end of the line; it was Jake Dennehy and her heart started to thump uncomfortably at the thought of further revelations. His first words reassured her.

'I've no real news. I've talked to the guy who did the Rio story but he's got nothing substantial on the woman. Nondescript was how she came across from the people he spoke to.' He paused for a moment and when he spoke again his voice was more tentative. 'Are you OK?'

Claire looked at herself in the mirror on the opposite wall. Was she OK? She looked strange, a creature of shadowed eyes and skin too dark for the hair above. 'I'm . . .' she hesitated. 'I'm fine, I think. Obviously I've got a lot to mull over but I can cope. I'm working again – that helps.'

'Have you thought over what I said?'

'I've thought about it.' She was fencing and they both knew it.

'The offer's still there when you're ready,' Dennehy said. 'I'll find out eventually anyway . . . but it's up to you.' His voice took on a more cheerful note. 'How are the mutts? You're not used to animals, are you?'

'How did you know that? I've never had a dog but I'm coping.'

He chuckled. 'The eyes . . . you looked as though you'd been put in charge of a herd of water-buffalo.'

Claire laughed. 'That bad?'

'Your eyes rolled when you were shepherding them through the door, as though you were hoping for the best. And when they actually went you raised them to heaven to give thanks.' It was such an accurate description of the way she had felt with the dogs at first that when she put down the phone she felt almost cheerful. It was true, she *was* coping. Not only that, she was finding the dogs rewarding. Especially when they obeyed her.

She finished getting their food together and put the bowls down on the floor between the questing snouts with new-found confidence. That first night she had expected them to take off her hand in their haste to get at the food, now she was in control. She stood over them while they ate and then let them out into the dark garden, all the while looking forward to the moment when, bathed and nightgowned, she could curl up with hot chocolate and chuckle over Stephen Gaunt's fax. But before she could do that, there was another task to perform, something she had been shirking but now felt ready to face. She collected the small parcel Gavin Lambert had given her on the day of the funeral and sat in the window-seat to look through it. Michael had referred constantly to his slim blue diary but Claire had never before seen inside it. Now she opened it with trembling fingers.

Each day was crowded with details in Michael's clear, beautiful hand: dates and times of meetings, important political conferences and constituency occasions mostly. She checked her own birthday and anniversary and found them there, but there was no trace of another woman except for Maeve's birthday on September 22nd marked with an NB and, on May 25th, a touching note, 'Mother died, 1972.'

There was a comb, an emery board, a neatly folded handkerchief, some loose change in a plastic packet and a folder containing several assorted credit cards and memberships of clubs.

At last she picked up his wallet. If there was anything of significance it would surely be here. All she found was a quantity of bank notes and a piece of white heather, which disintegrated as she pulled it free of an outer pocket. She had half expected a condom but there was not one there and she was about to return the wallet to the pile when her probing fingers encountered something in the very last compartment.

It was a photograph, a snapshot, and her heart began to pound as it came into view. But the face smiling up at her was her own, snapped on a sunlit beach the summer before their wedding. It was a very ordinary photograph. She could not even remember its being taken, and yet Michael had kept it all these years! As she put it back in place she felt a momentary triumph but it was short-lived. Her picture might have been in his wallet but hers had not been the last face he had seen before he died.

15

Once she had made up her mind to go to Kennerley Street, it had to be done quickly. It was five weeks since Michael's death and she wanted an end to the wondering.

She caught the nine-twelve train from Durham the following day, leaving Freda in charge of the animals, promising that she would be back to care for them in the evening. Now, as the train pulled out she looked at the city, the houses clustering below, the Castle and Cathedral proud above them, all held within the comforting arm of the River Wear. Durham was beautiful. She had thought that the first time she had come there, all those years ago, and it was true. As the Cathedral tower passed from sight and the train gathered speed her eyes filled, so that the winter landscape blurred. Whatever she had hoped for in those days, it wasn't what she had ended up with . . . she had hoped to be happy ever after and now she was on her way to a sordid little love-nest in what would probably turn out to be a run-down London street.

For the first time she regretted her expedition. She should have left well alone, let Gavin Lambert empty the flat and given up any idea of understanding Michael's infidelity. But even as she knew regret, she brushed it aside. She needed to understand why it had happened. If she didn't, she would forever see it as her fault and the idea of feeling guilty about anything and everything was no longer acceptable.

To divert herself she pulled out the fax she had received yesterday. Obviously Stephen — she always thought of him as Stephen now, which was strange considering she had never met him — obviously he thought of home at bedtime and breakfast time, a fact she found oddly touching. Maybe he had seen her complimentary postscript about his garden after all for after some inconsequential remarks about the animals he wrote: 'I'm glad you are enjoying the garden. It's a pity you missed the summer. I only hope there's a little colour there still and the primulas should be showing but before I left it was glorious. I sat out in the evening whenever I could this year and watched the swifts feeding above . . . such apparently aimless flight but it gets them their supper. They will be gone now, until the spring, but you will still have the others. I won't ask if you're feeding them, I've learnt my lesson. I am enjoying my spell here but I miss the garden, especially in the early evening.' Claire closed her eyes, imagining the summer garden, the slender flowers heavy with bees, butterflies on the buddleia, which seemed to be everywhere, the larkspur and lupins and irises . . . and cornflowers. She had found a half-empty seed packet in a drawer so he must grow cornflowers too.

She must have fallen asleep, thinking of flowers, for when she came to her senses the train was pulling into Peterborough. She bought a gin and tonic from the trolley and sipped it as the train sped on and the outskirts of London came into view.

Once or twice she opened her bag and fingered the brown leather wallet of Michael's keys. There were several unidentified keys attached to rings inside the wallet, two of them too small to be door keys, one the key to a Yale lock. If her prayers were answered it would open the door to the Kennerley Street flat. If it didn't, she would have to decide whether to ask Gavin Lambert for a key or go home unsatisfied.

As the train drew into King's Cross she gathered up her things and made her way through the remaining first-class carriages to the very front. The sooner she was in a taxi and on her way, the sooner she could put her mind at rest and get back to Durham, a prospect that was becoming more desirable by the minute.

Every time anyone looked at her she wanted to shrink back, sure she had been recognised. She tried to be rational, telling herself that it was arrogance to assume anyone was even remotely interested in her. All the same, she tried to avoid the taxi-driver's eye as she mumbled her destination and climbed into the back of the cab. Would the very name of Kennerley Street bring him up with a start? To her relief, he simply put down his flag, let out the clutch and pulled away without the remotest sign of interest.

She felt fairly confident about her mission until she was deposited on the pavement outside the Kennerley Street house. It was a rather decrepit, three-storey building with close-curtained windows that gave no indication of the various tenants' personalities. Which was Michael's window? Impossible to tell.

She mounted the step and to her horror saw that there were seven nameplates, each with a bell, and the outer door was operated by a combination lock which needed the right numbers punched into it. What on earth could she do about that?

She descended the steps and began to walk towards the corner shop, afraid to be seen lurking. The neighbours must still be interested in comings and goings at the scene of a sudden death, natural or otherwise. And which of the neighbours was in cahoots with the *News of the World*? If only she had Perdy here, or even Debs, who was not as brave as Perdy but could stand her ground when she had to do so.

She looked in the shop window, trying to look interested in the cut-price groceries and rather wan fruit displayed there, all the while casting surreptitious glances towards the house. There must be some way of gaining access. She couldn't come all this way and be thwarted at the last step.

She was getting desperate when she saw the stout black woman turn into the street from the opposite corner. She had a bag of vegetables in her arms and a child of two or three held on to her coat. The woman walked slowly to accommodate the tiny legs alongside her and then shifted the bag on to one arm, fishing in the pocket of her jacket with the other hand. 'She's finding her key,' Claire thought. If only . . . if only the woman lived at number nine! She began to walk towards the pair, trying not to meet the woman's eye, praying all the time that the ponderous steps would turn into the right gateway.

Her prayers were answered. The woman brought out a key, transferred it to the hand that clutched the bag and used her free hand to hoist the toddler on to the steps of number nine. Claire quickened her step to fall in behind mother and son as they reached the top of the steps. She held her breath as one plump, black, red-tipped finger punched in the combination . . . 5 7 9 3 2. She repeated it over and over as the door swung open and the woman passed through.

'Thank you,' Claire said, putting out a hand to stop the door from closing. The woman half turned but her smile was indifferent. To Claire's relief she continued on along the hall, leaving Claire free to speed up the stairs as the door clicked shut behind her.

On the first landing she took out her diary and wrote down the combination with a trembling pen. 57932. She had no intention of ever coming back here but it was best to be on the safe side. That done, she turned and looked. Two doors on this landing: if only she'd had time to check the name plates . . . not that Michael would have used his own name. Perhaps it was the woman's name blazoned there for all the world to see. She would check when she went out.

She tried the key in the first lock, holding her breath in case the door was suddenly flung open and an irate tenant confronted her. The lock did not give and she moved to the second door. Again, no luck.

The lock that responded to the key was on the next floor. She pushed open the door, drawing a deep breath and moving into the dim interior.

The gloom was caused by the fact that the curtains were drawn. She moved cautiously across the windowless hall and through the door towards the pale oblong that was the window of the living-room. When she pulled back the curtains the movement sent a shimmer of dust motes to dance in the sunlight. Already the room was taking on the patina of neglect.

Claire turned back to see a square, high-ceilinged living-room, furnished with the anonymous furniture that epitomises rented accommodation. There was every variety of veneer, every shape of leg, the only common denominator that it was all shabby and cheap. How had Michael, who was used to better, endured this place?

But as she moved about the room she saw that her first impression was only half the story. There was an expensive stereo system in one corner and when she moved closer she saw that the CDs reflected Michael's taste in music; Coltrane, Charlie Parker and a lot of the classics, Mahler predominant among them.

There was a framed print on the wall, a Dürer,

which she had seen before, in the flat he had occupied before their marriage. Her eyes pricked at the memory and she felt a furious anger, which was almost immediately replaced by a feeling of despair. She had wanted this flat to be a dump, a place where he could employ the services of a tart. But he had lived here. It was a home.

And not just a home for one. There were two Portmeirion mugs in the kitchen. A wooden wine rack held some good wines, and a half-empty bottle of port, which Michael loathed, stood on the shelf above the work-bench, next to a year chart. There was a date ringed . . . in June, circled in red. What did that mean? She pulled out a drawer. It held cutlery, not cheap but of an ordinary pattern. The second drawer failed to pull out. Was it locked? There was no keyhole so it couldn't be. She tugged at it, suddenly desperate to see what it contained, but it failed to budge until she exerted an upward pull on the handle and the drawer slid smoothly out on its runners. It held only kitchen implements, a tin-opener, a corkscrew, some knives and, of all things, a potato-masher. Had they really cooked here in between bouts of fornication? Sure enough, there were sprouting spuds in the cupboard and mouldering food in the fridge. Claire had believed she had left the foolish laughter of bereavement behind her, but now it came again, an irrepressible giggle that turned into a sob and was not pleasant at all.

She moved back through the living-room, noticing books on a rack, mostly non-fiction paperbacks, with a green pottery frog standing guard over them. There were two robes on the back of the bedroom door, kimono-style so she could make no estimate of the woman's size or shape, and the drawers held only a change of male underwear and a new shirt from Turnbull & Asser's, still in its wrappings. There were pink tissues in a box on top of the bedside cabinet, and a tube of handcream on the white-painted iron mantelpiece.

She sat down on the bed, feeling remote from it all. She had not known Michael at all; there was a whole other life here, sketchy but nevertheless powerful. She ran her hand over the cheap counterpane. Her husband had died in this bed, for all she knew in the arms of another woman. 'I never knew him,' she thought. And then a second uneasy thought intruded. Had she known the woman in the kimono, holding a Portmeirion mug and cleaning her teeth after sex with one of the two toothbrushes she found leaning together in a mug in the tiny bathroom?

The idea tormented her as she let herself out of the flat and pocketed the key. She met no one on the stairs and she was able to pause on the step and check the bell-push for the second floor flats. Two names, MacDonald and Fettes, the name of Michael's old school. He had always been sentimental about his schooldays.

She caught the five-thirty Pullman from King's Cross, settling in the dining-car, not because she was hungry but because she needed a drink and knew it would be foolish to drink on an empty stomach. She drank two gin and tonics and ordered a half-bottle of white wine to wash down the beef olives and assorted vegetables that were on offer that night.

While daylight lasted she looked out at the unfolding landscape but as darkness fell and the dining-car gradually emptied, she leant her head against the glass and relived the day. What had she gained? At least she knew now that it had not been some transient encounter that had killed Michael. He had cared enough for the woman to set up a framework for their meetings. 'He gave her time that belonged to me,' Claire thought. 'She stole part of my life.' And he must have been happy there. It had not been simply a bolt-hole for sex. They had spent time there together and that was what hurt; not that they had fucked but that they had laughed and cooked and read and argued. 'Things we did once,' Claire thought, 'and then did less and less.'

As York gave way to Darlington and Durham loomed, she knew she must find the other woman. Until she did that, she would know no peace. 'Where did I fail?' She almost put out a tentative finger to write the question on the window, steamed by her breath. If she found the person who had usurped her place in Michael's life she could bear it if she was beautiful . . . or talented and witty beyond belief. Yes, that would be bearable. 'But let her not be ordinary,' she prayed at last. That would be too much to bear.

16

Claire was tired after her trip to London. It was hard to summon up the energy to walk the dogs but she did it, knowing their afternoon walk with Freda would have been as brief as the cleaner could make it. Freda's note implied a day of overwork and torture but she had done her duty, coming back to feed the animals at the appointed time. Claire let them snuffle on the river bank for as long as she could and then whistled them up for home. The cat was perched on the bottom stair when she let herself into the house. 'Aoow,' it said, arching its back in reproof before stalking away.

'I'm glad you missed me,' Claire said tartly but she checked that Calliope had water when she filled bowls for the dogs. At least the cat had noticed her absence. She had expected the dogs' euphoric welcome. The cat was different and feeling small, as she did now, any attention was welcome.

She fell asleep as soon as her head touched the pillow but it must have been restless sleep for when she awoke the bed was in disarray and the luminous dial of her bedside clock showed four-twenty a.m. She lay for a moment, confused, before the subject of her dream washed over her. She had dreamt that she was making love with Stephen Gaunt. She had held his torso in her two hands as he entered her, felt his ribs and the muscles that activated his arms and shoulders, clasped him to her, wound her legs around his lean, muscular legs. He had murmured in her ear and she had turned her head until their mouths met, soft and moist and questing. And she had climaxed . . . most shameful of all, she dreamt of being brought to orgasm by a skilful lover. Humiliated she stepped from the disordered bed and went in search of tea. 'I don't even know what he looks like,' she thought as she scalded a tea-bag. She felt her cheeks burn and when she saw her face reflected in the glass door of the kitchen cabinet her eyes looked huge and unreal.

It was months since she had had sex. That was why she was having erotic dreams. She told herself this over and over again as she sat at the kitchen table, the dogs regarding her mournfully from their baskets either side of the radiator. Besides, you were not responsible for dreams, neither were they manifestations of subconscious desire. They were more probably brought on by indigestion, the cucumber sandwich she had consumed before bed or the beef on the train. If she had wanted to have an erotic fantasy it certainly wouldn't have been with a stuffy academic who left fussy lists and never cut his asters. If it had been Jake Dennehy now, she might have thought it was wishful thinking. She tried to summon up Dennehy's face but it wouldn't come. She made herself another cup of tea and went to the study in search of something to read.

For a while she studied the bird books, recognising one or two of her daily visitors, reading up on the swifts Stephen had talked about in his fax. Its Latin name was *Apus apus* and it had a sooty-brown coloration with a dull, white throat and sickle-shaped wings. It spent almost all its time aloft, sometimes asleep on the wing, and never perched on wires or aerials or roofs. It was in Britain from May to September, nesting under the eaves of older houses or in crevices. Its food was entirely insects taken on the wing and its voice a long, harsh scream.

Claire closed her eyes on a picture of the swifts above the summer garden, propelled on flickering wings above the buddleia and cotoneaster, nesting as evening fell, within the grey stone wall. It was a pleasant vision. She read of the kingfisher then and the Ring-ouzel, whose song was a harsh tac tac tac, but eventually she tired of birds and began to look for something else. She needed some light reading. Where would he keep his *Lucky Jim* or Tom Wolfe, always assuming he had them?

She was riffling along the shelves when she came to a section of bound theses. She pulled one out. *Cromwell's Commonwealth* by Stephen Gaunt. So he had been published, had he? She pulled out another, *Understanding the Interregnum 1649–60*. The third was

entitled *The Act of Oblivion*. Oblivion! Forgetfulness
– how pleasant that would be, to wake one morning
remembering nothing. In books and plays amnesia was
always portrayed as tragic but she had a shrewd idea
that it could be the answer to many people's problems.
It would certainly help her now. She opened up the
paper and read a few paragraphs. Obviously Stephen
Gaunt was a scholar of some distinction. She tucked it
under her arm and went back to bed.

Settling herself on her pillows, she began to read,
expecting a dry if impressively authoritative disserta-
tion. She found instead a fascinating picture of England
in the autumn and winter of 1659–60, demoralised
by insecurity and lawlessness as Cromwell's Commonwealth collapsed.

Republicans were falling out and conspiring against
one another while, in the Spanish Netherlands, the
young Charles II and his exiled court prepared for a
triumphant return.

The King was not a vindictive man. Moreover,
he was shrewd enough to realise that an orgy of
retribution would be a poor start to the Restoration.
His Declaration of Breda promised clemency and the
Act of Indemnity and Oblivion was introduced to the
House before the Royal party landed at Dover. The Act
made it a crime for any person to reproach another for
his actions between 1637 and 1660 and erased, from
the public memory at least, all acts of hostility between
King and nation during these years.

But the Bill's passage was slow and in July 1660,

Charles went to the House of Lords to urge all speed, calling the Act, 'a necessary foundation of that security we all pray for . . . if you do not join with me in extinguishing the fear which keeps the hearts of men awake and apprehensive of safety and security, you keep me from performing my promise . . .'

Claire pictured the handsome Charles, his face alight with the glow of good intention, begging his Parliament to forget the past. In the end there had been bloodshed and retribution for a few but at least the King had tried. Could she be as forgiving? And if she could, would it free her from that fear 'which keeps the hearts of men awake'? To consign painful things to oblivion was an attractive concept, but would it work in 1994?

She must have fallen asleep then for it was eight o' clock when she awoke and one of the dogs was barking to be let out. She hurried downstairs, fastening her robe as she went, and let the anxious dogs out into a rain-swept garden. The sky was the colour of gun-metal and the flowers and shrubs, so buoyant yesterday, looked suddenly diminished. winter was well and truly here. She went through to the kitchen to put on the kettle for tea and switched on the radio; but she was not really interested in what was happening in the wider world. Her own affairs obsessed her now, especially the need to know every detail of Michael's affair.

As she buttered toast she wondered why it mattered so much. Supposing she discovered the woman's identity, came face to face with her, what could she do or say? 'What was it like for you?' The flippant question served to remind her of her dream. She had liked it, had woken feeling content. Perhaps she could live again, love a man . . . she couldn't envisage ever trusting again. Could you love without trust? In any event, she must first tie up the loose ends.

'All my life I have been afraid,' she thought as she went in search of pen and paper. She had done so many things secretly, afraid to own up to desires or ambitions. She had even allowed her family to nudge her into marriage. Left to her own devices she would probably still have married Michael, but not so soon. And what part had her parents' machinations played in his proposal? Perhaps that was it, he had never wanted her at all. She had been forced on him because her father had influence in the constituency. Could that have been even remotely true?

She had always wanted to please him, that had certainly been true . . . and it had worked at first. Suddenly she *could* see his face and it was smiling, as he had smiled often in those early days. But she had always been afraid of rejection; she knew that now, or rather, was able to acknowledge it at last.

His death had not changed things. She had crept up to London yesterday like a thief, breaking into her own flat, for on Michael's death the lease had passed to her. Why hadn't she told Gavin Lambert? Why hadn't she phoned Perdy or Debs, stated her intention and gone ahead whether or not they approved? As soon as she had worked out what she was going to do she would ring them and tell them and nothing they could say would deter her. But before she said anything she must have a plan. If she was the least bit woolly they would destroy all her resolve.

She began with a list of possible women. At first, names cascaded through her mind but eventually she narrowed it down to six. The first was Stephanie Routh, Michael's Labour pair. She was not Claire's immediate choice as a *femme fatale*; on the other hand there had been that provocative perfume, the hint of cleavage. There was more to Stephanie than met the eye and some men were attracted to brusque women.

Secondly she listed Pamela Corby, the glamorous Conservative who had come to Michael's funeral and was helping Gavin Lambert to arrange the memorial service. She had seemed composed enough that day but if she had been Michael's lover she could hardly let it show.

The third name on the list was Maeve: boss—secretary relationships were notorious. Maeve had been at home that night when Claire rang her, but was Michael already dead then? Could any woman calmly discuss the whereabouts of a man she knew to be lying dead in the bed they had just shared? Claire decided the answer to that question was probably 'No' but left Maeve's name on the list anyway.

Madelena Dimambro came next. Her flat was above theirs in Kensington and Michael had often said she

had the best legs in London. She was rich and divorced
. . . but surely he could have used her flat? Why lease
Kennerley Street? Perhaps the risk of going in and out
of his own block would have been too great. She left
Madelena's name in place.

When she had finished she had added two more
names, her cousin Elaine, who came to stay with
them once a year to scour the London shops and
flirted prettily with older men, and Catherine Farrer,
Michael's only serious girlfriend before her, or so he
had said. She had never married and worked for her
brother. Old liaisons often came back to life – everyone
knew that.

For good measure she also added 'Unknown Journ-
nalist', remembering something Michael had said once.
'They're like flies round the honey-pot . . . they'll bed
anyone as long as he's a Member and they can pump
him for gen.'

She carried the list through to the sitting-room and
counted the names, seven of them if you counted a journ-
nalist. Seven women to be investigated or discovered. It
seemed a formidable task.

She heard a soft plop as the evening paper came
through the letter box. She left the list lying on
the coffee table and went to fetch it. There was no
mention of Michael but that didn't dent her resolution.
She picked up the telephone.

'Mr Dennehy? It's Claire Griffin. I've thought over
your offer and I've decided to accept it on one condition:
I want to meet you but I'll ask the questions. There are

some things I must check out and you can help. After that, I'll talk to you and to no one else . . . but it will be when I say.'

When he had leapt at the offer and she had put down the phone she marvelled at her own determination. A phrase came into her mind . . . *The mouse that roared.* Well, if that was roaring it had been easier than she had expected and he had agreed to everything she had proposed.

She was still feeling elated when the call came from Perdy, ringing from Deborah's phone. True to her new self she told Perdy exactly what she proposed to do. 'You're mad,' Perdy said flatly. 'You've made a list . . . a list of who? The odds against your knowing the woman are huge, Cleo. You're not thinking straight.' Deborah came on the line then, after a whispered conversation wth Perdy.

'Cleo? I can understand how you feel, darling. Heaven knows I can . . . but I have to say I agree with Perdy — you'd be wasting your time.'

Inside Claire, the new-found confidence trembled. It would be so much easier to give way, to consign the list to the boiler, to go back to her work and forget the dingy flat with its evidence of intrigue. 'I'm not up to this,' she thought and knew, in the same instant, that if she didn't at least try she would go on being anxious to please for the rest of her life.

There was a click on the other end of the line. 'Perdy's on the extension now,' Deborah said, 'so you can talk to both of us. Honestly, Cleo, if we thought it would work we'd help, you know we would. But it's hopeless.'

'I know the chances are slim,' Claire said, surprised and pleased that her voice was so steady. 'But I'm going to do it. I won't make a fuss, I just want to sound them out. I'll know if they're covering something up . . . if they're not, it won't make any difference.'

At the other end of the line, Perdy snorted. 'Grow up, Cleo. You're going to ring or call on women you hardly know — or don't know at all, I don't know who's on the damned list — and they're not going to guess something's up? You're mad! And don't expect any support or encouragement from me. I've only got one piece of advice — give up mad ideas and get a life!'

Even for Perdy it was harsh, and it was a relief when Deborah broke the silence. 'I won't say I won't help you, Cleo, but I'm just afraid that you'll get hurt. It'd be so much better to walk away from it all.'

'Don't do anything until we've talked,' Perdy pleaded. 'We'll come up or you come here — we'll make the time — let's talk, Cleo, before you go blundering in.'

Again she felt herself waver but the phrase came back . . . *the mouse that roared*. 'I'm sorry,' she said politely. 'I'll be very careful, I promise you, but I can't put Michael's death behind me until I've at least tried to find out what went on.' When she put down the phone she reached for the list and carried it to the study, where she had left Michael's briefcase.

Stephanie Routh's number was in his Filofax and, as

she had half hoped, it rang out four times and then gave way to an answerphone.

'This is Claire Griffin,' she said as calmly as she could. 'You did say I could get in touch. I wondered if we could meet soon: I have a feeling I want to talk to the people my husband worked with. It sounds silly, I know, but it would help. I know you're busy so I'll keep on ringing until I find you in.' She was about to say, 'I'm not in London at the moment,' when the message tape ended. It didn't really matter, she decided, putting down the phone. She had made the first contact. It would all have to carry on now.

'Winter is closing in,' Claire thought, as she tipped birdseed into the various containers and looked around the garden. A pink dahlia clung grimly on and here and there remained a single reproachful rose . . . but the odour and colours of decay were on the garden now. She looked at the birds, skitting about in the trees above her head. How could they be so cheerful with months of ice and even snow ahead? And when spring came, what then? Would she be settled in a new life, looking forward to some kind of future, when the birds were nesting? The thought of the list sustained her. She had made a beginning. That was what mattered.

When she had filled the containers she strewed some seed on the concrete path, as Stephen Gaunt had detailed in this morning's fax. 'I don't feed the larger birds until the weather gets rough. If you think it's time, put seed on the path but don't encourage the magpies. They can fend for themselves.'

She welcomed the faxes now, feeling somehow

comforted by Stephen's thinking of home when he had so much to occupy him over there. Without this sanctuary she might have been holed up in the London flat or in Yorkshire, the Press slavering at the door, or still imposing on Deborah and Hugh. It could even have come to the nightmare scenario — back with her parents. Yes, she had a lot for which to thank Stephen Gaunt. She would certainly leave him a fond thank you letter.

She restored the nuts and seeds to their cupboard and went to the telephone. If she was lucky, she would catch Stephanie Routh before she left for her office. The call was answered almost immediately.

'Claire, I was so glad to get your call. How are you?' She sounded as though she really cared and Claire felt a momentary tremor. If Stephanie had been Michael's mistress might it be better not to know? But Stephanie was already offering a meeting. 'Can you come here? Where are you? I know you're not in London, I tried your number. I'll be coming up to my constituency next Friday night; we could meet Sunday morning — Devening's not far away.'

So Stephanie was assuming Claire was in Yorkshire. All to the good! She thanked the MP warmly and said she would be in London on Thursday anyway. 'I know you're busy but half an hour would do . . . I don't want to impose.' When she put down the phone they had arranged to meet in the lobby of the House at two o'clock.

As she waited for Freda to arrive, Claire felt a

mounting excitement. On Thursday she would meet with Stephanie Routh and, with luck, she would be able to cross one name from her list. She wanted it not to be Stephanie. 'I like her,' she thought. If it was glamorous Pamela, the Conservative MP, it would be bearable. Michael could never have *loved* a woman like that so she would know the affair had been superficial. Stephanie was different: Stephanie would have mattered.

Freda was full of gossip when she arrived. According to her morning paper Roger Moore was going to leave his wife. She had always had a soft spot for him, ever since 'The Saint', but there was too much carry-on nowadays. People like him should set an example.

'I've something to ask you,' Claire said when the other woman's conversational flow slowed. 'I'm going to need some time away in the next ten days or so. Not for long periods and almost never overnight, but I was wondering if it would be possible for you to cover for me if I paid you – time and a half, of course, because it would be late afternoon or early evening.' Freda's brow had clouded at the mention of extra work but the clouds cleared magically at the mention of extra money.

'Well,' she said. 'I could do my best.' And as long as I get notice so I can leave his tea.' They hammered out a financial agreement. Time and a half for afternoons and double time if she had to see to the dogs last thing.

'That shouldn't happen often,' Claire assured her. 'And you must add on the time it takes you to come and fro. I'm very grateful to you for helping me out. It's to do with settling my husband's affairs or I wouldn't suggest it.'

'Don't you worry about it,' Freda said. 'Christmas is coming. I reckon the extra pay'll come in nicely so it'll work out all round.'

'Could we start on Thursday?' Claire asked and was relieved when Freda agreed.

She walked the dogs then, glorying in the deep layers of damp leaves beneath her feet, wondering once more if this had been a particularly beautiful autumn, as she believed, or if she was simply seeing it properly for the first time because the pain of bereavement had stripped blinkers from her eyes. At any event, the landscape was a joy; the dogs, looking back occasionally to make sure she was there, a reassurance. And on Thursday, less than forty-eight hours from now, she was going to *do* something! 'I am taking charge of my life,' she thought and the mere idea put a spring into her step.

She was sitting in one of the deep, chintzy armchairs, sipping the coffee Freda had brought her, when the phone rang. 'Claire?' Her heart sank as she recognised her mother's voice. 'I did think you might have telephoned before now.'

'I'm sorry, Mummy . . .' She was beginning to apologise when she changed her mind. 'I've got my hands quite full here, with animals to care for and my designs to finish.' She tried to keep her voice even. God forbid she should start to complain, as her mother always did.

'Oh well.' Her mother's tone was resigned. 'I'm sure we wouldn't want you to neglect your duties. I'll tell your father you're well. Is it a nice house?'

Her mother was not really interested in the Durham house and they both knew it. As soon as she decently could, Claire enquired after her brothers and allowed her mother's enthusiasm to wax. 'So Adam will go to the War Office in February,' she said at last. 'He'll need somewhere in London, Daddy suggested your place. He's already made enquiries around here for two-bedroomed bungalows for you, although of course you know you're welcome to come back home if you choose. We thought you'd rather not return to Devening.'

'I'm not coming back to Yorkshire,' Claire said flatly. 'I don't know what I'm going to do with Campden Street — or the other houses, come to that — but I'll probably stay in London. It makes sense with my work, and most of my friends are there.'

'I would have thought family bonds meant more——' Her mother was rapidly moving into her 'deeply wounded' mode. 'Still, if it's what you want . . .' She didn't say 'You've always been a difficult child' but the words hung in the air just the same.

When they had said goodbye Claire put down the phone, seeing that her fingers were white and stiff where they had gripped the handset. This roaring mouse stuff was all very well but it took its toll. All the same, once upon a time she would meekly have agreed to move back to a Yorkshire bungalow within earshot of her parents and then wept at the mere idea. At least she had nipped that idea in the bud. She clenched her fist and punched the air. 'Yes,' she said triumphantly. 'Yes.'

She rang the Golds then and assured them she was working hard and all was well. 'Just a tip,' Sorrel said before she rang off. 'Everyone, but everyone, is going to Vietnam nowadays. I wouldn't be surprised if that comes through next season.' Claire promised to think Oriental and then went into the study to set up her drawing-board in the light from its south-facing window.

She liked this room, with its air of slight untidiness, and Stephen Gaunt's life in pictures around the walls. Before she began work she studied them once more. It seemed that the eyes of the darker brother followed her as she moved along, but when she turned back the eyes of the fair-headed guy seemed on her too. She smiled at her foolishness and sat down to draw. She worked steadily until Freda popped her head around the door. 'I'm just off, then. Get yourself away on Thursday and don't worry about this lot. I'll see to them — that damn cat soon lets you know if you don't.'

Claire ate scrambled eggs on toast for lunch and then worked on until it was time to take out the dogs. When she got back she telephoned Perdy. To her relief the phone was answered almost straight away. 'Claire!' I was just going to ring you. How's tricks?'

'Fine,' Claire said carefully. 'I'm coming to London on Thursday . . . any chance of meeting?'

'Of course—' Perdy's agreement was heartfelt.

'Where and when? I've got an early-evening drinks thing but either side of that I'm yours.' They made arrangements to have an evening meal, with Deborah if she was free, and then Perdy cleared her throat. 'Coming up for any special reason?'

'I'm meeting Stephanie Routh,' Claire said, trying not to sound defiant and succeeding only in sounding self-important.

There was a low whistle at the other end of the line. 'You don't think she's the other woman, surely? She's an old boot.'

'She's not. She's not much older than you or I,' Claire said defensively, remembering the expensive smell of Stephanie Routh's perfume.

'So you do think it might be her?'

'She's on my list.'

'List? Cleo, you're not going funny, are you? You mean to say you've actually drawn up a list, solemnly put down names? I know you said it the other night but I didn't really think you meant an actual, written list.'

'Yes, I have written them down, people Michael knew . . . and liked—'

'Am I on it?'

'It's not funny, Perdy.'

'I know.' Suddenly Perdy was contrite. 'It must be awful for you and I'm a pig to make fun. But I can't get my head round you, of all people, cold-bloodedly compiling a list. It's not like you, Cleo, is it?'

'It hasn't been up to now,' Claire said carefully. 'People change.'

'Well,' Perdy said. 'It's your life. Will you ring Debbo or shall I?'

They agreed that Perdy would contact Deborah and Claire went back to her drawings, but she had hardly sketched a line before Deborah was on the telephone.

'You're not going to do anything silly, are you? Perdy says you've really got a list. A list of who, Cleo? You can't go round buttonholing every woman Michael knew. It could be anyone, darling, I mean, he must've known thousands of women—'

'I know,' Claire said. 'I know all that and I'll almost certainly fail, but I've got to try, can't you see that?' Max had appeared in the doorway and was regarding her, head on one side.

'I suppose so.' Debbo's voice was resigned. 'I suppose I'd be curious if it was me, but I still think it's asking for trouble. Still, if it's what you want . . . By the way, Perdy suggested Orsini's tomorrow night. Is that OK with you?'

Claire went back to work after Debbo had rung off but it was a relief when she could declare a good day's work done and watch some television. She walked the dogs last thing, shivering a little in the cold, clear air. The Cathedral loomed huge in the moonlight and the lamps around Palace Green wore hazy haloes. She felt tremulous but excited about what lay ahead on Thursday. 'I can be happy,' she thought. 'At least I think I can, once I've cleared away the debris.'

Back at home she made a corned beef sandwich and

washed it down with coffee. She had hardly eaten all day and that would have to change: she had work to do in the next week or two and work needed energy. She settled the dogs in their baskets and called for Calliope. There was no response but she thought she heard a faint miaow from somewhere as she mounted the stairs.

When she had put out her bedside lamp, praying for a good night's sleep, she wondered if Stephen Gaunt would fax her tomorrow and then hastily summoned up a picture of Sammy Gold instead. If she was going to dream tonight she didn't want another erotic dream. Once was quite enough.

18

As the countryside sped by and the counties gave way — Durham to Cleveland, Cleveland to Yorkshire — Claire avoided catching other passengers' eyes. Much to her relief, most of the pictures that had accompanied the *News of the World*'s exposé had been library pictures; Michael and she at the races, at a charity gala, on their wedding day. There had only been one picture of her taken since his death and in that her features had been mercifully indistinct and her hair its natural brunette colour.

Nevertheless, she had done what she could to disguise herself further before catching the train. Her eyes were shielded behind tinted polaroids and she wore more make-up and jewelry than she had worn as her former self. She closed her eyes behind the tinted lenses and when she woke up the train was entering Peterborough.

She took a cab from King's Cross straight to the House. Big Ben was showing one-fifty as they drew near so she was right on time.

It felt strange to be in the House, in the place where Michael had spent most of his time throughout their marriage. She stood in the lobby while Stephanie Routh was informed of her arrival, watching the faces come and go; some of them familiar, some obviously foreign. And then Stephanie was bearing down on her, holding out both arms, bending to hug her in that same scented aura, her eyes wide with surprise at the sight of her bleached hair. 'It suits you,' she said and let it go.

She took Claire's arm as they walked along the imposing corridors and then Claire was sinking into a deep armchair and Stephanie was presiding over the tea. 'I tried to reach you but when you were never in I realised you'd gone back to Yorkshire, which was the sensible thing to do. Sugar?'

When she had supplied them both with tea, Stephanie settled back in her armchair and looked expectantly at Claire. 'She's waiting for me to say something,' Claire thought, her mind suddenly blank. How could she broach the subject of Michael's infidelity? She was scrabbling around for an acceptable opening when Stephanie, seeing her difficulty, came to the rescue.

'I know how difficult it must be for you, finding out what you did. Michael's death was tragic and more than enough to cope with; the rest is just very sad.' Her eyes were large and brown and moist now – tears of sympathy or grief for a dead lover?

Claire nodded. 'I think that's why I feel so . . . confused. Why I need to talk to the people Michael knew, people who knew him. I feel as though I didn't really know him myself — can you understand that?'

'Yes.' The reply was instant and vehement. 'Of course I can understand it. I'd feel the same and I'll help if I can; Michael and I didn't see eye to eye on a lot of things — obviously — but we got on quite well. And I do know one thing: he loved you. He may have strayed — it's not uncommon in this business, as you've probably noticed — but he did love you, Claire. There was just that something in his eyes when he talked of you . . . you know . . . a kind of proprietorial affection that denotes real love. Not daft, Mills & Boon stuff but real love . . . a real relationship.'

'Was it?' Claire almost wondered aloud, instead smiling and keeping the question to herself. 'That night . . . when I was wondering where Michael was, I thought of ringing you.' She had hoped to draw Stephanie out about her whereabouts on the fateful night but the ruse didn't work.

'It must have been awful for you.' Stephanie reached across to pat Claire's hand. 'Who did you turn to?'

'Friends,' Claire said. 'I'm lucky . . . I have two of my friends from university here in London. Perdita Lawrence, the barrister . . . you may have heard of her? And Deborah Grant. She's an author.'

'I've heard of Perdita Lawrence. She was involved in the Stafford enquiry, wasn't she. When did you first find out about Michael?'

'The next day. We were going to report him

missing and then the police arrived. Someone had tipped them off.'

'Not till the following day? That must have been awful.'

Claire nodded. 'When did you hear?'

'That morning. When I arrived here it was going the rounds. I didn't believe it at first. I'd seen him the night before . . .'

Claire tried to keep her face impassive but she ceased to breathe. 'Come on,' she urged silently. 'Don't stop there.'

'He was just leaving,' Stephanie continued. 'We walked up to the gates together. A cab came and he told me to take it, he'd get another. I said I was going over his way, to Kensington, and could I give him a lift, and he said he'd something to do before he went home and was going in the other direction. I said something about it being nice to be finished early – nice but strange – and he laughed, and that was the last I saw of him. He closed the door and stepped back and my cab pulled away.'

She sounded so sincere but the woman in question would not easily give herself away. 'Were you going to a meeting?' Claire tried to make the question sound nonchalant but her voice sounded strained and it was a relief when Stephanie answered at once, obviously unconcerned.

'No, I was having a night off too; Michael said you were making a special meal. I was meeting a friend in a restaurant . . . one we hadn't used before. It was very good – you must let me take you there when you feel up to it.'

Claire opened her mouth to ask the name of the restaurant but before she could speak a messenger approached and murmured discreetly in Stephanie's ear. 'I'm so sorry . . .' She was rising to her feet. 'I've got to dash . . . but if you want to talk again, do ring me.' There was another warm, scented embrace and the meeting was over.

Outside, on the London pavement, Claire held up her hand to a cruising cab, trying to decide whether or not she could eliminate Stephanie from her list. She had seemed so genuine and open . . . but she was a clever woman. Michael had often said so and she'd had several weeks to get her story right.

As the cab drew away from the kerb and she settled back, Claire decided that Stephanie's name would have to remain for the time being. If there had been more time . . . if there had been no interruption . . . but that interruption could have been pre-arranged to extricate Stephanie from a tricky situation. No, Stephanie must stay for the time being even if the odds against it being her had lengthened.

She paid off the cab at her own door in Campden Street and fished for the key. The flat had been empty since the day of her escape in Hugh's car. She pushed open the door, expecting to find a pile of mail and papers on the mat, but there were only two letters, both postmarked Tuesday. She remembered then that Gavin Lambert had had a key and had 'taken care' of mundane matters. What had he done with her mail? There must have been some. She walked through to the kitchen to put on the kettle and then went into Michael's study.

The missing mail was there, piled neatly, but when she went through it she saw that there were only circulars or letters addressed to her. Anything for Michael had been spirited away. She sat down at the desk and looked in the drawers one by one. Had Lambert already gone through them? How far would he go to 'keep the lid on things', as he had termed it. And with the 'sleaze mountain' threatening to engulf the Tory party, why was he even bothering with her?

The bottom drawer held personal papers and she picked one or two out at random. There were things in there she might need; certificates, insurances, but she couldn't face them now. She took out the drawer and decanted its contents into Michael's spare briefcase. She would take them back to Durham and go through them at her leisure.

When she had replaced the drawer she reached for the phone. Maeve was still in the office she had used when Michael was alive and she readily agreed to meet Claire the next day. So far so good. Jake Dennehy was next, although she had to ring two numbers before she tracked him down. He too was enthusiastic about a meeting. 'Let me give you lunch . . . anywhere you like.'

'I can't make lunch . . . I'm meeting someone else.'

Some instinct made her keep Maeve's identity secret but Dennehy did not probe.

'Tea, then? The Meridien? I can be there at four.'

Claire pondered. She would have to leave for King's Cross at five. Mustn't spend too long with Dennehy or he might winkle out more than she would choose to tell. 'Make it four-fifteen,' she said.

It was strange to move around the silent flat. She contemplated putting on a tape but then she thought of the lovers listening to Mahler in Kennerley Street and changed her mind. She still felt a sense of wonder that something so dramatic, so sordid, had happened to her. The rest of her life had been a monotone: happy in parts but never sublime and never, to be fair, unbearable. Now it was shot through with colours too vivid for her liking.

It was a relief when she could begin to get ready for her meeting with Debs and Perdy. Orsini's was a restaurant they had often used and she trusted the proprietor. No one there would ring a newspaper or talk about her visit later. 'You're getting paranoid,' she told the bathroom mirror. Still, it paid to be careful.

In the bedroom she riffled through her clothes. The last time she had dressed for a special occasion it had been her husband's funeral. What should a grieving widow wear for an evening out? She settled on her black suit, the one Michael had bought for her in the Nice boutique. It was too good to throw away; she might as well face up to wearing it now. But when she zipped up the skirt she saw it had

227

dropped to rest on her hip bones. Had she lost that much weight?

She sat down at the dressing-table to check her face. Weight loss always showed in her face first. She was fingering her cheekbones – or rather the hollows beneath them – when her eyes fell to the photographs beneath the plate glass of the dressing-table. She had been so happy when she put them there, sorting them like a collage so that she had Michael in every mood: smiling, reflective . . . and lying, lying, lying. The last three had been taken last summer. The Kennerley Street lease was two years old. She leaned closer but the eyes in the pictures were discreetly veiled. Had he ever looked her straight in the eye? She couldn't, for the life of her, remember.

Perdy was waiting at their table, radiant in a black velvet jacket and white jabot. 'I made an effort to get here early, Perdy said, 'so I could have a drink ready for you.' There were Kir Royales waiting and Claire sipped the crimson liquid gratefully.

'Ta. It was a relief to see you already sitting here.'

They were on to their second drink when Deborah arrived, panting and looking flustered but remarkably glamorous. 'I made an effort,' she said, seeing their approving looks. 'You two always look so ruddy immaculate . . . you make me sick.'

'Well, you don't look wilted tonight,' Perdy said.

Claire nodded. 'You look brilliant, Debbo. You have such lovely skin . . . and your eyes are gorgeous.'

'Short-sighted eyes always look come-hither,' Deborah said, fishing in her bag for her spectacles. 'People can't read them — at least that's the theory. Anyway, enough flannel . . . although you can praise my hair; it cost a fortune.' It was piled high and fell in tendrils about the plump and pleasant face.

'Ta,' she said, when they both enthused. She perched her spectacles on her nose and opened the huge menu. 'Now . . . whatever I choose I'll want what you two have. If I do, will you let me pick?'

They talked as they ate and drank, of Deborah's children and the book on Francis Bacon that she was half-way through writing. They discussed Perdy's latest case and the restrictive practices of the Bar. 'They're so hidebound,' Perdy said, twirling a prawn aloft as she spoke. 'All they talk about is the Field Club or the Fencing Club or last weekend's houseparty or next weekend's houseparty . . . the same old round. They all get old before their time. I won't let it happen to me.'

'We are getting old, though,' Debbo said glumly. 'I'll be thirty-one next year and you two will be thirty. God, nearly half-way through. I'm not going to have a party next year. I told Hugh on my last birthday — no more, I said.'

'Do you remember your twenty-first?' Perdy said. 'We all got pissed and took off in that boat — it was nearly midnight and still light. I'll never forget it.'

'I used to have my parties out of doors when I was a kid,' Debbo said. 'June's not as sunny as it used to be, I don't care what they say.'

'That's rose-coloured spectacles talking.' Perdy was on her high horse. 'Statistics prove the climate hasn't changed that much—'

'Balls,' Deborah said politely. 'Tell her, Claire.'

Claire smiled and shrugged. 'Don't ask me. And don't talk about getting old and all this half-way-through stuff. I don't feel as though I've lived yet . . .' It was true. She had meant it as a pleasantry, no more, but as she spoke she realised that she meant it. 'My whole life has been an overture,' she thought. 'Now, something must begin to happen.'

Across the table her friends were shifting uneasily. 'Do you want to talk?' Perdy said.

'We decided we wouldn't if you didn't.' Debbo was looking strained. 'But, honestly, Claire, we hope you've dropped this idea of poking around.'

'Let it go,' Perdy urged. 'We know it's your decision and we're not trying to push you, Cleo, but—'

It was now or never. She put out a hand to both of them and smiled. 'I know you're doing what you think is best for me and I'm grateful, but I've made up my mind and I won't change it. Now, don't let's spoil this meal — it's the best I've had in ages. Catch their eye, Perdy, and get some more wine. We're none of us driving so we can have a good old booze-up and talk no more about problems. The first one to make a non-facetious remark gets the bill.'

They hesitated for a second, exchanging glances, but then Claire's will prevailed and it was a heady feeling. Her triumph lasted the rest of the evening, only evaporating when she was alone again in the flat, having turned down Perdy's offer of a bed. Memories of the night of Michael's death returned; sitting up, shivering, arms round her knees, waiting for dawn. How long would it take for those memories to fade?

She turned on her side and tried to think of the Durham garden, of cold, wet noses thrust into her hand when she was miserable, of birds flitting ghost-like through the bare trees. 'I'm going home tomorrow,' she thought, and then smiled in the darkness at her error. This was home and Durham only on loan. All the same, she would be there tomorrow, a thought so comforting that it lulled her into sleep.

19

Claire had intended to look through the papers in the briefcase while she drank her breakfast coffee but when it came to it, she couldn't face them. What did they matter after all, scraps of a life that was over. She felt uncomfortable in this flat now, the place that had once been home but now was alien. Gavin Lambert had turned off the central heating and although she had turned it on as soon as she arrived yesterday, the flat still had the chill feel of a place where no one lived.

She sat at the table, nursing her cup in both hands, weeping quietly for the loss not only of a husband but of a way of life. There was nothing here for her now. She wanted to be back in Durham. She missed the dogs, she even missed the arrogant, aloof cat and the clatter of the fax machine. The blue tits would be at the nuts now, the great tits pushing them aside, the chaffinches an orangey cloud in the apple tree. But that life was not her life. It belonged to someone she had never met and probably never would.

In the end, she decided to get out of the flat as soon as she could, get done what must be done and get back on the train. She spent a little while going through clothes and underwear and toiletries, supplementing what Perdy had packed for her all those weeks ago. It would be wonderful to have more choice and not have to rinse things out every single night. Afterwards she showered and made up her face and put all her bags ready in the hall. There was a formidable pile and for a moment she contemplated abandoning the briefcase. But sooner or later she would have to clear out this flat to put it on the market. Might as well make a beginning while she was in Durham, with time on her hands.

She phoned a cab and when it arrived summoned the driver to help. 'King's Cross,' she said as she climbed in. She checked the bags in at the luggage office and then caught a second cab to Kennerley Street, alighting at the corner and making sure the coast was clear before she mounted the steps and punched in the combination.

She had intended to collect up all personal items and remove them from the flat and she did make a beginning but before long she realised she couldn't really face it today. Besides, she would need containers, bags and boxes for all the things that would need to go. There was far more here of a personal nature than she had imagined.

As she moved from room to room, she realised how long and how often this flat must have housed the lovers. They had had a life here and it showed. She felt an almost frightening sense of inferiority. Michael had played Mahler and drunk wine with her but not often and she had always had a sense of his doing it because she expected it, whilst he was really longing to get back to his working life.

He had *chosen* to come here, with the faceless, nameless woman. He had played Mahler and drunk wine from choice . . . and he had done it often. Claire began to cry, tears of misery until her nose ran and rivulets of mucus threatened to invade her mouth. She fished in her bag for a tissue but there were none and she moved to the bedroom, remembering there were tissues on the bedside cabinet there. The tissues were in place, but as she wiped and then blew her nose she realised something had been missing from the living-room. What had it been? She walked back into the room and looked around. It was the small green ceramic frog she had noticed on her first visit. Who had taken it, and when?

She moved around the flat, desperately trying to visualise each room as it had been when first she saw it. The year planner that had hung on the kitchen wall was gone. There had been a date ringed there . . . in one of the middle months . . . but nothing else: she had even turned it over to make sure nothing was written on the back. Now it was gone. Why? Who would take such trivial things; a china frog, a cheap . . . no, a free calendar, for there had been the name of a business firm emblazoned across the top. And if anything else was missing it was something so inconsequential that she had not even registered it. What had the firm been called, the firm on the calendar? She racked her brains but couldn't remember.

Suddenly she felt in desperate need of a drink. It was only ten o'clock and her stomach was empty, which made drinking foolish, but she felt a certain wry satisfaction in selecting one of Michael's wines from the rack, a 1990 Taja Jumilla. She tugged at the drawer which held the corkscrew and then, remembering the knack of opening it, lifted the handle and pulled.

The wine was fruity and soft and she drank two glasses before reason reasserted itself. There was a gadget in the drawer for extracting air from an open bottle and she capped the wine and put it in the fridge. She would have to come back here before long and empty the fridge of its pathetic contents; you couldn't dump the debris of another life on prospective tenants. She rinsed her glass under the tap and stood it upside down on the drainer. It was two hours before she was due to meet Maeve. How was she going to fill them?

In the end she fled Kennerley Street and took a taxi to Selfridges, wandering from department to department, fingering beautiful garments just to look involved, examining magnificent china or complicated toys, wondering as she did so if life would have been easier now with a child in tow. She patronised two of the coffee shops and sighed with relief when at last she could go through the ornate and imposing doors and step into a waiting cab for the drive to meet Maeve.

She had to wait half an hour, sipping Perrier, before

Maeve arrived, spouting apologies and shrugging out of her coat at one and the same time.

'You've dyed your hair,' Maeve said, patently shocked.

'Yes,' Claire said but felt no need to explain.

'Oh well,' Maeve said, obviously taken aback. 'A change sometimes does you good.' They both ordered pasta but while Claire toyed with penne, Maeve demol-ished her spaghetti carbonara with evident pleasure. They talked pleasantries for a while, about Claire's sojourn in Yorkshire — with friends, to explain why she could not be contacted at the constituency house or her parents' home — and then of Maeve's beloved little boy. But at last Claire managed to bring the conversation round to the reason for their meeting.

'I wanted to talk to you, Maeve . . . it's strange, but I feel this need to piece together Michael's life, to understand him . . . to understand what happened.' Maeve's eyes dropped then and Claire could see that the loyal secretary wanted to avoid anything even remotely controversial. She rushed to reassure. 'I don't mean the flat, or any of that . . . but you were such a help that night — oh, I know you couldn't actually do anything — but just knowing I could ring you was a comfort.'

Maeve's face cleared. 'I wish I could've done more. What sort of thing do you want to know . . . do you mean Michael's routine?' She chattered on about an MP's workload while Claire looked into the nice, open face opposite and decided Maeve was incapable of deceit. Except that deceivers always had nice,

237

open faces. They couldn't get away with it, other-wise.

'I didn't bother you that night, did I? I mean, ringing you when you'd just got in?' She had wanted to find out what time Maeve had arrived home that night but Maeve was too busy reassuring Claire she had not been a nuisance to part with any information. When the lunch was over and Claire had turned down Maeve's offer to pay, she had gleaned only two useful pieces of information: the name of Maeve's nanny and the fact that she lived in Fulham. If anyone could prove what time Maeve got home it would be the person who had charge of her child.

Claire took another cab to the Meridien, dropping Maeve off at the House as she did so. The amount of money she was spending on taxis was alarming but this was too important to skimp. If she wanted to carry out her duty to Stephen and the animals he had left in her care, she couldn't be away from Durham for long. Packing in as much as she could when she was in London, or any of the other places she might have to visit, would be essential.

Of one thing Claire was sure: she had been right to try. Progress was slow — two people interviewed already and little or nothing to show for it as yet — but just doing something had made her feel calmer, more in command of her life. Even if she never found the woman, never worked out why she had succeeded where she, Claire, had failed, she would feel better for making the effort.

Jake Dennehy was waiting in the Meridien lounge, rising from his armchair to greet her. He ordered Darjeeling, she Assam. He tucked into the finger sandwiches and scones and cream while she pleaded a pasta lunch and refrained. While he ate he listened as she outlined her plan and her intention. 'I don't want to confront her or punish her, I just want to know who she is and see if I can work out why it happened.'

'These things do happen,' he said. 'No discredit to partners, men sometimes stray . . . so do women.' He added the rider quite bitterly and Claire wondered briefly if he had been the victim of unfaithfulness himself. In the centre of the room the harpist was playing 'Send in the clowns', the strings tinkling gently, their notes lingering on above the tea-time chatter.

'I am trusting this man with my innermost secrets,' she thought suddenly. 'He's a journalist, he'd betray me for the sake of a good headline.' Would tomorrow's sensation be 'Wronged wife has list?' But she needed his help and you had to risk things sometimes. As if he had read her mind, he grinned.

'You're wondering if you can trust me, aren't you?' Claire nodded and he continued, 'Well, there's no answer to that. I do my best but I'm a journo when it comes down to it: I want a story. I'll get one in your case . . . it's only a matter of time, but I genuinely – cross my heart, on my mother's grave . . . all that stuff – don't intend to do you down. I can't and won't exaggerate or distort and I don't move till I'm sure.' He took a sip of his drink. 'I'm spending quite a lot of time in your neck of the woods at the moment . . . fishing, yes — that part's true — but I'm also nursing a story: political corruption at local level. I could've gone public three months ago but if I had done I'd have exposed the little fish and given the big fish time to cover their tracks. So I've written nothing. Not even a "watch this space".'

Claire bit her lip but only for a moment. 'OK. Well, I don't have anything new or explosive so don't look too eager. I have a list of names . . . possible names: women Michael knew and might have . . . might have had a relationship with.'

'I don't suppose you're going to show me this list of yours?' he said.

Claire nodded. 'You're right, I'm not. But I want to know if there were any journalists Michael was friendly with — well, not friendly — you know what I mean.'

'A hard-faced Fleet Street hack . . . he'd hardly have it away with one of them, but—' He was looking thoughtful. 'Ellie Ferris — she's with the Beeb — he had dinner with her about three months ago. At the Gay Hussar . . . I saw them there. I don't want to make too much of it . . . we often share a meal with politicians.' He grinned. 'They talk more after a pie and a pint.'

'Anyone else?' Claire asked. Michael had never mentioned an Ellie Ferris, or a meal at the Gay Hussar.

Dennehy was shaking his head. 'No one in particular . . . there are a lot of women journalists in or on the fringes of the Lobby — it could be any one of them but I can't think of one in particular . . .

most of them are dogs. Who else have you got on the list?'

It was Claire's turn to grin. 'No you don't. I ask the questions at this stage, remember? You get to know what I find, when and if I find it.' But as they talked on she wondered if she should show him the list. Roaring mice needed all the help they could get; they couldn't afford to be too scrupulous. Besides, if she could find the woman, so could he – or any other journalist. So it would come out anyway, sooner or later.

'Supposing I show you the list,' she said. To her relief he didn't lean eagerly forward.

'I look at it,' he said. 'Perhaps I tell you one or two names are no-noes. Perhaps I add one or two.'

Claire reached in her bag and took out the paper. He accepted it and sat back to study it. 'You can forget Stephanie Routh,' he said.

'Why?'

Dennehy shrugged. 'No reason, she's not the type. Anyway, she's otherwise engaged.' So he knew something about Stephanie that ruled her out but wasn't about to share it. She liked him for that and it was a relief to forget Stephanie.

'What about the others?'

He had finished the list now and raised his eyes. 'Pamela Corby? Possible, if you think Michael might have fancied her. His secretary? I doubt it. That sort of thing's common knowledge. The Italian lady, your neighbour . . . I wouldn't know.'

'How do you know she's my neighbour?'

He grinned. 'I know everything about you.' It was said jokingly but for some reason she flushed as he continued, 'The other names are strange to me but I'll check them out.' He took out a pen and notebook and looked at her. 'OK if I copy them?'

Claire nodded: it was too late to draw back now. 'Elaine is my cousin. You can leave her to me, but Catherine Farrer lives in Wetherby and works on her brother's stud farm.'

'I'll check her out,' Jake said.

'Tell me something,' Claire said suddenly. 'I know why I want to know – I need to know. But why this continuing interest from the press in Michael's story? He's dead . . . and he was only a PPS. I doubt if many people had heard of him before, and yet you're still keen.'

'The public's endless appetite for sleaze,' Dennehy said. 'And that's the sad truth.'

They parted at the door of the Meridien as she stepped into a cab. 'I'll be in touch,' he called as the commissionaire closed the door and Claire settled back in her seat to wonder whether or not she had done the right thing. Suddenly she thought of her mother: 'You always were impulsive, Claire.' It was true. But not as true as it was going to be. In the dark of the cab she gave the clenched-fist gesture of triumph and then shrank back, terrified she had been seen in the rear-view mirror.

King's Cross was crowded and it took ages to find the trolley she would need for her bags. She was piling them on when she felt a touch on her shoulder.

'I hoped I'd catch you.' It was Perdy and Claire felt a surge of pleasure at the sight of a friendly face. 'Wish we had time for a drink,' Perdy said. 'Still, at least I got to say goodbye.' She wore a black-and-white check coat over the black skirt and white shirt she wore for court and her face was flushed in the cold air.

'You look lovely,' Claire said simply and Perdy laughed and put up a hand to her blond and now slightly tousled hair.

'After a day in court? Take off the rose-coloured specs, Cleo. And take care of yourself.' At the door of the train she hugged Claire before handing up the bags one by one. 'Take care . . . we'll be up when we can. Don't do anything silly.' They waved to one another until the train pulled out of the station and Claire settled back for the journey north.

20

Claire spent the day after her trip to London in a state of confusion. What, if anything, had she achieved? She had got little or nothing from Stephanie or Maeve. As an interrogator she came a poor second to Clouseau. And she had given much too much away to Jake Dennehy. Once or twice she had looked at the case of papers she had brought back with her but the very thought of sifting through remnants of Michael's life was unpleasant and she let it go.

When she went to bed that night she found it hard to sleep and in the early hours of the morning she gave up the struggle and went downstairs to make tea. The dogs' enthusiastic greeting was a comfort. She sat, elbows on the kitchen table, hands clasped round the warm mug, while both dogs regarded her, eyes bright at the thought of a moonlit walk. 'Not now,' she told them. 'But later on . . . I promise you we'll have an extra-long walk.'

When she had breakfasted and briefed Freda on the

needs of the day she put the dogs in the car and drove out into the surrounding countryside. She made for the sea and found herself in the fields above Seaham Harbour. On the horizon the white-capped sea was steely grey and as she looked around it seemed that winter had bleached the landscape. The hedges were devoid of colour, the grass bleached as though burnt, the sky every shade of grey, a gleam of water here and there where the earth had been furrowed. And while the tracing of bare trees against the sky was beautiful it was a bleak beauty, devoid of warmth. It was almost impossible to believe it would be green and abundant next year. In the weeks she had been here the year had died. What would 1995 hold for her? She turned her face from the wind and saw that a farmer had already started to plough, the newly turned earth a rich, dark brown again amid the lacklustre stubble of the unturned ground. That was farming, always pressing forward.

A flock of wood pigeons swooped suddenly, a great scarf of colour waving across the landscape, blue-grey turning to white as bellies flashed. Claire felt her throat constrict at the sight of such abandon. How wonderful to be able to soar and wheel in concert. She whistled up the dogs and turned for home.

Freda was still full of the lottery when they talked over coffee. Everyone she knew had won ten pounds, or so it seemed. 'What would you do if you won the jackpot?' Claire asked. The answer was instant.

'£1,000 to each of the kids, a bungalow, a Vauxhall

Astra and a good holiday. And the rest in the bank,'
Freda said. 'I wouldn't call the Queen my cousin if
I had that.' Again Claire was seized with envy:
how wonderful to have a formula, a blueprint for
happiness.

'What about you?' Freda asked and Claire could only
shrug and talk vaguely of perhaps buying a villa in
Europe somewhere, trying to inject a little colour into
the story for Freda's sake, but the older woman's eyes
were full of sympathy.

'Things'll pick up,' she said. 'You'll see.'

Claire could see that Freda thought her life aimless.
'I can't really think at the moment,' she said. 'About
the future. But I will. I've enjoyed being here . . .' She
was on the point of saying 'again' but bit it back. It
had been agreed at the beginning that it would be wiser
not to let anyone know she knew Durham from student
days. Better stick to the story.

'There isn't a nicer city,' Freda said complacently.
She folded her hands across the front of her flowered overall. They were nice hands, work-roughened
but well-shaped. 'I've lived here all my life, except
for three months down the Midlands. Jack went
for the work but we didn't take to it. You've got
everything here, history, scenery — they say it's cold
but I call it bracing. And people come from far and
wide for the Cathedral . . . and not just that. Take
the bridge out the back—' She gestured with her
head in the direction of the back garden and the
elegant high-level Kingsgate foot-bridge beyond it.

'The chap that designed that did the Sydney Opera House too.'

'Ove Arup . . . he did the structural design,' Claire said.

'That's right,' Freda said. 'Silly name but he was probably a foreigner. He won an award for that bridge and he was prouder of it than any of his other things. They put wreaths on it when he died a year or two back. 1988 it was. When Jack left the buses.'

The phone rang and Claire stood up. 'I'll get it. I must get down to work anyway.'

It was Jake Dennehy on the other end of the line. 'How are you?' He sounded as though he cared and Claire steeled herself. Mustn't let him soften her up.

'I'm fine,' she said. 'Have you managed to find out anything?'

'Got your list there?' She took it from the desk and reached for a pen.

'Fire away.'

'I think you can forget the secretary.'

'Maeve?'

'Yes, we checked. She was home by seven that night.'

'How do you know?'

'The nanny . . . don't worry, she didn't know why we were asking. We said we were researching TV habits. The guy I put on it is good. No progress on any-one else, so far. I'm concentrating on Pamela Corby.'

'What about Stephanie Routh?'

'I said you could forget her.' Again, he wasn't saying why the Labour Member was out of the running.

'Why?'

'Take my word for it. I'd be after her if there was the least possibility. Now, I've got our stringer in Leeds on to the ex-girlfriend.'

They talked on for a while and then made their goodbyes. 'I'll be in touch,' Dennehy said and was gone. Claire drew a neat line through Maeve's name but she left Stephanie Routh in place and wrote Ellie Ferris in the space for Unknown Journalist. One down, six to go. She was making progress.

Elation made her bold. She put out a hand to the telephone and a few moments later she was through to Catherine Farrer. There was a forced sympathy in the cut-glass tones on the other end of the line but she could tell that her call was unwelcome. What she could not be sure of was whether Catherine's veiled reluctance to talk to her was the product of guilt or simply because, as the wife of a dead and tarnished MP, Claire was of little or no value as an acquaintance.

She trotted out her story of needing to talk to the people Michael had known and came up against a wall of indifference but her new-found strength enabled her to persevere. When she put down the phone she had an appointment at Catherine's home for eleven-thirty a.m. the following day. 'But I must be out of the house by twelve-fifteen, Claire . . . it's unfortunate but I have an NSPCC lunch in Devening. I'd cut it if I could, you know that, but I'm on the committee.'

Claire thought over what Catherine had said. Her mother was on the NSPCC committee, therefore she too would be needed in Wetherby. That was just the time to call. She dialled her parents' number and told them she was paying a flying visit to Devening to pick up some warmer clothes and would look in on them.

'I'm out to lunch,' her mother said fretfully. 'Does it have to be tomorrow? I'd like to see you but I can't just cut and run at the drop of a hat . . .' She didn't tut-tut at Claire's lack of consideration. She didn't need to, it was implicit in her tone.

'Don't worry,' Claire assured her. 'I have to be back in Durham for five. I'll call by at about three and if you're not there, you're not. I'll be coming again.' It took an hour and a quarter to drive from Devening to Durham so she would have to take her leave at three-forty-five. She could stick it out for three-quarters of an hour.

As she put down the phone she heard the fax machine ring. It must be the middle of the night where Stephen was − either he was an insomniac or he was having some late nights! She waited as the sheets rolled out. There were two of them, closely written. She read the first few lines.

'I caught an international weather report tonight: you're cold over there, it seems. I hope you're keeping warm. There are extra blankets in the chest in the guest-room and a plug-in heater in the garage. You may find fieldmice there too − they come in at this time of year.' She tore her eyes away from the rest. She would keep it for later, when the house was battened down for the night and she and the dogs could enjoy it together.

There was a sudden loud 'miaow' from the doorway. Calliope was there, back arched, tail erect. 'Did you say, "Me too"?' Claire asked. 'Oh, very well, if you behave yourself.' She paused suddenly. She was talking to a cat. A week or two ago that would have seemed like incipient madness. Today it felt perfectly OK.

Having saved the fax for bedtime she eagerly snuggled down to read it. 'I have an apartment here with a view over the city and every mod. con. known to man but unless I am immersed in work my mind wanders constantly to Durham. Do you know those lines of Gray's? "I have one of the most beautiful vales in England to walk in with prospects that change every ten steps, and open up something new wherever I turn me, all rude and romantic, in short the sweetest spot to break your neck or drown yourself in that ever was beheld." And in addition it was the first place to produce mustard! How about that? But although I miss the place dreadfully, it comforts me to think of you there, drawing the curtains against evening, stoking the fire . . . I do hope you've been lighting the fire — there's plenty of wood in the shed. Light a fire for me so that I can think of you there; Max and Brutus at your knee, safe in the warmth while a good English wind howls outside.'

As if on cue, the wind raced down the street outside, rattling the window-frame. Claire was smiling as she put out the lamp; all men were children at heart. Tomorrow she would light a fire and put his mind at rest. As she composed herself for sleep she also composed her reply.

'You will need to go scouring for wood when you return for I have been prodigal with flames leaping up the chimney.' In fact she had relied on the central heating but there was time to change. 'I sit here and imagine myself as a distinguished academic resting after a hard day's wrestling with young minds. In fact, all I have done is feed and walk your animals. How do you fit it all in?' She would have said, 'You must teach me,' but that would sound like a come-on and that would never do.

21

As Claire drove along the AI, the Cleveland Hills on her left, the Pennines in the distance on her right, she tried to work out what she would say to Catherine. She would have to think up something more substantial than a need to talk about Michael. His former girlfriend would have little or no patience with that.

She visualised the woman as she drove: Catherine was an elegant blonde of about thirty-five with a Sloaney perfection about her. Michael had joked about her and called her horse-mad but that might have been simply a way of disguising his true feelings. Catherine was attractive in a brittle way and at ease on social occasions. 'As unlike me as it's possible to be,' Claire thought. Did that make her more or less likely to be the one? It was hard to imagine Catherine making love to Mahler but you never could tell what desire would do to people.

She slowed the car as traffic from the AI9 filtered in on her left. It was not too late to turn and head back to Durham. Instead she put her foot down and watched the needle climb on the speedometer. The sooner she got it over the better. Last night she had dreamed of sex again, beautiful and strange with an unknown man. Except that she had known him in her dream, had melted into him – or rather let him melt into her – as you only did with a beloved. The sex had been not wild but sweet, so that she had woken with that same satisfaction; a feeling of both mental and physical contentment which had persisted into the morning, although she could remember only vague portions of the dream and never, thank God, the face of her dream lover. She tried to tell herself it had been Michael but she knew it had not.

The signs for Devening loomed up and she took the slip road. To her relief there was no sign of any of her neighbours as she drove along the street of detached houses and swung her car between the tall hedges of her own drive.

Inside, the house had the same air of neglect she had detected in the London flat. And yet they had been away from this house for longer stretches and when they came back it had always been welcoming. That was when she had come back with Michael. Now, it was almost as though the house knew its owner was dead and had given up the ghost with him. Legally, Claire might now be in charge but there was no welcome here, no sense of belonging.

She hurried up the stairs and took one or two items from the wardrobe, enough to make her visit look convincing if her mother needed proof. There were some letters on the mat and she stuffed them into her bag before going through to the study. There was just enough time to look through Michael's desk before she went to keep her appointment.

But once more the masses of papers defeated her. She left the drawer that obviously held constituency matters and decanted the contents of the remaining two into the suitcase, on top of her clothes. She had not yet touched the papers she had brought back from London: now there was a second batch, she must get down to it without delay.

The thought of being back in Durham by the fire, Max at her feet, destroying one by one the paper relics of her former life, was immensely cheering. She took a last look round and then went out into the winter sunshine, seeing the patina of neglect upon the garden, wishing there was already a 'For Sale' sign there and that she was done with it. 'Soon,' she promised herself. 'Soon I'll have finished the list, emptied the houses, finished my work for Sammy and Sorrel.' She would be free then, free to do anything she liked, even back-pack round Australia if she chose. She turned on the engine and threaded the country lanes that separated Devening from Wetherby.

When she pulled up at the pillared portico of Catherine's house she felt quite calm and confident. She would not beat about the bush. She would mention the night of Michael's death and persuade Catherine to tell her her whereabouts. Simple. And she had no doubt Catherine would be waiting, coffee tray at the ready, anxious as always to show how much better she would have filled the role of MP's wife than Claire.

Catherine was waiting in the hall, coral cashmere sweater belted over a dog-tooth check shirt in grey and white. 'Do come in. You've changed your hair – how nice. And let me take your coat. I thought you'd like some tea. Or would you prefer coffee?'

'Tea would be fine,' Claire said, handing over her coat.

For once, Claire did not have to initiate the questioning. As she poured gracefully, putting the milk in last, Catherine spoke of Michael. 'You said that you wanted to talk to people who knew Michael well. I *did* know him well, as you know, so I suppose it's his background you want filled in.' She handed Claire a cup. 'We grew up together, of course. His father and mine were partners . . . when his parents were killed Mummy and Daddy simply stepped in. People did in those days. Daddy was a trustee of his inheritance but they saw him through all the highs and lows and hardly touched his trust-fund. He was like a son to them – I suppose that's why people thought of us as a couple . . .'

'Until you spoilt it.' She didn't have to say it. It was there, in her hostile eyes, in the set of her mouth, in the way she crossed her dark-clad legs as she spoke.

'How long is it since you met?' Claire asked.

'Five years, six perhaps. You were there; it was

my brother's wedding so it was six years — Philip
married in 1988. Michael wanted me to visit you both
in London . . . and he wrote when Mummy died, but I
never actually saw him after the wedding.'

'Were you engaged to Michael?' As if on cue,
Catherine looked down at her ringless hands.

'Not officially. Everyone just assumed it — but I never
did. We were both free. He made his choice—'

The finality in her words had a ring of truth about it.
Catherine would never ever have dallied with Michael
in a London flat. She bore him too much of a grudge
for that.

Her smile grew wider and more brutal. 'It must have
been dreadful. I know what it was like here . . . he was
a good Constituency Member. He'll be hard to replace.'
She looked down at her cup. 'Actually, they've just
found a candidate — not that they'll be asking anything
of you when it comes to the by-election—'

'Except that I keep away,' Claire thought wryly.
'Mustn't have Death's head at the feast.' For a crazy
moment she thought of asking what Catherine thought
it would be worth to keep away but the hysteria
soon passed.

As Claire was leaving, Catherine smiled a thin smile,.
'I shouldn't let it hurt you too much . . . that he
was unfaithful, I mean. We all have to rise above
such things.'

Catherine's smile suddenly became genuine. 'I'm
seeing your mother today. We've felt so awful for
her . . . she's a splendid woman.'

'But I'm the widow,' Claire thought. 'Why no sympathy for me?'

As if on cue, Catherine bent to peck at Claire's cheek. 'And of course for you. The whole thing is so unfortunate . . . but time heals. Cling to that.'

As Claire steered the car along the winding roads she pondered over that statement. Did time heal? Could anything ever be the same again?

She had intended to spend the time until she called on her parents in sorting things at her own home but half an hour there had convinced her otherwise. Instead she drove out of Devening until she found a pub that did food. It was one of a chain and the menu was predictably ersatz but there was a cosy booth she could sit back in and watch the other diners and the antics of the waitresses in their brown-and-white gingham dresses and minuscule pinafores.

She had forgotten the paralysing slowness with which time passes when you are alone. She had finished her scampi and chips before ten minutes were up and had to make her dessert and coffee last for ever. When she could sit it out no longer she window-shopped in Devening for the last half-hour and then drove to her girlhood home, to find her mother still in her charity lunch finery.

'I've hurried back. I hope they've managed without me.' Her tone implied that they couldn't possibly have done so and it was all Claire's fault.

'Have you decided what you're going to do?' her

father said when they were seated. 'I know you wanted to get away from it all but it has to be faced sooner or later.'

'Will you go back to teaching?' That was her mother, making teaching sound one degree better than prostitution.

'I can't go back to it, Mummy,' Claire said, feeling awkward. 'I never took the teaching diploma. Had you forgotten?'

'You know what I mean. You have a degree. You're qualified.'

'That's a matter of opinion,' Claire said tartly.

'Now, now . . . you know what your mother means.' Her father's eyes strayed to the clock as he spoke.

'Do you want to be rid of me?' Claire thought. 'Or do I imagine it?' What was certain was that she could never confide in them. Shock-horror would be their one reaction to the idea that she was tracking down the other woman in Michael's life. They drank tea from Minton cups and made polite conversation and it all seemed like a scene from a Rattigan play.

As she drove back to Durham she tried to remember if she had ever had a rapport with her parents. When she was very small, perhaps. In some distant past she could remember being on her father's knee, her mother bending over her cot . . . but once she had become ambulant they had expected her to be a 'brave girl'. Well, she was being a brave girl right now, even if her method of showing it would send them both into shock.

The phone was ringing when she got home and the

259

dogs were barking furiously. She punched in the number to still the alarm system and snatched up the receiver. It was Jake Dennehy but she had to drop her car keys and put her forefinger in her free ear before she could hear him.

'So you got back OK? I checked out the Ellie Ferris business. She was in Dublin that night. I know that for a fact. But I did pick up one piece of scuttlebutt. Did Michael ever mention Patricia Connaught?'

'No. I never heard that name. Who is she?'

'She's the deputy editor of *Westminster Scene*. I've asked around. She and Michael were on good terms. That's all I heard — they were close but no more than that. Apart from that, I'm coming up to Durham tomorrow . . . can we meet?'

She agreed to have dinner with him the following evening but after she had put a match to the fire and gone through to check the dogs' water bowls she wondered. For a working journalist he seemed to have a lot of free time: was he coming up to work on the corruption story, or was he concentrating on her . . . was she his real assignment? That was how tabloids operated. Michael had told her how they targeted people.

She put it out of her mind as she set about feeding the dogs. She would think about it after a good night's sleep . . . and she meant to make sure she got a good night's sleep. No sexy dreams tonight — she wasn't up to it.

She had intended to sit by the fire and work on

the papers she had brought back from London after supper but when she went into the study to collect the briefcase she found a fax awaiting her. She picked it up, feeling a frisson of pleasure at the sight of a whole sheet covered in Stephen Gaunt's spidery writing. What had he to say tonight? She paused only to cross Catherine Farrer and Ellie Ferris, the journalist, off her list, substituting Patricia Connaught, then she carried the fax through to the living-room, where she could curl up by the sparking fire, the dogs heavy on her feet, doors and curtains closed against the world outside.

Tonight he was being more provocative than nostalgic. 'I see the Tory party are in trouble again.' He was referring to the resignation of the Vice-Chairman of the Conservative party, Patrick Nicholls, who had made a scathing attack on Britain's fellow-Europeans. 'He says the French have the nerve to represent themselves as a nation of resistance fighters when in fact they were mostly collaborators. Which makes him a courageous man if not a wise one. And Germany's contribution to Europe has been to plunge it into two world wars. Harsh if true. As for the lesser countries, he says they assault our ears with the banging of their begging bowls. I like it. I'm not sure I agree with it but no one could say it was grey. Nicholls for PM, perhaps? Discuss.'

She sucked her pen to compose her reply. Stephen didn't know anything about her so she could write freely. 'I rather like my politicians grey. It makes for a quiet life. There are other professions to supply colour to the national scene. Thespians? Or academics, perhaps? Discuss. But not tonight; I'm going to bed. Good-night from us all.'

22

Claire took two sleeping tablets and slept heavily, waking with a feeling of futility. She was making a fool of herself, behaving like an idiot looking for a needle in a haystack. In the last few days of checking off her precious list she had looked closely into three faces. All that had looked back at her from Stephanie and Maeve was genuine sympathy and concern. In Catherine's case there had been no hint of guilt, only that same bitterness she had always shown. Four names left: Elaine, Pamela Corby, Madelena Dimambro and the journalist Patricia Connaught. Who was to say she would fare better with them?

She went downstairs in her nightdress to let out the dogs, still filled with a sense of hopelessness. The dogs stretched and yawned and padded slowly into the weak sunshine, to look out over their territory like lions surveying the jungle. She stood for a moment, shivering and miserable, the sight of the dying garden almost unbearable, and then felt a small, furry shape twine in and out of her bare ankles. 'Calliope!' She bent to give the cat a stroke of thank you but with an 'Aargh' of no thank you it was gone, stalking past the dogs to be lost in the browning foliage. Claire shut the door and went back upstairs in search of her dressing-gown.

As she ate her toast she thought again of the list. She must have been mad to think that out of all the women Michael might have known, she could target the one who mattered. A proper list would contain hundreds of names, thousands even. And she had been naïve enough to list six or seven.

But as she went upstairs to get dressed she knew she must carry on. Foolish and time-consuming it might be, but going through the list was all she had; the urge to check off those particular names the only thing that was keeping her going. And in spite of Jake's assertion that Stephanie could be discounted, Claire still wanted to see proof.

As she set up her drawing-board, one ear cocked for Freda's arrival, she caught a glimpse of her reflection in the mirror above the fireplace and was momentarily startled by her fair hair. She hated being blonde, not least because it was a symbol of the way in which her life had changed. A month ago she had inhabited an ordered world; now she was a bottle blonde, playing at being a private eye while living in someone else's home. Except that what she had thought an ordered world had been a sham too, no more real than her present existence.

As she began to finger the fabrics and then to sketch,

optimism reasserted itself. If she could satisfy herself that none of the women on her list had betrayed her, that would be something. She liked Stephanie Routh, had played childhood games with Elaine – that was why Michael had got on so well with her, because of Claire's childhood affection for her cousin. Once she knew who it was not, she would cease to care so much about who it might have been. That was the theory she must cling to. She fell to work and by the time Freda brought in her coffee she had a satisfying sketch to show for her efforts.

She carried her coffee through to the study and dialled Elaine's number. 'Claire! I was just thinking about you.' Claire was glad her cousin could not see her, for a blush suffused her cheeks. Elaine had been thinking about her? If she knew what Claire's own thoughts had been she would not have sounded so affectionate.

They joked about telepathy for a while and then Claire got down to the purpose of her call, all the while aware that while Elaine was trying to be sympathetic and supportive, her mind was elsewhere. 'I keep thinking about that night,' Claire said. 'The night Michael didn't come home. I almost rang you.'

'I wish you had . . . I'd've come straight up to London.' Elaine sounded so sincere.

'Were you in?' Why beat about the bush? When you were recently bereaved you could say and do anything and be excused.

'That night?' Did Elaine sound evasive? There was

a pause and then she spoke. 'I was out . . . not that I wouldn't have got your message. The machine was on.' She did sound evasive! All of a sudden, the reality of what she was engaged in came home to Claire. If it was Elaine, what would she do? How could she bear it?

'Elaine? You sound strange.' She had to know. She felt tears prick her eyes . . . she had never really suspected Elaine – she had added her name to the list for padding to make up numbers . . . to be perverse and list the most unlikely people!

'Well, actually––' At the other end of the line Elaine was drawing in her breath. 'I didn't want to tell you yet . . . it seemed wrong, somehow, to be so happy when you were so sad, but . . . well, the truth is, Peter and I are engaged. He proposed that night – I would have telephoned you the next day to tell you but Uncle Howard rang with the news. I haven't mentioned it since because you were so unhappy––'

Elaine had been in love with Peter, her tennis partner, for ten years. 'How wonderful,' Claire said and meant it. She could cross Elaine's name off her list, consign the whole thing to the fire in fact, because this proved how foolish the whole thing was. 'How wonderful!' she said again and gave herself up to discussing wedding plans.

In the event she did not burn the list. She crossed off Elaine's name and sat, tapping the pen against her teeth, wishing she had not let Gavin Lambert take Michael's address book, which might have yielded so much information. At last she picked up the telephone and rang Madelena Dimambro and then Pamela Corby's office to arrange to meet them when next she was in London. She rang Patricia Connaught's office, too, only to find that she was out of the country and would not return before next week.

She walked the dogs then, taking them down the steps into the woods along the river, the cold wind on her like a benediction. Here, in the woods, winter did not seem as bleak as it had in the open. If she forgot about the list — forgot Michael, even — she could stay here, find a job, stay within the comforting horseshoe arms of this river. She would have to leave North Bailey but there were other places. Except that memory was the one portmanteau you couldn't put down; it had to be carried for ever, strapped to your wrist like a diplomatic bag, tugging at you when you tried to get away. The least she could do was sort out her memories before she embarked on a new . . . and hopefully more tranquil . . . life.

She made a plate of tiny cucumber sandwiches when she got back to the house. While the kettle boiled she checked the animals' water and then carried coffee and sandwiches through to her drawing-board. Only leisure wear to do now and the collection would be complete.

By the time the ache between her shoulders forced her to stop it was three-fifteen. She was leaving for Jake Dennehy's hotel at seven o' clock. Hours to kill! She fetched the briefcase from the study and began to go through the papers.

There were some important documents, certificates

and insurances, and she put them on one side for perusal later. Others were obviously political and she regretted her impulsive jumbling up of the drawers. Some things – old cards, letters from her and her parents – she read and reread, tears trickling down her cheeks. Michael had kept small tokens of her affection . . . she had mattered. She wiped her nose on the back of her hand in the end and carried what she had managed to discard out into the garden. There was an incinerator there and she dropped the papers in before going back to the house to fetch some matches.

It was good to stand there in the open air, the papers turning to ash, the scent of smoke in her nostrils. When the fire was away she picked up fallen twigs and leaves and added them to the blaze, wondering all the while if Stephen Gaunt would be grateful. There had not been a fax this morning. Perhaps he had begun to enjoy America and was losing his preoccupation with home. The foolishness of this conjecture when there had been two faxes yesterday brought a smile to her face. 'Honestly, Claire,' she said aloud and laughed again.

She began her preparations for the evening with a long, slow bath, her hair put up in pin curls, her face smothered in cream. Her skin felt old nowadays, old and dry. When she got out of the bath she rubbed a hole in the steam on the mirror and looked at herself. 'I look a mess,' she thought and when she put on her grey Caroline Charles suit the waistband fell almost to her hips and the jacket drooped at the shoulders.

Even her grey Roland Cartier shoes felt slack when she slipped them on but she walked into the hotel with her head held high: she had absorbed enough from Michael to know you kept your end up in front of the Press, friendly or otherwise.

Jake Dennehy did not behave like a Press man tonight. Across the table in the restaurant he talked amusingly of books and films and people in the public eye. As Claire listened, smiling, she tried to guess how old he was. There were crow's feet at the corners of his eyes . . . age or laughter? The hair at his temples was cut short but the stubble was greyish. He was probably in his early forties. There was no sign of a wedding ring on the strong fingers that twirled his glass and he had never mentioned anything about his background.

It was in the moment when he was telling her a funny story about Dudley Moore that she realised she wanted to go to bed with him. The thought was so shocking that she excused herself from the table and sought refuge in the powder room. She wetted her hands under the cold tap and splashed her face. What had happened to shame? To decency? 'I am going mad,' she thought, seeing a long, spiralling descent into degradation and the madhouse.

But she still went back to the table and when his eyes met hers, she held his gaze and saw there only a calm recognition of the changed atmosphere between them.

They went upstairs after coffee, carrying two balloons of brandy, and in the darkness of his room, curtains open to reveal a cold and starry sky, they made love. She closed her mind to reason, her heart to decency, and simply enjoyed the release sex gave her, for it was good sex, gentle and tender and prolonged. Afterwards he held her, saying nothing, just hugging her gently with a rocking motion, unaware that her head was filled not only with grief but with the sound and words of Dylan's 'Lay Lady Lay', the music that had made the whole thing possible because it meant lost virginity and, more important, shut out the sound of Mahler.

23

Claire was waiting to alight when the train drew in to King's Cross. As the taxi carried her towards Campden Street she thought about the day ahead. At one o'clock she was lunching with Madelena Dimambro. She had suggested taking her Italian neighbour out somewhere but Madelena had been adamant: 'I cook for you . . . please. I will love it — you will love it.' So it was pasta with Madelena and then she would have time to do one or two tasks in her own place before going over to the Meridien for tea with Pamela Corby — The Glamorous Conservative as she had now become in Claire's mind.

The MP had hummed and hahed over the meeting but relented at last . . . 'I must _make_ time, you poor thing.' There had been a hint of a suggestion of calves'-foot jelly and victuals for the poor in the MP's voice that had grated but the meeting must be endured. Claire was dedicated to crossing off every name, though she was now far from sure that she would learn anything helpful.

After the Meridien, she was meeting Jake in the American bar at the Savoy for one drink before she caught the train home. At the thought of Jake her cheeks flamed: how could she have been so crazy . . . so shameless? She had heard that bereaved women acted out of character: now she was proving it.

Madelena drew her over the threshold with coos of delight and all-enveloping Latin embraces. 'Poor Claire . . . oh, you are thin.' Her eyes took in Claire's dyed hair and shock was swiftly followed by pity. 'You have changed your hair. Good, good – it's good to have change.'

Madelena's poodle sat regarding them solemnly, its head cocked on one side, as they ate antipasto followed by spaghetti carbonara. It was easy to get Madelena to talk about the night of Michael's death; the woman was hungry for the details of what had happened and happy to chip in. Her financier husband had deserted her two years ago. Now she lived an affluent but aimless life and gossip was a joy to her.

By the time they had finished their Amaretto and macaroons Claire knew that Madelena had been at home that night. She had played two hands of poker with Cecil Courelle, from the fifth floor, and he had left at ten-thirty. 'So I could have come to you . . . you could have come to me.' As Madelena talked her ample bosom heaved above her taut little waist. 'She is well corseted,' Claire thought, 'but she's got a wonderful body just the same.' The blond hair was well-cut and glossy above the professionally tanned face with its huge and limpid eyes. If the lids were beginning to droop, if there were lines now from nose to chin, it seemed only to add a certain world-weary charm to Madelena's countenance.

'She could have been the one,' Claire thought. She was older than Michael — forty probably, or forty-five — but still a beautiful woman. But if she was covering up involvement with Michael would she give such an easily disprovable alibi?

When she left Madelena's flat, with promises to keep in touch ringing in the air, Claire mounted the stairs to the fifth floor. She had her story ready: someone claimed to have rung her doorbell on the night of Michael's death. Had he heard anything around seven-thirty? But there was no answer as she repeatedly rang Cecil Courelle's doorbell and in the end she had to carry her frustration down to her own flat.

The flat seemed even more forlorn now, taking on a somewhat hang-dog air, as though it knew it had been deserted. 'I will never live here again,' Claire thought, 'except for long enough to empty it and put it on the market. I'm finished with this place.' It was frightening. Eight years of her life wiped out in a single night.

What would she remember of this place? The first heady months of marriage: nest-building, getting things the way she wanted, waiting for Michael to come home, with everything prepared so they could play at being in love? The thought shocked her. 'Play at being in love.' Why had she said that, used those words? 'I did love him. I was loved.'

She tried to remember the hills above Eze, love uninhibited in the Riviera moonlight . . . but the memories of all the nights she had spent alone in this flat superimposed themselves and another image intruded . . . two toothbrushes leaning together intimately in a glass in the bathroom of a flat he had shared with someone else.

She was splashing her eyes with cold water when Deborah arrived. 'How did you know I was here?' Claire asked, amazed. Debbo moved past her and went towards the kitchen.

'Is the kettle on? I rang you and your Freda answered . . . when she said you were in London I just hoped you were here so I came on spec.'

They drank coffee either side of the kitchen table, with a companionable silence between them – which can only exist between old friends. 'You're awfully thin,' Debbo said at last. 'Are you eating?'

'Yes. But I also exercise two dogs three times a day.'

'If I thought I could lose weight, I'd buy out Battersea Dogs' Home,' Debbo said. Her plump face was flushed this afternoon, her newly washed hair adrift around her temples.

'I'd hate you thin,' Claire said truthfully. 'It looks good on Perdy – absolutely right – but you wouldn't be you if you were skinny.'

'Just don't say it's my nature,' Debbo said. 'Hugh says "Why diet? It's your nature." It drives me wild! My nature is a cross between Kate Moss and Joan Bakewell. It's my metabolism that belongs to Roseanne Barr.'

Before they left they hugged one another in the hall. 'Come back soon,' Deborah said. 'You know it's open house Chez Grant. I just wish I could come to you more often . . . still, if you're still there the week after next I'll come. Hugh's mama is coming to stay, she'll adore having the kids to herself. We'll see if Perdy can make it too but I'll come anyway.'

'Stephen is due back soon,' Claire said. 'And I must be back here for the memorial service. Still, we'll see. It would be heaven if we could have one more weekend there. It was so like old times when you came before.' There was nostalgia in her voice and Deborah patted her hand.

'We'll be happy again, Cleo, and not just for a weekend. Hang in there, Griffin. It'll all work out given time.'

Deborah drove her to the Meridien, piloting the BMW expertly through the London traffic and pulling in to the kerb in front of a rank of taxis. 'Goodbye, Cleo,' she said. 'And do be careful!'

The top-hatted commissionaire helped Claire out of the car and through the revolving doors. She hurried through the foyer and into the comfort and serenity of the Meridien tea-lounge, where a harp tinkled gently in the background, and supercilious waiters hovered to make sure all was well.

Pamela Corby was half an hour late but her apology

was brief. 'You're still here – good. I'd've hated to have come on a wild-goose chase. I don't want eats . . . just tea. Now, how are you?'

If Claire had hoped for sympathy she was to be disappointed. Pamela managed to make Michael's aneurysm seem like an act of pure selfishness. 'We've had so many of these things lately. That's the trouble with being in power for fifteen years – every little misdeed mounts up. "Wait till you've been in government for fifteen years," I tell the other lot. Not that they ever will be. But these affairs keep hitting the papers. I don't know, it's hard on those of us who just keep our heads down and get on with the job. What are you going to do? Did I hear you were a lecturer?'

'Teacher,' Claire said. 'But I never qualified.'

'Oh . . .' Pamela's blue eyes were raking the room in search of a VIP.

'Everything about her is squeaky-clean,' Claire thought, looking from the superbly cut bob to the determined line of the chin, the French-manicured nails, the neat if bony knees in their navy stockings. 'By Currie out of Bottomley,' Claire decided, struggling to suppress a grin, for there was a distinct note of the nanny about the other woman and the hand that idly tapped her thigh could well have been holding a cane.

'It was good of you to come,' she said, regaining her composure. 'I wanted to talk to the people who were closest to Michael—'

Pamela's eyes widened. 'We were colleagues. I wouldn't say we were close.'

'I didn't mean close friends, I meant more a proximity. That last night, you were there for the debate, weren't you?'

'Yes. Michael was just in front of me. I remember he turned round just before the House rose, and I thought how well he was looking. Happy . . . as though he was going somewhere nice—'

'We were going to have a special meal,' Claire said. 'Because he was coming home early . . . it was a joke, you know — it didn't happen often so we were going to celebrate it.'

'Being the spouse of an MP isn't easy,' Pamela said. 'Harry often says that if he'd known what he knows now when I stood for the Council he'd have locked me in my room.'

The idea of anyone subduing Pamela threatened to bring another smile to Claire's lips. Instead she cleared her throat. 'Did you leave as soon as you left the Chamber?'

'Yes. I don't believe in hanging about . . . and anyway I was meeting someone.'

'Someone?' Was the someone Michael, Claire wondered. Aloud, she said: 'Were you meeting another Member?'

Pamela looked surprised at Claire's question.

'It was Cicely Longburrow. You remember Cicely? Went down at the last election. She'd just been selected for Langthorne — a pity really, she'd've been perfect for Devening. Still, of course, she couldn't foresee . . . none of us could.'

How remiss of Michael not to die before Cicely picked the wrong constituency, Claire thought. Aloud she said, 'Where's she living now? I'd like to congratulate her on getting a new seat . . . well, on the chance of one.'

'She's still in Cheyne Walk. I don't remember the number. You can drop her a line through me if you like. I'll see she gets it. And now, let me pay for this tea—' But Pamela was still ferreting for her credit cards when Claire paid the bill.

'I must rush. Can we share a cab?'

Claire pleaded the need to freshen up before she went on and Pamela exited, her walk as seductive as that of a super-model and guaranteed to draw every male eye in the room.

Claire waited for a while and then slipped down to the ornate powder room to check that she did not look too wild-eyed and abandoned for her meeting with Jake. She buttoned her silk shirt to the neck and blotted her lips till almost no touch of colour remained. But even as she stared into the mirror her cheeks grew rosier, her eyes more febrile. Why had she agreed to this meeting?

But it was too late now. He was waiting in a corner seat at the Savoy, champagne in a bucket and a display of canapés at the ready. 'What's this?' Claire said weakly.

'Sit down,' he said. 'And stop blushing. It becomes you, but you look as though you might combust.' He smiled. 'Did I ever tell you I like the new hair? It makes you look less like the Dark Lady of the Sonnets and more like a woman of the '90s.'

, She had wanted to talk to him about Patricia Connaught, to keep the conversation on a business level, but somehow they fell into exchanging the pleasantries of lovers — drifting out, when the time came for her to leave to sit side-by-side in a black cab as it threaded through streets lit up for Christmas, with lamplight gleaming on the wet pavements.

'I'll ring you,' he said as he handed her into the train. She wanted to say something sensible, something to restore an atmosphere of calm between them, but it was Jake who spoke. 'I know who you remind me of,' he said. 'Celia Johnson . . . all eyes and lips and *Brief Encounter*.' He shut the door as she moved to a seat, lifting her hand as the train began to move, holding it there till he became no more than a speck at the end of a platform and then the train was out of the station and he was no more.

24

Claire was awake before daylight, anxious to get up and out to buy a paper. Last night Jake had phoned to warn her that his corruption story would break today. She had been taken aback for a second. Was this how the call would come when her own story was about to unfold? And was that what she wanted? She felt awkward with him now. If she never went to bed with him again he would be her one and only one-night stand. Alone, in her own bed, she winced at the thought of what she had done. Groaned and turned to hide her face in the pillow at the knowledge that she wanted to do it again!

It had been good to be held in a man's arms. Good to feel arousal, accommodate her limbs to his, move with him so that each could deliver a gift to the other. And afterwards, before sanity returned, she had known peace, an all-pervading peace. If she was honest, the fact that she did not love him had added to the sensation. She had not felt obliged to worry about him. No 'How was it for you?' She had been selfish and she had enjoyed it. 'I am no longer a nice woman,' she thought. It would have been unthinkable once; now she could take it in her stride.

In the shower she tried to think ahead and plan the day along sensible lines. She would walk the dogs and buy a paper but as soon as she got back to the house she would go straight to work. She would keep at it, pausing only briefly for a sandwich lunch and a look at the paper. Hopefully, Jake's article would be a balanced one. If not, she would have to reconsider sharing information with him. When the truth came out it must be in as unsensational a way as possible.

After lunch it would be back to work until it was time to walk the dogs again. After that, she would watch TV or have a hugely hot and lengthy bath – with pads on her eyes and gunge in the water, as they suggested in magazines. And she would not . . . not, not, *not* . . . have randy thoughts. She dressed in a sensible gingham shirt and jeans, topped with a big woollen jumper, and boiled herself an egg as a sensible start to a sensible day.

She walked the dogs until they began to look back at her, a sure sign that they had rid themselves of the pent-up exuberance of the night, and then she collected a copy of the *Globe* from the newsagent. It was there on the second page – 'Northern council in corruption probe' – above Jake's byline. The council concerned was Barrington and if Jake had it right they had committed every crime in the book: nepotism, bribery, fraudulent conversion, collusion between all the parties to ensure jobs and sweeteners for the boys – and their wives and mistresses. There were pictures of the guilty parties scuttling from their cars, holding newspapers or briefcases to hide their faces. She folded the paper discreetly and made her way home, thinking all the while of the people . . . wives and lovers, friends and colleagues . . . who would open that paper today and be stunned by what they read there. In the past, she had not believed spouses when they disclaimed all knowledge of any wrong-doing. Now she knew you could be in the dark about things that happened close to home.

She wondered if perhaps Freda would raise the subject – the authority concerned was only a few miles from Durham – but Freda had another interest, the enormous rise in salary of the Gas Board executive. 'Half a million pounds a year . . . or as good as,' she said. 'And my man responsible for a whole college and not much over £100 for a flat week once the taxman's had his bite.'

When she had finished lambasting the Gas Board chief she started again on Roger Moore, whose extra-marital affair was still rumbling in the tabloids. She was inclined now to be a little more sympathetic to the screen idol. 'You can never tell in a marriage,' she said. 'It's not always the one that strays who's to blame. You need to be a fly on the wall to know the truth of it.' Inside, Claire's indignation stirred briefly, only to be replaced by doubt. Had she been to blame?

Perhaps she was past her sell-by date as far as Michael was concerned. Perhaps he had not fallen deeply in love with another, but simply grown tired of her.

In an effort to escape from this hypothesis, she threw herself into her work and the prescription worked. Not only did she forget her troubles, but her designs for leisure clothes were good, the lines lean and yet flowing enough to give ease of movement. One, a satin and velvet blouson top over reed-thin ski-pants, was so good that she decided to recommend it be made up in three colour-ways. She had placed slanting pockets just above waist-level and the zipped front extended into a graceful cowl that hung at the back to elongate and grace the wearer's neck. 'Not bad,' she said, when she had pinned on the swatches. 'Not bad, at all!'

Over lunch she reread Jake's exposé. It was well-documented and restrained but deadly in content. The life-style of councillors and officials was detailed and costed and their sources of extra income listed. He ended with a demand for answers to questions.

How would he end the piece on Michael's other life? At least there would be a picture of the other woman. She could see it in her mind's eye now, the face furtive, the brows down as whoever she was tried to avoid the camera's eyes. Claire felt a sudden, vicious pleasure at the thought. Let the bitch see how she liked having her face in the papers.

But the face she had conjured up was the face of a stranger. What if, instead, it was someone she knew?

Someone familiar . . . who had kissed her cheek on meeting or sat at her table?

She wiped her mouth, carried her crockery to the draining board and went to the phone to ring Sorrell Gold.

'I'm coming back to London for Michael's memorial service. It's on the 12th. If I haven't delivered before, I will then, I promise.'

It was growing dark when she laid down her pencil, time to give the dogs their second walk of the day. Something drew her to the phone when she was dressed, the dogs yelping and weaving around her at the prospect of the open air. She dialled Dennehy's number but there was only an answerphone and when she tried his home number there was a machine there too.

As she walked the dogs she told herself it was for the best. Her relationship with Jake was maturing too quickly. Like a puffball . . . and everyone knew what happened to them! She had started the day determined to be sensible and so far it hadn't gone too badly. Tonight she would get out all the papers she had brought from London and sort them out and tomorrow she would have a satisfying bonfire of things that no longer had relevance to her life.

But by the time she had done the evening's chores and poured herself a dry sherry, the desire to sort through the papers had left her. Once or twice she checked the fax machine, in case something had slipped through unheard. There was nothing. She went to the bedroom window and drew back the curtains to gaze out on the night sky and the silhouette of the Cathedral. The Rose Window seemed aglow but whether from reflected street lamps or from light within she could not be sure.

She was thinking of Stephen and wishing for a fax full of nostalgia for the summer garden when the doorbell rang below. She knew it was Jake even before she saw the bulky figure on the step. He moved into the hall and the taxi that had deposited him moved away down the road. 'Well,' she said. 'This is a surprise.'

He shut the door with one hand and reached for her with the other but when a kiss of welcome turned into a kiss of passion she struggled free. 'Not here,' she said. 'It's not my house.'

He followed her into the kitchen and she poured him a beer. 'I wanted to see you,' he said. 'And the train seemed the answer. Anyway . . .' he shrugged out of his coat and sat down, 'you can cross a couple of names off your list. Madelena Dimambro was exactly where she said she was. In her own flat. But there was more than a bridge game going on.'

'Not Cecil?' Claire said, genuinely shocked.

'Cecil,' Jake said and grinned. 'There's life in the old dog yet.'

'How did you find out?'

'The gentleman is a cad, I'm afraid. He boasts of his conquests. And I'm almost sure we can forget Pamela Corby. I still need confirmation but I think she can go too. So that leaves— ?'

She did not dare to mention Stephanie Routh again. Not when he had been so adamant she should be forgotten. 'There aren't many names left,' she said. I've seen Catherine Farrer and I'm pretty sure it's not her. And my cousin Elaine is definitely out. I still haven't found out where Patricia Connaught is—'

'I'm working on that. Does that mean we're down to one?'

She almost said, 'Two with Stephanie,' but stopped in time. 'One or two thousand, I suppose. Perdy and Debs always said the list was useless.'

'We don't know that yet.' He stood up then and reached for her again but this time she was ready for him.

'I can't do . . . anything here, Jake. Are you staying overnight?'

He nodded. 'I've got a room at the Ramside.' She turned to her handbag, where it lay on the dresser, and took out her car keys. 'Take my car. Check in and come back for me.' When he had gone she walked up the stairs, shedding her clothes as she went. In the shower she gave herself up to the water's flow, banishing thoughts of what lay ahead. He had had condoms last time so he would this time. Thank God for safe sex. And yet . . . and yet . . . if she had a child . . .' She put up a hand and turned the water to cold. If she was going to have lunatic thoughts she deserved to be shocked back to sense.

She was still shivering when he came back for her. They didn't talk much on the way to the hotel but he must have noticed how cold she was for he folded her into the bed and then, when he too was free of clothing, he knelt to take her thin, frozen feet and warm them one by one with his mouth.

25

There was a comprehensive article in the morning paper, concerning the involvement of the Al Fayed family with prominent politicians. Beside such matters Michael's story had paled not only into insignificance but to oblivion. Sipping orange juice at the breakfast table, Claire pondered the events of the previous evening. 'I must be mad,' she thought but knew, even as she thought it, that she would sleep with Dennehy again because it made her forget, for a little while, that she had not been enough for the man she had married.

In the study she took out the papers she had brought back from London and Devening and began sorting through, taking an almost vicious pleasure in consigning most of them to the pile for the incinerator.

She had almost emptied the briefcase when she came across a torn piece of paper. There was type on one side but it was the telephone number scribbled on the other side that held her attention. The numbers were in Michael's distinctive hand, no doubt about that: 0476 599342 . . . not a London number. She lifted the receiver and dialled but the number rang out again and again with no answer. Frustrated, she went in search of the telephone directory and looked up the code. Malden-le-Hyde, a small town in Shropshire. Who lived in Malden-le-Hyde and why had Michael kept their number? She dialled it again with no response.

Her every impulse was to sit by the phone and press the recall button till she got an answer. All the doubt she'd experienced at the breakfast table was forgotten now that she had what might be a new lead. She tried to tell herself that it was foolish, a matter of no importance, that Michael would carry the number of his lover in his head . . . but what if he had scribbled it on their first meeting and kept it because it was to become important?

When Freda arrived she managed to discuss the day's arrangements sensibly and then took the dogs out for their morning walk, cutting down Bow Lane to the river bank, letting the dogs nose and scuffle among the leaves that now lay in a damp layer beneath their feet.

As she walked she tried not to dwell on the number. She would keep on trying till she got satisfaction but until she did she mustn't let it get out of proportion.

She went over the remains of the list in her head. Stephanie Routh's restaurant must be identified and checked, whatever Jake said. Madelena she could forget, and Pamela Corby she had already dismissed, even without Jake's assurance. Pamela would not take risks, not even for love. And the bitterness in Catherine's words had been both chilling and convincing.

But she would keep on chasing the elusive Patricia Connaught and soon, very soon, she must go up to Cumbria and see to the cottage. The sooner it was on the market the better and it would be madness to go back to London without sorting it out.

As she whistled up the dogs and turned for home she felt her spirits lifting at the thought of shedding property and cutting herself free from her former life. You could go on for ever looking for reasons. Best to walk away.

She rang the mystery number again as soon as she got back to the house but there was no answer so she tried Patricia Connaught's office. Patricia was still away but expected back next Monday. She tried the 0476 number once more to no avail and then went to the kitchen in search of a drink. Freda was still there, Stephen Gaunt's silver laid out before her on newspapers spread on the kitchen table. 'Coffee?' Claire asked and was rewarded with a gracious inclination of the head.

'He'll be back in no time now,' Freda said, pulling off her rubber household gloves as Claire put down the mug. 'By, it's flown.'

'Does he spend Christmas here?' Claire enquired and launched Freda into full flow.

'He loves Christmas . . . "Let's have the carols out, Freda," he says, every year.' She saw Claire's look of puzzlement and explained. 'He's got bells for the tree, well . . . they play "Jingle Bells", "Sleighride" . . . "Oh Little Town of Bethlehem" is his favourite. And he has a crib, Baby Jesus and all the animals. He had them when he was a bairn and he wouldn't part with them. Half of them's peeling but when I offered to touch them up for him he wouldn't have it.'

'So he stays home for Christmas?'

Freda shook his head. 'Off on Christmas Eve . . . him and the animals. Down to Cheshire, to his brother's place. He loves his nephews, but enough is as good as a feast, he says. Mind, he has those boys in the summer. Two weeks or more while their Mam and Dad go off. He takes them all over. And then he has the girl from his brother's first marriage. She's fourteen, and what a madam, but he puts up with it.'

'Has he never married himself?' Claire asked.

'No,' Freda said. 'He's had his chances but he hasn't bitten.'

So the fussy professor was a doting uncle. Smiling, Claire carried her second cup of coffee out to the garden. It was cold now and she clasped both hands around the cup for warmth. There was a late-blooming lupin clinging on but most other things were gone. Only the winter jasmine emerged triumphant. Soon it would be time to leave all this and, whatever the state of the garden, she would miss it.

When the chill began to strike through to her bones she went indoors and tried the mystery number again. To her delight she got the engaged tone. Someone was there! She scrambled eggs and ate them quickly before trying the number once more. It was still engaged and her hopes rose. Any moment now she would know whether or not it had any significance.

She had to ring twice before she got the ringing tone. The next moment a woman's voice said, '0476 599342.'

'Who is that, please?' Claire held her breath. What if the woman said, 'What's it to you?' She did not expect the answer she received.

'Jane speaking. How can I help you?'

Jane? Jane who? Claire took a breath and plunged in. 'I've been given some numbers . . . the thing is, I've muddled them up. Are you Askham School?'

'This is Elite Motors, madam.'

'Oh.' Claire sought desperately for the right question. 'I believe you do car-hire?'

'No, madam – we specialise in classic cars.'

'Of course,' Claire said, suddenly remembering Michael hankering after an old Bentley. She smiled wryly as she made her excuses and put down the phone. A wild-goose chase. She had spent a whole day chasing moonbeams. She was screwing the paper up when some instinct made her straighten it out and turn it over. She had never looked at the type. Now she studied it.

It was part of a letter, carelessly typed, informally written. The right-hand half of the page was missing so all she had was a collection of half-lines. The first one said: 'I will be there by eight,' and then, 'we can have a few . . .' Claire read on: '. . . wonderful, I can't wait.' It was a letter from someone looking forward to a meeting. 'A few' what? Whatever the few were — hours, embraces — they would be 'wonderful'.

But it was the last two lines that held her attention: '. . . as we both know, darling,' and 'but C always was'. Darling? Who was darling? Michael, obviously, if he had kept the remains of the letter. And she, herself, was C — who 'always was'. Was what didn't matter. What mattered was that the woman — for it was a woman, she knew that beyond a shadow of a doubt — the woman knew her, had known her for long enough to know what she 'always was'.

She realised that she had held a clenched hand to her mouth, realised it because her teeth were bruising her lips. She reached for the list and spread it out. Which of them had 'always' known her? Stephanie Routh and Pamela Corby she had known for eight years, Maeve for seven years; and Madelena Dimambro had only known her for two years, which was not 'always'. Cousin Elaine would have done but she was out of the question. Catherine Farrer would fit. She need not consider Patricia Connaught, for they had never met. Stephanie, Pamela and Catherine. Three women, already half dismissed, reactivated now by the scrap of paper.

She felt shaken by the discovery. Who would type a letter? Lots of people. People who didn't want to leave incriminating handwriting. She poured herself a whisky and water and sipped it like medicine.

She was still trying to come to terms with the

note when the phone rang. She had always felt she must know the woman. What had changed? It was the 'always' that made the difference. It was not a passing acquaintance; it was someone who had 'always' known her.

She picked up the phone, to hear Jake Dennehy on the line and immediately she clenched her free fist, digging her nails into her palm. She must be careful not to give too much away until she was sure. When he asked how she was she said 'fine' and would not be provoked or cajoled into another word. She might have let him know her sexually but some things were too intimate to share. It was a relief when she could plead pressure of work and put down the phone.

She worked until it was time for the evening walk but her mind was not on fashion. The dogs made straight for the kitchen when they got back. Claire would have followed them had Calliope not prevented her, winding in and out of her legs in an ecstasy of welcome. When Claire was able to free herself she gave each animal a tit-bit to stay its hunger and went to check the fax. There was only one page but the important thing was that Stephen was coming home in two weeks' time. 'Do I want to meet him,' Claire thought, 'or do I want to run away?'

She had finished feeding the dogs when the phone rang. It was not Jake again as she feared, but Gavin Lambert and he was not in a happy mood.

'Forgive me if you feel I'm overstepping my brief,

but I believe you're checking out some of the women your husband knew.'

'Who told you that?'

'That's not important. What *is* essential is that we shouldn't attract any more attention to what happened. The Press have had a field day. Why give them more?'

'I'm not interested in giving the Press anything.' It was a lie but she hadn't the strength to stand her ground at the moment.

'Well then, I don't see the point—'

'The point is I need to know, Mr Lambert. For my own peace of mind . . .' No, that was not the phrase. 'So that I can put it behind me. Surely I have that right?'

'What makes you think you can find out? The police have tried and failed. You haven't anything like their resources or their expertise.'

'How do you know they've tried to find her?'

'Because they enlisted my help. Not that I could give any. They gave up because it was a pointless waste of resources. Your husband's death was not a crime.'

'Do you know?' she asked bluntly.

'What do you mean?'

'Who the other woman was.' she said shortly.

His answer was equally abrupt. 'No.'

Later, in bed, Claire thought about his words. She had nothing and no one on her side. She had traipsed up and down the country and achieved nothing. Instinct might tell her it had not been Catherine Farrer but where was the proof? She was beginning to think that Stephanie Routh was the most likely candidate, but proving it was another matter and Jake had been adamant that Stephanie was not in the running. In fact, Claire was wasting her time. The harder she looked, the less she discovered.

And there remained the question of who had told Gavin Lambert. Had the mystery woman made another phone call? Was it someone she had already seen? His 'No' had been convincing but he would die for the Tory party, never mind lie for it.

Suddenly she wanted Jake, wanted him to turn up on the doorstep as he had done last night. 'I want him . . .' she thought. Or did she just want a man, any man? 'When I am old I will probably pay handsome young men to tell me I am young,' she thought. She put her hands to her head and squeezed, as though to force out any wickedness. 'You're being difficult, dear.' She heard her mother's voice, calm as always but this time spot-on. Widows were not supposed to have needs, except for a pension and a puppy to soak up left-over love. 'You're letting the side down, Claire,' she said aloud. 'It's not on, old thing. Not on at all.'

To banish uncomfortable thoughts she put on the light and reached for Stephen Gaunt's paper, *The Act of Oblivion*. When at last she put out the light, the events of 1994 seemed less important than they had been before.

26

Claire took the dogs with her on the trip to Cumbria, enjoying the idea of setting them free in so much space! They were obviously used to car travel, leaping into the back seat, as they always did, and settling down at once.

As she drove she thought of Gavin Lambert's letter, which had arrived that morning and was nestled now in her handbag. It contained the same strictures he had used on the phone: 'It would be foolish to pursue matters better left undisturbed; counter-productive to alert the Press; sleeping dogs should be left to lie . . .' She looked at the sleeping dogs in the rear-view mirror and smiled wryly.

The last two paragraphs were concerned with Michael's memorial service. It was to be held in London on December 12th as arranged, and any special requests she had would, of course, be incorporated. It added the fatal rider that her father and Adam had been 'most co-operative.' Claire could just imagine!

She made for Bishop Auckland when she left Durham and then followed the A688 to Barnard Castle, spotting the magnificence of Raby Castle in the distance. A few moments later she had joined the A66, the road that would take her up into the Pennines.

Above her the sky was a cold blue and filled with the white streaks of high-flying aircraft making highways north and south. In harsher times the hills that ranged before her would be mantled with snow but there was none today.

But the countryside was becoming less lush; the winter trees were dark amid fields raped of their crops and turning black. Sometimes she passed grey stone houses, rubble-walled and sturdy, and there seemed to be miles of dry-stone walling, held together as if by magic but really by the skill of the hands that had built it.

On either side of the road the fields were higgledy-piggledy, uneven shapes and smaller than those further south. They were dotted with sheep cropping the winter grass but as she drove on, the rocky outcrops that signalled the moors became more frequent.

Seen from a distance the Pennines seemed gentle but now their vast range was becoming clear. Why had they chosen a cottage here? 'How bleak it is,' she thought, as dark clouds gathered over Arkengarthdale. Suddenly she was afraid. She had never been up here alone before and without Michael the road, with its snow markers either side, seemed sinister.

It was a relief when she could turn off and go down

into the folds which hid her destination. Only a few more miles to the cottage. A quick look around, a visit to Mary Lindsey, their neighbour, and then she could roam with the dogs while it was still light before taking the road home. She didn't want to do the whole trip back to Durham in darkness.

As she opened the door she steeled herself for the same odour of neglect that had affected the other places she had shared with Michael, but in fact the cottage seemed more welcoming. Sun streamed through dusty windows and the dried flower arrangements on the deep window-sills gave the cottage a lived-in air.

She pushed open the bedroom door, saw that all was well and went into the kitchen. That, too, was as it should be . . . except . . . she moved towards the sink, seeing the washing-up bowl upturned as she always left it, the tea towel hanging from the handle of the grill. It was the dishcloth that attracted her. It was draped neatly over the taps. She never did that: she usually wrung it out and left it on the draining board. She tried to remember whether or not Michael had washed up the last time they had been here — and then decided it didn't really matter.

A few moments later she was striding down the field path and past the copse, until the chimneys of Mary Lindsey's house showed above the hillock. 'You should've telephoned,' Mary said, waving agitated, paint-covered hands in greeting. 'I could've given you lunch . . . as it is—' She gestured at the gouache on the easel. 'I'm so absorbed I forgot to eat.' They were there:

the hills, the lowering clouds, the very atmosphere of Cumbria.

They settled in the window-seat, mugs of Cup-a-Soup in hand. 'I was so sorry,' Mary said. 'I'd've come up to London if there'd been time to arrange it, but I just can't get away when I like, as you know. What with the animals and things.'

'I know,' Claire said. 'And I was grateful for your letter.'

'It was so awful,' Mary said sympathetically. 'I didn't hear about it until the next day — I was devastated. I was at the theatre . . . they were doing *Brigadoon* in Kendal — quite good apart from the tenor — I didn't get back until eleven, but you could have phoned me then. Not that I could have helped much at such a distance.'

Looking at Mary, the spitting image of Susannah York, fair hair tied back above a deep blue painter's smock, Claire wondered if she was capable of deceit. The blue eyes were almost transparently honest, the expression open. 'Michael was having an affair,' she said suddenly.

Mary's eyes dropped. 'I know. I saw something in the papers. It's almost impossible to believe.'

'She can't look me in the face,' Claire thought. 'She can't meet my eyes.' Either Mary Lindsey was guilty or she knew something. She had never considered Mary as a possible 'other woman'. Not Mary of the honest eyes.

It was an effort to kiss Mary's cheek in parting, to

wave as she walked through the gate and away from the cottage, a relief when at last she was over the hillock and out of sight. Would Michael have come up here when Mary couldn't come to London? Was it Mary who had washed up and draped the dishcloth? There had been a similar cloth ornamenting the taps in Mary's own kitchen. And Mary had known her since they bought the cottage in 1988.

She walked the dogs for an hour then, alternately weeping and fulminating, and yet she still felt uncertain. Mary knew her, yes . . . but well enough to write, 'C always was'?

Once she had given the exhausted dogs a bowl of water and some of the biscuits she had brought with her, she set about making a mental inventory of the contents of the cottage. She would keep the oak chest from the bedroom and the patchwork counterpane . . . the rest of the bedroom furniture could go. The nursing chair in the living-room was antique and a family heirloom: she must keep that. And the cuckoo-clock, long since silent, had been a gift from Debbo and Hugh. If she hadn't had the dogs she might have got it all into the car. As it was she would have to make other arrangements.

They had never left much at the cottage, bringing things they needed with them and taking them away again, so it did not take long to go through drawers and cupboards, leaving what might sell, piling rubbish in the centre of the kitchen floor. She would give the key to an estate agent and ask them to deal with everything and the local council would take the rubbish if she telephoned them. The harder she worked, the less she thought about Michael . . . about Mary . . . about anything.

She gathered up an armful of the discarded household goods and carried them out to the outhouse. There was a bin there – might as well fill it first and pile the rest of the stuff neatly by it. She struggled to free a hand to lift the lid and was about to decant her armful into the bin when something bright at the bottom of it caught her eye.

She put down the things she was holding and reached in. It was a gleaming gift tag that sparkled among the debris in the depths of the bin, still attached to wrapping paper by gilt string. Whatever it had contained, it had been small. Jewelry probably, or expensive perfume. She turned the card over, seeing Michael's familiar scrawl, seeing what was written there. 'For P, whom I love.' She felt a sudden sourness in her throat, a ringing in her ears.

'For P.' Who was the P in Michael's life – the one who could write 'C always was'? Not Pamela Corby, whom she hardly knew. Not Patricia Connaught, who had not 'always' or ever known C.

Claire sat down heavily on the dry-stone wall, feeling the rocks move, not caring if she fell and the wall toppled with her, as she suddenly remembered Perdy teasing Michael, and him responding; saw that lovely face, the fair hair tumbling around it, in Michael's bed, in Michael's heart . . . while all the time he was lying to his wife.

It had to be Perdy. It all fitted, even Perdy's calm that morning when she had come to support Claire. She had not hurried to ring the police because she knew Michael was already dead and there was no need for haste because she had already tipped them off before she arrived. The pieces were fitting together now. Perdy had not wanted her to investigate, Perdy had said 'move on', because she knew what was there to uncover.

She pictured Michael and Perdy alone in the small cottage, where she and Michael had once been happy. Waking in the morning to the heady silence of the countryside, huddling by the open fire at night, glasses in hand, revelling in being a million miles from any, where or anyone. And what hurt most was not that Michael had been unfaithful; it was that Perdy had betrayed their friendship. It ought not to be that way but it was. She felt such anguish that she screamed aloud and had to cover her mouth with her hand to subdue it.

It seemed possible now that she thought about it. Not only possible but plausible. But what if she was wrong? Suddenly she remembered Mary Lindsey and the painter's unwillingness to meet her eyes. She went back into the house and dialled Mary's number.

'Mary . . . Michael was here, wasn't he? In the summer – alone . . . without me. I mean with someone else.' Too late to beat about the bush now. 'I have to know, Mary.'

There was what seemed an interminable pause and then she heard a sigh at the other end of the line. 'He came with your friend . . . the one you went to university with. They didn't know I'd seen them; he never let me know they were there. I think it was only one night – two at the most. I was painting above the copse. I saw them there.'

'Thank you,' Claire said and put down the phone.

The dogs paced the back seat on the drive home, alerted by her weeping as Brough and Bowes and then Spennymoor flashed by and the towers of the Cathedral came into view.

She had downed two whiskies and was brewing coffee when the phone rang. For a moment she contemplated letting it ring. What if it was Perdy? What could she say? 'I need time to think,' she thought. In the end she lifted the receiver and waited to hear the voice on the other end of the line, ready to put it down if it was Perdy. To her relief it was Deborah who spoke.

'Is that you, Cleo? Oh good . . . are you all right? You sound choked up. Everyone's going down with bugs. Still, Perdy and I are coming this weekend—'

'No.' The vehemence of Claire's own voice shocked her. Did Deborah know? Was she, too, a traitor? 'No. I don't want you to come – well, at least, not Perdy. Can you come alone?'

There was silence for a moment. 'It'd be a bit awkward,' Debbo said at last. 'We've planned to come together. I could cry off but I could hardly say, "Don't you come." What's the matter, Cleo?'

'I can't talk about it now . . .' Tears were overtaking her, the whisky wreaking havoc in her brain. She heard Deborah suck in her breath and then let it out in the low whistle that meant she was thinking hard.

'I'll come up tomorrow, on an early train; I'll let you know which one. I'll say I'm going to the library to research. No one'll know. I'll have to be back by night-time but at least we can talk.'

When Deborah was gone Claire dialled Perdy's number, ready to put down the receiver unless it was the machine. She heard the mechanical voice and left her own message. 'I have to go away for a while, Perdy. No use ringing me here. I'll be in touch.'

When she had put down the phone and switched on the answerphone, Claire made her way upstairs and into the master bedroom. She opened the doors of the wardrobe and buried her face in the garments that had taken on the shape and smell of Stephen Gaunt. When her sobs subsided she took down one of his sweaters and, clutching it like a favourite toy, crept beneath his duvet and curled up, like a child, in the womb of his bed.

27

Claire was waiting on the platform when the train came into Durham station. Deborah's normally contented face looked strained and Claire felt a pang of guilt. 'You must've got up at the crack of dawn,' she said, as she helped Deborah alight. 'How did you manage with the children?'

'Left it all to nanny.' Debbo linked her arm in Claire's and swung her leather bag on to her shoulder. 'They think I'm browsing in the British Library. No one knows I'm here . . . so let's get to your place and sort this out. Why don't you want to see Perdy, of all people?'

'I thought we'd get lunch somewhere first,' Claire said. Freda was still at the house and she wanted to talk to Debbo without eavesdroppers.

'All right,' Debbo said. 'Anywhere you like . . . just tell me what's going on.'

They sat in an almost deserted restaurant and ate from the à la carte menu, neither of them noticing much about the food for even Deborah lost her usual appetite as Claire outlined her story.

'I went up to Cumbria yesterday. I wanted to look over the cottage . . . you know I'm putting it on the market. And I went to talk to Mary Lindsey.'

Deborah looked up from her plate. 'Is she on your list?'

'No, but that's not important now. I went to see her and I could see she was uneasy; not guilty . . . just on edge. I came away eventually and started to tidy up. I knew I couldn't take everything; I had the dogs in the car. But I thought I'd work out what I wanted to keep, get rid of the rubbish — that sort of thing.' She paused, trying to keep the narrative in sequence, aware of Deborah's mounting impatience on the other side of the table.

'So?' Deborah said. 'What happened? You sounded devastated last night and you don't look too good today.'

Claire slid her hand into her bag and produced the wrapping paper and gift tag. 'I found this,' she said. Deborah took it and examined it for a moment. When she looked up, there was apprehension in her eyes.

'Who's P?' she asked. 'Was there a P on your list?'

'Yes . . .' It was Claire's turn to be impatient. 'But that's not anything to do—' She broke off, remembering that Deborah didn't know about the all-important scrap of paper. 'I found . . . I didn't tell you, there wasn't time — I found a piece of a letter among Michael's papers. It was from the woman . . . obviously from her to

Michael. She said something about me . . . "C always was" . . . so I knew she knew me, had known me for a long time. So the P on that tag has to be someone I know well.'

There was silence for a moment and when Deborah broke it she spoke slowly, as though the words were painful to enunciate. 'You can't believe it's Perdy.'

'Who else?' Claire said. 'I couldn't believe it at first. I felt vile for even thinking it, but when I thought it over, it fitted.'

Deborah was shaking her head. 'I can't believe it, Cleo — not Perdy . . . she's not capable of such deceit.'

'Where was she in May or June?' Claire asked. 'I've narrowed down the times Michael could have gone up to the cottage without my knowing. He was away two weekends then; once in Brussels, once at a seminar on energy. At least that's what he told me.'

'That's when she went to Paris,' Debbo said triumphantly. 'She couldn't come to Emlyn's birthday because she was in Paris — I remember that, and she sent the Snoopy cake. That was May, so it couldn't've been her. She's not that keen on men, well, you know what I mean. She can love them and leave them. She could easily have resisted even if Michael had been keen. And she was just "good old Perdy" to him . . . as she is to Hugh.'

'How do you know she was in Paris and not in Rio? You don't, do you? And I thought I knew Michael and I didn't,' Claire said. 'How can I be sure I know Perdy?

How can you be sure? She'd hardly have told you about it, would she?'

'I suppose not . . . but it still beggars belief. What are you going to do?'

'Scratch out her eyes,' Claire said icily. 'That's what wronged wives are supposed to do, isn't it?'

'You couldn't make a scene . . . it'd be beneath you.' Debbo's large eyes were alarmed behind her spectacles and Claire smiled bitterly.

'Nothing is beneath me now, Debs. I'm a wronged wife. I can wallow in it as much as I like; spray-paint her car, cut up her clothes, make all the scenes in the world, and all I'll get is invitations to be on chat shows.'

'Seriously, though, how will you face her?'

'How will she face me, Debs? That's the real question. At the moment I've got the answerphone on so I needn't pick it up if it's her. But that won't work for ever. I know what I ought to do — give her a chance to admit it . . . but I just can't face it. Can you understand that?'

'Yes!' For the first time that day Deborah's tone was definite. 'Yes, I can understand it. And with the service coming up . . . keep out of her way, Cleo. Until you're sure. I still think you could be wrong so don't rush in. I'll help, I'll think up a story. When do you leave here?' She was back to her old self, arranging, comforting.

'Thank God I've got you,' Claire said and reached to squeeze her friend's rounded arm.

They walked the dogs by the river in the afternoon,

each of them a little misty-eyed with memories of this riverside when life had been easy. 'I must catch the train,' Debbo said at last, checking her watch. 'Let me know when you're coming back, Cleo. We must stick together now. You'll have to face her eventually but I'd leave it for now. She told me you left her a message that you were away. She believes it but she's worried.'

Claire watched the train until it was a dot at the end of the line and then she went back to the house, where Max was waiting, head on one side, obviously aware that something was wrong. Claire sat down on the settee and let the mongrel clamber up beside her. Not to be outdone, the boxer lumbered over and planted his huge, mournful head on her knee. 'I'm all right,' she said. Max's head cocked again, as if to say, 'Oh yeah?' She sat there, revelling in the feeling of being the sole object of their attention, until the fax machine started. Stephen must be ready to leave for his day's work.

There was no particular message in the fax. It simply spoke briefly and nostalgically about an English garden.

'I know most things will be done now but I think of the fallen leaves with affection. I used to curse them when I had to sweep them up. The greatest joy of the winter garden, though, is the birds. I swear they say, "He's coming," when I take out the seed. But you'll surely have heard them for yourself.'

She put the fax aside and went to prepare food for the animals. They were noisily licking their dishes when the phone rang. 'I'm here, at the hotel,' Jake

Dennehy said. 'Will you come to me or shall I come to you?' She knew that if she consented to see him they would go to bed.

'I'll come to you,' she said.

She spent a long time in the bath, crying quietly and wiping her tears with a face-cloth. She was remembering things Perdy had said. 'He'll be all right, so let's not panic.' And all the time she had known he was dead. And at King's Cross she had been blunt. 'Take off your rose-coloured spectacles, Cleo.' That said it all.

When she got out of the rapidly cooling water Claire looked at herself in the mirror. It was a vacuous face, a face ripe for having egg on it. 'Moron,' she said aloud. And then, louder, 'Cretinous idiot.' She understood now why people in trouble lacerated their flesh. She wanted to take a knife and cut weals into her arms, striking till the blood ran and mingled with her tears.

Instead she poured herself several generous drinks and then put on the sexiest garment she could find, a black crêpe dinner dress that Perdy had packed for no obvious reason. Her eyes were red and swollen but a mauve shadow and violet eyeliner worked wonders. When she was ready to leave the house she looked the part she had written for herself on this occasion, the role of a woman who was going to have sex for sex's sake.

But all the while she lay in Jake's bed, making the statutory moans and grunts of satisfaction, she wondered why she had ever thought this would solve anything. The image of betrayal was too strong to permit of any other emotion. She could not climax and when he had held himself back for as long as he could he shuddered and groaned, his breath coming in laboured pants until he rolled over and lay on his back.

'What's wrong?' he said at last, and when she did not answer, he raised himself on an elbow and looked down at her. 'Come on, you can tell Daddy.'

'There's nothing to tell.' He gave her the old-fashioned look she deserved and she shook her head. 'I need to think. I told you I'd tell you, if I told anyone. But not now, not yet.'

'So you know?'

She nodded.

'For sure?'

She nodded again, expecting him to continue the interrogation in the hope of making her crack. Instead he put out a hand and stroked the hair from her forehead.

'I can wait,' he said. 'You take your time.' And then his hand was moving, tracing her lips, her throat, circling a nipple, moving to stroke her belly with gentle movements before it went down to part her legs and enter her so gently that she ceased to care about perfidy or betrayal and gave herself up to the single joy of being alive.

28

Jake drove her home at two a.m. As they entered the Peninsula the Cathedral reared above them, eerie in its floodlit splendour. Claire looked sideways at Jake and saw that he too was moved. 'It's magnificent, isn't it?' he said. 'I must see inside it one day.'

He had been tender tonight and understanding. There was a human being in there but the outer hide was Pressman and she musn't forget it. Tonight she had desperately wanted to tell him about Perdy but it wouldn't do. A blonde barrister was a sub-editor's dream; she could see the headlines now. Once Jake knew, he would use it. He had been honest about that so she couldn't tell him yet. This was too important — too devastating — to be subject to impulse.

He kissed her good-night at the door, a gentle, almost formal kiss on the temple, and stood until she was safe inside and shooting home the bolts on the door.

Claire slept fitfully, disturbed by dreams, and woke an hour later than usual. Jake was calling for her again at eleven and she hurried to finish her chores so that she would be ready when he arrived. If he had to come in and wait there was the possibility of Perdy ringing and leaving a message on the answering machine and if she didn't answer Jake would know something was wrong. She deeply regretted telling him she knew . . . it had been in a weak moment when she was consumed with guilt for not returning his passion. There was nothing worse you could do to a man than be cold. Her mother had made that clear, in one brief pre-wedding lecture. Enthusiasm was mandatory! It was only now, when she so often thought uncomfortable thoughts, that Claire asked why that should be so. She had needed an excuse for not responding and she had given too much away. She mustn't make things worse, so keeping Jake away from the answerphone was absolutely vital.

She was at the window when she saw his car coming up North Bailey and by the time the rented Audi rolled to a halt she was at the door. 'Where shall we go?' he asked, looking approvingly at the thick oatmeal sweater she wore over a paprika shirt and trews.

'You've never seen the Cathedral,' she said. 'You can't go back to London without seeing it this time.'

They left the car and walked up on to Palace Green. In daylight the Cathedral was just as magnificent, the Castle more threatening. 'The only northern fortress never to fall to the Scots,' she told Jake. The octagonal keep would have been spectacular had it not been dwarfed by the Cathedral's towers; twin towers to the west, four to the east and a central tower that climbed massively towards the sky. 'It's beautiful in spring,' Claire said, thinking of daffodils nodding among the flat, grey tombstones. They stopped at a grave and Jake read the inscription aloud.

'John Chaytor, Colonel of the Royal Engineers, who died the eighth day of February, AD 1862, aged 61 years.'

'I wonder who he was?' Claire said. 'He must have been special to lie here, so close to the Cathedral.' They turned and walked together towards the door, a door that seemed too small for such a huge building.

'So that's the famous Sanctuary knocker,' Jake said, looking at the fierce head. 'One touch and you were safe, or that's the theory. Do you think it's true?'

Claire smiled. 'Probably not; given the lawlessness of the times I can't see them suddenly falling back because of a door—'

'What about the power of the Church?' They were inside now, the pillars to the right and left of them grey and massive and patterned in herring-bone or diamond or whatever had appealed to the mason. They walked down the right-hand aisle and paused before the miners' memorial. Jake read the inscription aloud. 'Remember before God the Durham Miners who have given their lives in the pits of this county and those who work in darkness and danger in those pits today.'

The surround was seventeenth-century woodcarving, made up of cupids and vineleaves and tiny carved figures of workers toiling for their keep. 'And now there are no mines,' Jake said. 'God bless the Conservative Government for that.'

They moved into a pew and bowed their heads. She was not sure whether or not Jake prayed and she twisted her gaze to have a peep. His face was impassive: he might have been communing with God or just waiting for her to finish and stand up. She gave up trying to figure him out and prayed for herself. 'Please, God, make it easy. Make it fall into place.' She couldn't ask for it not to be Perdy. Even God could not undo what was already done.

Afterwards, they went into the Castle. Above their heads standards hung like spiders' webs. The Castle wasn't wearing as well as the Cathedral but it was impressive in its own way. Men had stood guard here so that the Cathedral would be secure.

'I know now why you came to this city,' Jake said, as they emerged into the open air.

'I was happy here once,' Claire said. She had not realised how sad she sounded until his hand closed on her arm and he squeezed it gently.

'You'll be happy again,' he said. 'Hang in there.'

He drove her out of the city then, weaving the Audi along country roads until they found a pub that served lunches. Claire watched him while he went to the bar to order. He was a big man, tall and wide-shouldered with a large head. She liked his rather battered face; the lines of humour at the corners of his eyes, the smile that went more to one side than the other, but what was happening between them was too sudden. If anyone had told her eight weeks ago that she would go to bed with someone she had not then met, she would have scorned them with laughter. And yet, in the aftermath of bereavement, she had been more uninhibited than she had ever been as a student, a time when you were supposed to be a libertine. The others had mocked her for it then. 'I'm being selective,' she had said and Debbo had translated 'selective' to mean 'plain, bloody slow.'

They ate toad-in-the-hole with french beans and sautéed potatoes and conversation became more and more difficult. There were only two topics in the forefront of their minds — sex and the mystery woman — and both those subjects were taboo as far as Claire was concerned.

It was a relief when he looked at his watch. 'I suppose I'd better get going if I'm going to make London at a decent hour.' She didn't invite him in when they got back to Stephen's house.

'Keep in touch,' he said.

'I'll be back in London next week. I'll ring you.' She turned her face slightly so that his farewell kiss landed on her cheek.

It was the night that bell-ringers practised. They rang out as she walked the dogs at eight-fifteen. In the floodlighting, the winter trees were a silver tracery above the quiet gravestones, the Cathedral towers shining white against the dark night sky. A lamp burnt at either side of the sanctuary door and the pavements around Palace Green were thronged with students moving busily here and there. She saw their faces in the lamplight, unbelievably young and vulnerable but confident too, full of expectation as she had once been.

She had a sudden unbearable vision of Perdy then, laughing at life, her hair in a defiant pony-tail above her Afghan jacket. No hint of the gulf that would come between them.

When she got back to the Bailey she looked up at the Rose Window, a flat black flower in the light stone now. A window needed light behind it as an eye needed a soul. She let herself into the house and settled the dogs, intent on doing some work before she went to bed, but she could think of nothing but Perdy and the confrontation that must come sooner or later.

As if to divert her, Calliope appeared, suddenly anxious to play. She pounced and retreated, rolled on her back, kneaded the arms of the sofa with delicately arched paws . . . but when Claire reached for her she drew away. 'You're nothing but a tease,' Claire said. 'A trollop.' The cat's head went back and her eye gleamed agreement.

'Aoow,' she said, which Claire translated as, 'It's the only way to live.'

'Your master didn't fax today,' Claire told her sternly. 'Just when I need him, he deserts me too.'

She lay awake long after she had put out the light, imagining Michael and Perdy together. Had it been Perdy's beauty, for she was beautiful? Or her love of argument – Michael had so loved a verbal tussle? In the end she concluded that it had probably been her own inhibitions that caused the affair. She had never said no to anything Michael suggested during love-making but she had never been the initiator. And now she had thrown all those inhibitions – which she believed might have wrecked her marriage – out of the window to have sex with a stranger. She had known Jake Dennehy for a few weeks, had spent only an hour or two in his company before going to bed with him. She felt her cheeks flush in the darkness but her shame was not for lack of inhibition but for the way in which she had used him.

She tried to tell herself that he was a man of the world, taking sex as and when he found it, but in her heart she knew that she meant a little more to him than that. It was a thought that made her feel ashamed but it was also a comforting one. 'I have to stop being selfish,' she thought and turned on her side to try to sleep.

29

A longer fax than usual arrived on the morning before her day of departure.

'It's good to think I'll soon be home,' Stephen Gaunt wrote, 'but I hope it doesn't mean a total farewell from you to Max and Brutus. Calliope I except; she gives allegiance to no one, but I know my mutts well enough to know they will miss you. If they have thrived – and you tell me they have – it is because they have felt at home with you. Come back and see them one day, and see the garden in other guises. Autumn to winter is not the most uplifting of seasons.' There was a hint of spring in his words and Claire felt cheered. But she would not come back; that would not be wise.

She talked to Deborah on the phone in the study. 'I'll be leaving at about eleven so I should be at the flat by five. And no, I'm sure I'll manage; I know what I'm wearing to the service so that's taken care of.' They seldom talked of Perdy nowadays, except when Debbo explained how she was holding her at bay.

There had been four calls from Perdy, each getting gradually more anxious until last night her voice had rung out frantically. 'Please ring, Cleo. I can't track you down. I've tried everywhere, and can't understand why you're not returning my calls. I'm worried about you, please ring.' And Claire had listened, marvelling at the extent of the woman's perfidy.

'I had to tell her you were coming back,' Deborah said now. 'She knows you'll be there for the service. And she knows something's up, wants to know why you are ringing me and not her . . . that sort of thing. Still, I'll cope.'

Claire thought of the various messages from Perdy. Sooner or later there would have to be a confrontation but not yet. 'I'm living a day at a time,' she said. 'I've got to get myself out of here, that's the first step.' Her eyes fell to the hyacinths she had taken from the cupboard that morning. She would take the ones that were already flowering with her and leave the china bowls of later bulbs as a thank you for Stephen. A hint of spring.

The phone rang almost as soon as she replaced the handset. It was Jake, ringing to check she was OK, and she reassured him. 'I'll be in London tomorrow. We'll talk then.' She was crossing to the door when the phone rang a third time. She left it and listened as the answerphone came on.

'Cleo?' It was Perdy. Claire stood for a moment and then, as her friend started to leave a message, she walked away.

* * *

326

In the afternoon, before the light faded, she drove to St Mary's and parked. The grounds were full of students moving busily back and forth, clutching books and portfolios. Mary's had always been keen on women studying science subjects, so most of them lacked the more dreamy air of the arts undergraduates.

Claire walked on, past the white posts with their white chains, towards the path that led to the science labs and the main road into town. They had walked down that road, arms linked, so many times and come back euphoric — not so much with drink but with freedom. Her eyes filled suddenly, remembering having to run when they were late, remembering laughter and lamplight in the ancient trees . . . and now she was older and wiser and had forgotten what lamplight through trees even looked like.

On her left a group of male students were punting a ball about in the mud amidst cries of enthusiasm, but they went unnoticed by the young women passing by. Claire looked at their comfy, shapeless clothes and the books hugged close to their chests and remembered looking and feeling the same. Nothing had changed and yet everything had changed. But she could still remember and identify with their eagerness. People said university opened doors but it was horizons it opened up, if only you had the sense to see them.

She was looking at the winter sun setting behind the trees, when she heard a girlish voice behind her, saying, '. . . because we like to confront things, don't we?'

'I have never confronted anything in my life,' Claire thought. 'Until now!'

When she got back to the house the dogs were all a-quiver. 'All right,' she said. 'Let's go.' She would walk them again tomorrow, before she left, but this would be the last time they would pad through the dusk together and the thought was painful. 'I feared them when I came here,' she thought. 'And now—' It was silly to say you loved animals; her mother had told her that years ago. 'But I *do* love them,' she said defiantly and aloud, with only the trees to hear.

As a bonus she walked them up on to Palace Green. She had intended to walk round just once for the dogs' sake, drinking in the glowing splendour of it all as she went. But as she came abreast of the Cathedral door she heard singing – a young treble's clear voice soaring above the music. It was a carol, a relatively unknown one but one she loved: 'Jesus Christ the Apple-tree'. They must be preparing for Christmas; well of course they would be with little more than two weeks to go.

She stood for a moment, the dogs at her heel, drinking in the music, before she noticed another solitary listener. A boy, jeans-clad and muffled against the cold, stood a few yards away. His face was raised towards the sky, his figure turned to stone by rapt attention. She saw light reflected from his spectacles and then, as if he had noticed her staring, he turned and smiled and she saw that he was Japanese.

They did not speak. There was no need. The music died away and they went their separate ways.

After the walk she packed up her drawings. She would deliver to the Golds the day after the service and she knew they would be pleased. She chuckled suddenly. If she went on like this she might begin to believe in herself; but never again in her judgement. 'Perdy was my rock,' she thought. 'And all the time she was paper.'

Her mother telephoned at five-thirty. 'Daddy and I will come up on the morning of the service. Peter and Rachael will be with us and Adam will come straight to you. I hope you realise how good it is of Peter and Rachael to come over; they've had to make arrangements for the children and arrange leave – I hope you appreciate it.' Claire promised a display of gratitude towards her brother and sister-in-law as soon as she saw them and agreed with her mother that she must be both brave and dignified at the service, as befitted a woman with her background. 'One hopes it will all go smoothly,' her mother said. 'Daddy says the horrid fuss is over now. I hope he's right.'

Claire knew she should feel guilty at what she was withholding. If – when – she told Jake about Perdy it would be headline news. She pictured the page, the photos of both of them, together and apart. It would last for a day or two and percolate to the local Press. 'I really ought to feel guilty at what I'm going to do,' she thought as she put down the phone. 'But I don't.'

*　　*　　*

It was dark now and she stood at the bedroom window to look down on the moonlit garden. She would miss its frost-bitten grandeur, miss the tits and the chaffinches, miss the winter jasmine spitting golden defiance at the grey winter skies.

When she went back down to the study she had a good look again at the photographs. She had never discovered whether Stephen Gaunt was the bespectacled one with the kind mouth, or the blond Adonis with muscles. She would never know now and it didn't matter. Somehow he had become substantial, an invisible man who made his presence felt. She was tempted to take the blue cashmere sweater for a keepsake but in the end all she took were his faxes and a copy of his paper on the Act of Oblivion, which she had made for herself using the fax machine.

As she packed everything carefully in her bag she asked herself if she was deliberately leaving before he came back in order to keep him a shadow. She could easily have stayed, handed over the keys herself, instead of through Freda. She could have asked Freda to identify him from the photographs. Why was she doing neither of those things? Perhaps because it was safer to care about a creature of the imagination than a real man.

When she was ready for bed, her bags packed and ready at the bedroom door, she looked at the clock. Midnight here, four o'clock in San Francisco. She went down to the fax machine.

'Thank you for today's fax,' she wrote. 'The gratitude is mine, I assure you. I was sad when I came to Durham: your house and animals have healed me. And you have been a companion too — I have never sparred by fax before, and find I like it. Thank you.' When she had transmitted it, she looked at what she had written in wonder. Was she healed? Sometimes she didn't feel like it.

She put out the lights, mounted the stairs and lay down for her last night's sleep under Stephen Gaunt's roof.

Claire felt genuine regret at saying goodbye to Freda and it surprised her to realise how much the older woman's comings and goings had lent an ordered pattern to her life at a difficult time. But it was the sight of both dogs, sitting upright in the hall — for once not leaping about at the prospect of a walk — that brought tears to her eyes, tears that flowed when Calliope appeared from nowhere, arching her back to yowl disgust at Claire's desertion.

'I will never see this house again,' she thought, looking around the sunlit hall. She had left Stephen a note of thanks and her fax number in case of queries but he would soon forget she had ever existed.

She had bought a hand-knitted cardigan from a shop in the Market Place as a farewell gift for Freda. She handed it over now and smiled as the large, capable, worn yet beautiful hands caressed the skilful blending of colour and texture.

'I can't take this . . . it's beautiful. You shouldn't

have — it's too good to wear. It's like a painting.'

'Nothing's too good for you,' Claire said, suddenly finding words. 'I couldn't have managed without you, you know.'

Freda was shaking her head and fishing in her pocket for a handkerchief and when she had blown her nose they hugged. Only for a moment, though. Neither of them, as Freda would have put it, was given to show.

'Goodbye,' Claire called from the car. Freda had retreated to the window to keep the dogs from running into the road. They were there, either side of her, solemn at the farewell and then Calliope appeared, treading daintly in front of them to spit defiance at the deserter as she drove away. 'I mustn't cry,' Claire said, and managed a gigantic but bracing sniff as she left the Peninsula behind.

The sight of Durham, its towers and keeps and huddled houses, was so nostalgic it was a relief to be out on the road at last, the miles slipping by. Wetherby, Doncaster . . . she stopped at a service point near Doncaster and ate a sandwich lunch to fortify her for the last hundred and sixty-five miles, and managed to slide into London just ahead of the rush-hour traffic. By five o-clock she had carried her bags from the car to the lift and was safely inside her own flat.

There were three messages on the answerphone, one from Adam and two from Perdy. She listened to the voice of her former friend pleading for a response. 'I'll leave my machine on, Cleo. Just tell me you're OK, and what you want me to do on Monday.'

Monday was the day of the memorial service. Perdy would be there. 'How will I handle that?' Claire wondered and could find no answer. She would have to deal with it when it happened.

The phone rang as she finished her unpacking and once more she heard Perdy's voice. 'If you get in in time, Cleo, give me a ring. I'm due at the Reform Club at eight but I could call in for a quick drink beforehand.' And then after a pause: '. . . Are you OK, Cleo? For God's sake, I must find out what's wrong. I wish I knew where you were. Please ring me.'

The thought that Perdy might call on spec as she went out to her meeting filled Claire with terror. To open the door and see her standing there . . . it was an unbearable thought. She picked up the telephone and rang Deborah. 'Can I come over for a while, just an hour or so?'

Five minutes later she was in a cab and speeding towards Hampstead but as they threaded through the lamplit streets she acknowledged that sooner or later the confrontation would have to come. It needn't even be a confrontation.

'I know.' That was all she would need to say, 'I know,' before walking away. For ever!

The Grant house was dressed up for Christmas, a nativity scene in the hall, streamers hanging from every nook and cranny. 'I don't believe in it all but that's not to say they shouldn't choose for themselves,' Debs had said, the first year the Virgin and Child had appeared. Debs was so reasonable; even now she was trying to bridge the gap between two friends she valued and Claire admired her for it.

After dinner they sat in a living-room covered with tinsel, and drunken home-made snowmen who lurked along the mantelpiece, and Claire tried not to envy her friend's domestic bliss. Hugh perched on the arm of his wife's chair, his freckled face soft as he looked down at Deborah, his hand straying occasionally to touch her arm or shoulder. 'Men,' Deborah said, raising her eyebrows to Claire, half in embarrassment, half in pride. In the corner Daniel and Fiona squabbled over who should dress the higher branches of the tree, and baby Emlyn had just been carried upstairs in his father's arms and was sleeping contentedly in his 'den'.

'Of the three of us,' Claire thought, 'only Debs has found true happiness.' For she knew in her heart of hearts that Perdy would have paid a price for her deception. 'She must have loved Michael very much to do that to me,' she thought and tried not to think about the fact that Michael must have returned that love or the affair would not have lasted. How long had it gone on? Would she ever know and would it help if she did?

Questions, questions. She was tired of questions. All she was sure of was that she must face Perdy before she spoke to Jake. For old times' sake, she mustn't read it in a newspaper.

*   *   *

There was another message from Perdy on the answer-phone when she got home. 'You've got me really worried, Cleo. And Debbo is no help. I hoped there'd be a message waiting. What's up? Please ring, even in unsociable hours. Love you, Perdy.'

Claire fell asleep almost immediately, to dream of being pursued. But the dream that woke her, sweating gently, was so erotic that she felt her cheeks flush in the darkness at the very memory of it.

31

Deborah was on the phone before nine o' clock. 'What are you going to do today?'

'I told you,' Claire said, trying to assuage the anxiety in her friend's voice. 'I'm going to do some shopping. It's ages since I went to Oxford Street on a Saturday.'

'You can't shop all day,' said Deborah, ever practical.

'Try me!' It was bravely said but by eleven she had exhausted Selfridges, moved on to Debenhams and tried on an 'Imelda' number of shoes. She had coffee in an Italian sandwich shop and couldn't believe her watch when she saw she had only taken five minutes to drink it.

She took a cab to Westminster Bridge, giving the destination before she had worked out why she wanted to go there. Above her, Big Ben looked more squat than it did in pictures. She looked at the building that had swallowed up her husband and tried to re-assemble the chicken and the egg theory.

Were politicians unfaithful by nature, or did the

job subvert them? You had to have a large ego to put yourself forward – perhaps that was it? But the woman in the flat had not been an ego-trip; she had been a life. Life with Perdy . . . which had been more satisfactory than life with Claire.

Around her, on the pavement, people were hurrying, going places. 'I am the only aimless person in London,' she thought, and tried to think of infidelity again because it was marginally less hurtful.

The year 1994 would surely go down in parliamentary history as the year of the affair. It had begun with Tim Yeo and there had been others before Michael. The tip of the iceberg; she knew of twenty or more scandals on both sides of the House. Did that make them unfit for office? Michael had worked hard, whatever else he had done with his life, and he had been jubilant about the prospect of peace in Northern Ireland.

She held up a hand to a cruising cab and gave her home address. Cowering in fear of Perdy was marginally less terrifying than being out on the street, prey to her own thoughts.

There were messages from Jake and Perdy on the answerphone when she got home and one from Gavin Lambert, giving her his private number in case she needed him tomorrow. 'Otherwise, I'll see you on Monday. I know you want to come with your friends but if you change your mind—'

She had arranged a long time before to go to the service with Perdy. 'Let me know where you are?' said the voice on the machine. Oh, Claire, where in

God's name are you? I'm getting frightened now and Debbo is frantic.' So Debbo had chickened out and was disclaiming any knowledge of her whereabouts. That made sense. At least it meant that Perdy wouldn't grill her for information. And there was no reason why Debbo should fall out with Perdy. 'This is my battle,' Claire thought.

The message from Jake was simple. 'I'll ring until I get you. I've booked a table for tonight. Somewhere you'll like.'

She felt overwhelming relief at the thought of getting out of the flat when darkness fell. You couldn't disguise a lit window and she couldn't spend all evening in the dark. She poured herself a gin and tonic and looked at her watch. Ten minutes past two. Now that it was mid-December it was dark at tea-time; if she was made-up and ready by then she could sit in the darkened room with perhaps the TV for illumination, turned down low so no one would know she was there.

But the skulking had to stop, and soon. 'After tomorrow,' she promised herself. After the last formal action she'd perform as Michael's wife. Then she would tell Jake everything and bring Perdy's professional house of cards, so carefully built up, tumbling down. Except that in modern Britain you didn't suffer for adultery: look at David Mellor — it had made him a media star. All it would do would be to attach a tag to Perdita Lawrence, barrister at law. Whenever she was mentioned, however prestigious the reference, they would mention the link with Michael. Perdy would go far. 'I am making Michael immortal,' Claire thought wryly and reached for the gin bottle again.

In the bath she thought about Durham. Stephen Gaunt would be back in his house now, sitting in the chair, his feet on the well-scuffed rug, with Max's head on his knee and Calliope close by. The cat had been faithful. 'I think she quite liked me,' Claire thought, 'but she was his cat and she wasn't about to forget it.' And faithfulness did matter; it was a virtue. Say what you would, it still made sense to cleave to someone.

She closed her eyes and tried to summon up Palace Green in her mind's eye. The late-afternoon sun would be touching the towers now, setting behind the old library, and students would be hurrying here and there in readiness for a Saturday night out, just as they had in her day. She sank lower in the water, thinking of how many of those eager faces would be Oriental. The University of Teikyo! Who could have foreseen a Japanese campus in 1985?

She tried to work out whether or not she minded this invasion. Durham was such an English city. What had the poet Gray called it? 'One of the most beautiful vales in England . . . with prospects that change every ten steps, and open up something new wherever I turn—'

She had run back to Durham and it had not let her down. It had part-healed her with its beauty and tranquillity but most especially with its hold on life. If those earnest young Orientals wanted to partake of the image of Durham, who was she to begrudge them?

The water was cooling and she levered herself to her feet, covering herself lavishly with her lotions and perfumes.

As she dressed in sheer stockings and a short, black, silk cocktail suit she laid out a very different outfit; charcoal barathea with frogging and a calf-length skirt – the epitome of Tory dressing for a solemn occasion. When she was finished she outlined her mouth in cerise. She would use a blush-pink lipstick on Monday morning, but no mascara or eye-shadow then. It was quite possible she would shed a tear. Not even her mother would object to a tear or two on such an occasion and the pictures would come in handy when Jake did his exposé. 'Oh God,' she thought suddenly, shocked at her own flippancy. 'Don't let me be like this. I don't want to be like this.'

She was waiting on the landing when Jake arrived. They met on the stairs and he took in her outfit and mood at first glance. 'OK,' he said, taking her arm. 'It's OK now.'

The cab threaded its way to Kensington High Street and turned left. 'Where are we going?' Claire asked.

The streets were less thronged than on weekdays. Life ebbed from London at weekends, whereas it flowed into Durham from outlying districts which sent their young on a pilgrimage to find fun as their ancestors had done centuries before.

'Are you listening?' She turned to see Jake regarding

her quizzically. 'I don't know where you were just now but it wasn't in this cab. You asked where we were going.' The cab was turning and she saw Harrods ahead, lit up like a Christmas tree. 'We're going to Turner's.'

'I've never heard of it,' Claire said.

'You will. It's becoming the place to see and be seen in . . . and the food is good, which is not always the case. You'll recognise the owner, he's on TV a lot – he has the patter but he knows his food.'

They were in Walton Street now. She knew and loved this long row of interesting shops, filled with jewelry and antiques and extravagant lampshades. Turner's was small and elegant and had an air of affluence about it. The décor was blue and gold and there seemed to be impressive-looking bottles every-where. They had a corner table and she felt secure and safe with her back against the cushioned seat.

'The food here's French but with a British influence,' Jake said. 'You'll like it.' The waiters had greeted him like an old friend so he must come here often. She glanced at the other tables, recognising both an author and a TV presenter. So the media had adopted it – that meant it was sure to succeed.

She looked around again. There were some rather fine lithographs on the walls and copies of Turners, which was a nice touch. Her eye rested on a bronze figure, a naked woman, poised by the window. She was enjoying the lines of the figure, its abandonment, when she realised that the diners at the table below it were looking in her direction. She felt herself blush. Had they recognised her?

She looked away and then, unable to resist, allowed herself a peep. One of the diners was Stephanie Routh, smiling now at Claire and inclining her head in greeting. Her companion was a woman in her thirties, pale, blonde, elegant, smiling too at Claire. As she looked over she saw Stephanie put out a hand to the other woman's arm and let it rest there. It was an intimate gesture and a loving one. Claire smiled and turned away.

'Stephanie Routh is over there,' she said.

'I know.' Jake's eyes were on Claire's. 'That's Tessa Evans with her. They share a flat.'

The waiter was placing their Kir Royales before them and Claire was glad of the interruption, which allowed her to collect her thoughts. So Stephanie Routh was gay. If only she had known that earlier. 'You might have told me,' she said.

Jake shrugged. 'It wasn't relevant.' What had he said, right at the beginning? Something about not betraying decent people. He had known about Stephanie, could have made it a story if he'd wanted. Whoever the other woman was, she was undoubtedly someone of importance. Two high-profile gay women – and he had not betrayed them, even to her.

He was smiling down at his glass and then he looked up. 'Why haven't I used it? What's the angle? That's what you're thinking, isn't it? Well, she doesn't queer-bash so she's not a hypocrite. She loves where she chooses, so do I. There are dozens of stories in and around the Palace of Westminster; you and I both know that. Most of us Press hacks go after the whited sepulchres; the men — and women — who thump the purity drum and indulge their liking for little boys or other people's wives in their spare time. Other people's husbands too nowadays; women Members will put the boys in the shade given time. Anyway, less of the morality and more of the menu. I can recommend the crab sausage — and what Turner can do with scallops you wouldn't believe.'

She saw the proprietor then, recognising him as the deft-fingered, fast-talking chef who graced one of the morning TV programmes and popped up occasionally in the evening. 'So that's Turner,' she said, glad of the opportunity to change the subject, for what Jake had said had made her feel uncomfortable.

As she ate a mouth-watering *Côté de boeuf* and sipped the Caronne St Gemme Jake had chosen to accompany it, she thought about hypocrisy. She had been bitterly hurt by Michael's unfaithfulness, devastated by Perdy's betrayal. But how spotless was she? She had used Jake Dennehy, had sex with him long before any emotion other than lust had come into play. That she had done it to assuage pain was some excuse but not enough. 'He's too nice to be used,' she thought and steeled herself to smile and talk so as not to spoil his meal. That was the least she could do.

'How's the beef?' he asked. 'It's one of the dishes he's famous for.'

346

'It's heaven,' she said and smiled to emphasise her words.

In the cab he reached for her hand. 'Enjoy it?' he asked.

'Very much.' She put her other hand on his. 'But I want to go home, Jake . . . alone, I mean.' She looked towards the driver and was glad to see he was wearing ear-phones and moving his head in time with the music.

'I like you very much and I don't know what I'd've done without you at times in the last few weeks. But it's been too quick. My fault; I wanted it – I still want it. But I want even more to get my breath back, to get to know you when we're not involved in something unhappy. Can we do that?'

The cab was turning into Campden Street. 'Let's get out. We'll talk then.' He paid off the cab in spite of her protestations but, to her relief, he didn't press her to let him come in. Instead he took her hands and then lifted an index finger to smoothe the hair from her brow.

'What about tomorrow?' he said.

'I need space, Jake.' She put up her hand to touch his cheek. 'I'm grateful to you, grateful in a lot of ways, but I need time to think.' She lowered her eyes. 'You probably won't believe this but I don't make a habit of leaping into bed with strange men.'

'I do believe you,' he said, so quickly that she laughed aloud.

'Was I that bad?'

'Far from it. I like you a lot, Claire. More than I bargained for, to be truthful.'

'Give me some time, Jake. I don't regret the last few weeks but now I need to do some thinking.'

'Get a good night's sleep then,' he said. 'I'll see you at the church.' He didn't kiss her. They grinned at the joke about church and moved apart, and he stood watching as she mounted the steps and opened the door.

'Good-night,' she said. He lifted his hand and did not turn away until she had shut the door and peeped out from the side window.

32

When Deborah rang in the early morning Claire was ready to be honest and say how much she feared the sight of Perdy on her doorstep. 'After the service I can cope, even welcome it. I want it all behind me, Debs. But not now, not before.'

'Come to us,' Debbo said, but Claire was not going to impose her own problems on her friend's family.

'Tell you what,' Debs said, ever practical. 'I told you I'd help you clear the Kennerley Street flat. We'll do it today, so that when you walk out of church tomorrow you really will be finished with the whole sorry mess.'

'You can't leave Hugh and the children on a Sunday,' Claire said, but Deborah only chuckled.

'You should hear yourself. You sound like the Lord's Day Observance Society. The lunch is all prepared. And Hugh is taking them to Greenwich anyway; he's been promising them a river trip for ages.

The day spent alone seemed to stretch before Claire like an eternity. 'All right,' she said. 'If you're sure.'

So here they were on Kennerley Street, punching in the combination, mounting the stairs, turning the key in the lock. 'It's not much of a place, is it?' Deborah said, looking around her.

Today the love-nest looked even more drab. 'Let's get it over with,' Claire said, and began to get out the refuse bags and boxes she had brought with her. They worked steadily and had cleared and tidied the living-room when Claire remembered the wine she had left in the fridge.

'Goody,' Debbo said as it glugged into two giant goblets. They stopped work for a while, easing into chairs opposite one another, slinging legs over arms and relaxing.

'How long had Michael had this place?' Debbo asked at last.

Claire shrugged. 'I don't know, exactly. A long time. I could ask Gavin Lambert; he'll know everything, I suppose.' With Debbo there, the flat had somehow lost its gloom.

'What do you want me to do next?' Debbo said, looking around her. 'It's not what I expected. It looks as bad as our place.'

'Your home is lovely,' Claire protested but Deborah had been right. This flat, for all its shabbiness, did look lived in. 'Let's drink up and get it over with,' Claire said. 'Can you go through the drawers in the bedroom? Sling out rubbish, keep anything you think was Michael's. I'll go through it all before we leave and ditch everything probably, but I'd like to see it first. I'll do the hall. It shouldn't take long.'

'Would it help to know when it started?' Debbo shuffled up in her chair. 'It might have been a flash in the pan . . . that night could have been a one-off.' She was trying to play it down but they both knew the flat had been more than the scene of a one-night stand.

Claire shook her head. 'It must have begun in the summer, if not before. I remember there was a calendar in the kitchen — one of those year-at-a-glance things — there was a date ringed in the middle of the year. May or June. Perhaps that was their Red Letter Day; the day love struck? But I think it was longer, perhaps as long as a year. The calendar has disappeared, along with one or two other things. I must ask Gavin Lambert about it, though why he should want a calendar, goodness knows.'

'I still can't believe it.' Deborah pursed her lips and narrowed her eyes. 'It would be so awful if you were wrong about Perdy, Cleo. After all, you had a whole list of candidates, and none of them was completely cleared.'

'None of them had the initial P — except a journalist called Patricia Connaught, and she doesn't count. We've never met so she doesn't know me. The same goes for Pamela Corby, whom you met at the funeral; she couldn't really say what I was like, Debbo, we've hardly met. That note said, "C always was . . ." That's the remark of a friend, or at least a close acquaintance.'

'Yes,' Deborah said slowly. 'That's true. All the same, I'd go easy when you speak to Perdy, just in case.'

They talked on for a while until the bottle was empty, and then Deborah levered herself to her feet. 'Nice as it is to loll about drinking wine, we ought to get on. I'll get going on the kitchen. I presume you want the fridge turned off and things like that?'

'Yes, please.' Debbo went into the kitchen but as Claire stood up the rack of wines caught her eye. She picked out a bottle of Château La Berrière, a Muscadet she knew Debbo favoured, and carried it through to the kitchen. 'We might as well drink this while we work,' she said. 'Less to carry away.'

Debbo had already rinsed the glasses and put them upside down on the drainer. She picked them up again as Claire said: 'There's a corkscrew in the drawer.' She was about to follow with instructions on the trick of opening it but Debbo had already moved to the drawer, lifting the handle and pulling it out in one smooth movement.

Claire might not have registered it if it had not been for the sudden terrible stillness of the figure before her. As it was, time seemed suspended until Debbo turned, her mouth stretched in a rictus of embarrassment, her eyes looking like stones behind her spectacles.

'Shall I pour or will you?' she said.

Claire didn't answer for a moment. It seemed as though the kitchen, the stove, the canisters, the sunlight coming through the window, had all suddenly became part of a dream . . . a nightmare. If she waited, she would wake up.

'Give me the bottle,' Debbo said, but her tone was uncertain.

'How did you know about the drawer?' Claire's own voice fell upon her ears like the voice of a stranger. 'If you've never been here before, how did you know about that drawer?'

'Oh dear,' Debbo sighed. 'That wasn't very clever of me — not clever at all.' And then, as Claire tried to cope with the teeming implications of what had happened, she continued: 'If you could see the look on your face, Cleo. You always did think everyone was playing by the rules; it comes from having all those brothers, I suppose. Too much cricket.'

A terrible confusion had overtaken Claire. Debbo had known how to open the drawer, therefore she must have been here before. And yet, when they had entered the flat she had looked around her, behaving for all the world as though she had never laid eyes on the place. 'It's not much of a place, is it?' That's what she had said.

A mixture of emotions was crossing Deborah's face; embarrassment, regret and a dawning resignation.

'Yes, Claire, it was me. You never even considered that did you?' Deborah shook her head sadly. 'You always overlook us, you shining ones, but we have our triumphs too. Because we have to work harder, be more, know more. You thought P stood for Perdy; it stood for Pandora, actually . . . that was Michael's name for me because, he said, I opened up a box of delights for him. We were lovers for two years, Cleo. Almost three.'

Claire thought of Deborah in the last few years, almost always pregnant or feeding an infant with breasts that spilt over with milk. She gagged suddenly, thinking of her with Michael, until a fresh and more dreadful thought overtook her.

'No,' Deborah said firmly, as though reading her thoughts. 'Emlyn is not Michael's child. I was careful about that. It would have been messy!'

Suddenly Claire remembered Deborah laughing on the phone that night. 'You talked to me,' she said, thinking of Michael lying dead in the bed Deborah had just vacated. 'You made jokes about Postman Pat, Deb. You said Michael was on his way. And all the time . . . you said ring if he doesn't turn up . . . but you knew he was dead. You even laughed when you said goodbye.'

Deborah's eyes had narrowed. 'God, I was scared getting out of that flat. I knew I had to get away . . . right away, before anyone found out.'

'Why didn't you call a doctor?' Claire said dully.

'Because he was dead, Cleo. Don't have any doubt about that. He died instantly, if it's any consolation. Just sat up suddenly and gasped and that was that. I made sure and then I ran.'

'Did he say anything?' Claire said. 'Before he died.'

Deborah had kept hold of her glass. Now she twirled it defiantly but the look on her face was one of misery. 'You mean a last remark? "Rosebud," like Citizen Kane?

Sorry, I shouldn't be flippant but nothing . . . absolutely nothing in my life has prepared me for this situation. Why did you have to dig, Cleo? I tried to stop you — I asked Gavin Lambert to stop you, or try to — but you had to go on.'

Inside Claire shock was giving way to anger. 'You let me think it was Perdy. You encouraged me—'

'No, I didn't,' Deborah interjected. 'I knew Perdy could prove it wasn't her. I couldn't say I knew it wasn't Perd; I kept saying, "Don't jump to conclusions." But you were so stubborn, Cleo. I never thought you had it in you.'

'Why did you let me wait all night? You knew for hours and you let me go on waiting. Why?'

'I had to wait to ring it in . . . I needed time to think — and I couldn't change anything. I should have taken more time; as it was, I had to go back to the flat after the funeral to get some of my things. There was a green frog Michael had given me and my birthday was ringed on the calendar, for God's sake. I did it for a joke, in case he forgot we were going up to the cottage. I thought you'd be sure to twig when you saw the date, but then you never even considered it could have been me, did you, Cleo?'

She held out a hand. 'We might as well have the wine; I could do with a drink. We had such fun at the cottage—' She put in the corkscrew and expertly pulled the cork. 'I thought we'd tidied up . . . the wrapping paper was an oversight.'

Once more the face of treason rose up in Claire's mind

but this time it was Debbo, not Perdy, who looked into her face and swore allegiance. 'I'll help you Cleo. You can rely on me.' How could anyone say that to someone they had betrayed?

Deborah poured two glasses of wine and put one in Claire's unresisting hand. 'Why did you do it?' Claire said. 'You and Hugh are happy.'

'Yes, we are. But you and Perdy have always patronised me, Cleo. "You look thinner, Debbo. You've got lovely skin, Debbo." Be honest, you thought I was lucky to get Hugh but I think I could have had anyone if I'd put my mind to it. And I like finding out if I can do it or not. It does no harm usually . . . it's over in a second. Michael was different.' She drank deeply of her wine. 'So what are we going to do now?'

An overwhelming tiredness had come over Claire. She put down her glass. 'Just go, please. That's what I'd like you to do.' And then as Deborah gathered up her things. 'You've been such a bitch. I can't take it in, not now.'

But as Deborah was quitting the room Claire had one last question. 'Why did Michael do it? Didn't he love me at all?' The minute she had asked she regretted it. She wanted neither information nor consolation from Deborah.

'Of course he loved you, Cleo. Perhaps too much. "I don't deserve her," he said to me once. He loved you . . . and he respected you. But he could relax with me.'

When Deborah had gone Claire went around switching

things off, desperate to be gone from this place. She left the bags and boxes behind her, walking aimlessly along the Edgware Road until she could flag down a cab.

'Where to?' the cabbie asked.

She gave the Campden Street address and climbed wearily into the back. They were passing Scotch House corner when she leant forward and told the driver to change direction. There was only one place she wanted to be right now, however difficult explanations might be.

'Thank God,' Perdy said when she answered Claire's ring on her bell. She drew her in over the step. 'I was on my way round . . . I thought you'd turned funny or something. I can see you're upset but at least you're in one piece.'

'I've been such a fool, Perdy.'

'Hang on a minute while I fix us a drink. Whatever it is, Cleo, we'll sort it out.'

But when the story was told and Perdy's initial disbelief had been dispelled, she had only one thing to say.

'Oh Cleo, Cleo . . . how could we both have been so blind?'

33

Claire was awake long before daybreak, listening to the traffic gathering pace in the street outside. She thought of what Perdy had said last night.

'I could forgive her the affair — just — but I couldn't ever forgive her these last few months of deception. Encouraging you on a wild-goose chase, letting you believe it was me. That's real deception, Cleo. I find that hard to forgive.'

Now that it had sunk in Claire was surprised at how little anger she felt. If she believed Deborah — and why should she? — Michael had placed her on a pedestal; Deborah had provided something more earthy, more titillating.

But if that was Michael's motive, where had Deborah's lain? In simply taking what belonged to someone else, someone close? You didn't expect Deborahs to be traitors. The very name breathed honest respectability. And yet Debbo had lied and lied, to her husband, to her friends . . . perhaps even to her lover. Who could tell?

'I am not cold,' Claire said aloud. 'We never knew one another, that was all.'

It was just light when she heard the fax machine ring. There was half a page covered in Stephen Gaunt's handwriting, with the heading, 'Durham'. He thanked her for the bulbs. 'They are such a harbinger of less grey times. I long for February when the daffodils will be out around the Cathedral.' She thought of the ancient stones. John Chaytor would have his daffodils soon, and the forsythia would be out in the North Bailey garden.

His next words shook her. 'I knew you had had your troubles. If we helped in any way, I'm glad.' So Deborah had lied about that too, saying she had not revealed Claire's secret and yet telling Stephen everything. The fax continued: 'Hopefully, the service will be cathartic. When you are ready, come to us again.'

She put the fax in a drawer before her family began to arrive but the word 'cathartic' lingered in her mind. 'Catharsis: a cleansing.' She hoped he was right. It would be good to put away the remains of the past few months.

Perdy arrived in plenty of time to help with Claire's parents. She wore navy with pearls at her neck and her fair hair was drawn back into a chignon.

'It still seems hard to believe——' she said, her one reference to Deborah. 'I suppose we'll meet in future years and smile coldly, as though we hardly know her. Right now, it seems incredible that we were ever friends.'

360

The Halcrows arrived then, with Adam hot on their heels. Perdy handed out sherry and kept up small talk until it was time to leave for the church. 'Is Deborah meeting us there?' Mrs Halcrow asked and Perdy stepped in.

'Chicken-pox,' she said. 'Right through her family. It's terribly sad . . . she's mortified. But she always puts her children first.'

There were only a handful of journalists at the church. 'We are old news,' Claire thought wryly. 'Now it's someone else's turn to suffer.' She saw Jake as she got out of the car and then, in front of her, Stephanie Routh with the woman she had been with at Turners.

'This is my friend, Tessa,' she said and the other woman smiled.

'Thank you for coming,' Claire said 'It means a lot to me to have both of you here.'

It was a crowded church; she sensed rather than saw that as she walked down the aisle, her eyes fixed on the window behind the altar – a glory of red and blue and gold. They sang 'Crimond' and 'O love that will not let me go' and as the music echoed round the church Claire mourned not only the loss of her husband, but the loss of a friend. But she did not mourn the passing of a childhood that had gone on for far too long.

She half listened as Gavin Lambert read from the Gospel according to St John. The words were comforting but Claire couldn't help thinking of Sunday school. In those days she had believed because she was told to and then, when she was old enough, she had become a disbeliever, feeling that was now her privilege. 'But I've never decided for myself,' she thought. Perhaps she would be able to now.

The vicar was speaking of the bonds of marriage, the void that the death of husband or wife must leave. His eyes flicked to Claire and then away again.

'I was Michael's wife,' she thought. And suddenly she could picture him as he had been in Eze; the winter they went to Chamonix; at Christmas each year when they decorated the house; on official occasions when he had spoken proudly of her as 'my wife'. What had Stephanie Routh said? 'A special look in his eye when he spoke of you.'

Whatever had happened, Michael had chosen her. And he had not cared that she had not given him a child because it was the partnership that mattered, not the fruit of it; the photograph in his wallet had been proof of that.

She was smiling as she let him go, peace made between them.

When it was time to leave she saw them there, in the back row, Hugh's face tortured, Deborah's defiant. So Hugh had known, or at least did now. As she walked past them she inclined her head to their tremulous smiles and then she was out in the sunshine and people were splitting into groups, some to talk of the sadness of death, others of the impending by-elections in Dudley and Devening.

Pamela Corby's voice was prominent. 'We'll take a terrible beating,' she said, 'but it will all come right at the general election.' Claire moved on. She had had enough of politics to last her several lifetimes.

In the church, as they had played 'Crimond' she had remembered her wedding day, when love was there for both of them. That was what she would remember. The rest would be consigned to oblivion, or the nearest to oblivion she could manage.

Now, with Perdy at her side, she spoke to Jake Dennehy, seeing Deborah and Hugh melt away into the passing crowds as she did so. Jake was looking at her expectantly and for a moment her resolve faltered. But only for a moment. 'I can do anything I like,' she thought. 'I can even change my mind if I choose.'

She put out a hand and rested it on his arm. 'I'm glad you're here, Jake. I wanted to tell you that I'm giving up. I don't care who the woman was. She's history.'

His brows came down. 'I thought you knew?'

'I thought I did. I was wrong.'

'You'll need to find out sooner or later,' he said. 'It doesn't do to leave things undiscovered.'

Claire smiled. 'Haven't you heard of the Act of Oblivion?' He shook his head in incomprehension and she smiled again. 'Never mind. I'm going away for a while. I'll call you when I get back—'

'Where are you going?' he asked.

She felt Perdy's hand at her elbow. 'I'm not sure,' she said. 'Probably somewhere warm. I'll let you know.'

But as she walked towards the car she was not

thinking of sunshine. She was thinking of bulbs break-ing through the cold Durham earth. Of a mongrel dog and a cantankerous cat and a garden that was always giving you surprises.

'It's a pity you missed the summer,' Stephen had said. But summer would come again and swifts would return to swoop above a garden where people drank wine and dreamt dreams and all was as it should be. She turned for one last look at the spire outlined against the sky and then she stepped confidently into the waiting car.